It's Complicated

Shoma Narayanan is a banker who is also India's first *Mills and Boon* author to be published internationally. Her books are quick, zingy reads featuring feisty, independent women and sexy, super-hot men—happy endings guaranteed!

It's Complex!

SHOMA NARAYANAN

Published by
Rupa Publications India Pvt. Ltd 2014
7/16, Ansari Road, Daryaganj
New Delhi 110002

Sales centres:
Allahabad Bengaluru Chennai
Hyderabad Jaipur Kathmandu
Kolkata Mumbai

Copyright © Shoma Narayanan 2014

This is a work of fiction. Names, characters, places and incidents are either the product of the author's imagination or are used fictitiously, and any resemblance to any actual persons, living or dead, events or locales is entirely coincidental.

All rights reserved.
No part of this publication may be reproduced, transmitted, or stored in a retrieval system, in any form or by any means, electronic, mechanical, photocopying, recording or otherwise, without the prior permission of the publisher.

ISBN: 978-81-291-3116-4

First impression 2014

10 9 8 7 6 5 4 3 2 1

The moral right of the author has been asserted.

Typeset by Saanavi Graphics, Noida

Printed at Replika Press Pvt. Ltd., India

This book is sold subject to the condition that it shall not, by way of trade or otherwise, be lent, resold, hired out, or otherwise circulated, without the publisher's prior consent, in any form of binding or cover other than that in which it is published.

To

Padma, Alice and Rita

1

'Black buck', Nikita moaned, as she opened her eyes. A vaguely familiar voice said 'What?'

'Killed a black buck,' she said, slowly and painfully. 'Like Salman Khan.'

'Oh, I get it,' the voice said, sounding relieved. 'Not a black buck, you almost killed me, not to mention a couple of pavement dwellers.' Her eyes widened in alarm, and the voice added hastily, 'Relax, we're all fine. And so are the black buck, you've just got your Salman Khan comparisons a bit mixed up'.

Nikita nodded and shut her eyes again. Salman was a nice guy at heart, she'd known that ever since she'd watched *Maine Pyar Kiya* when she was in primary school. He was misunderstood, that's all—it was so easy to lose control of your car, if you just dozed off at the wheel for a few seconds. The car!! Her eyes flew open, and she sat up, ignoring the sharp pain shooting through her middle.

'My car!' she wailed, struggling to get off the bed. 'What happened to my car?' A couple of faces swam into focus— one evidently belonged to a doctor—as if the white coat and stethoscope weren't enough, he was also wearing a name tag that said in block capitals DR SUHAS REDDY. The other face was familiar, and obviously belonged to the vaguely familiar voice.

'I know you,' she said accusingly. 'You're the unemployed hot guy in 405.' Her voice sounded slurred, and she wondered what was in the drip that was going into her arm. Saline? Mind-altering drugs? Painkillers?

The hot guy looked faintly embarrassed, and the doctor started flapping around trying to get her to lie down again.

'You've bruised a few ribs; you're lucky nothing's broken, but I don't want you to move until we're sure you don't have concussion.'

'But my car…'

She gave the nameless hot guy an appealing look, and he responded nobly, though what he said was less than reassuring.

'It's being towed to a garage.'

'*Which* garage? How badly is it damaged?'

The doctor was shooing the man out of the room, and he called out over his shoulder, 'It'll live, but you'll get a hefty repair bill.'

Nikita gave an anguished little cry as the doctor firmly slammed the door behind the man.

Once outside, Jai ran a hand through his hair. It was pretty late at night and he hadn't eaten . He'd done as much as he could for Nikita, still, he could hardly abandon her at the hospital even if she didn't know his name. He grimaced. The 'hot unemployed' remark had stung. Of course she'd been doped out of her mind with painkillers, and had probably said the first thing that came into her head, but it still rankled.

Maybe there was someone he could call, a friend or relative of Nikita's who could come over and look after her. Her handbag was with him, he'd taken it from the car along with her laptop bag after dragging her out, and for a second he wondered whether he should open it. He went as far as unzipping the black leather bag, but stopped when he looked inside and saw the mindboggling number of things. God knows what she'd think if she knew he'd been rummaging around in it.

Twenty minutes later, the door opened, and Nikita walked out. She was pale and a little groggy, but completely in control. She looked a little surprised to see him.

'Oh, you're still here,' she said. 'I'm so sorry, the doctor took ages to let me go.'

'I had your bag,' he said, gesturing towards the handbag that he'd put on the seat next to his.

'Of course,' she shook her head once as if to clear it. 'How stupid of me, I'd even forgotten I'd need to pay.'

She took the bag from him, and settled her bill at the nurses' station. Even with her spiky blue-black hair in disarray, and sporting a spectacular bump on her forehead, she was striking to look at. She wasn't pretty exactly—her features were just a little too sharp, and her body a little too thin. The first time he'd seen her, he'd thought her eyes were her best feature. Almond-shaped with thick short eyelashes, they normally sparkled with life and what he suspected was a rather bitchy sense of humour. Right now, she looked like she was in pain and her eyes were dull with fatigue. Still, he could hardly take his eyes off her.

'How're you feeling?' he ventured.

Nikita shrugged. 'Shaken up. And my arm hurts pretty badly, so does my head, and there are bruises on my tummy where the steering wheel hit it.'

There was a pause, and then she said diffidently, 'Thanks for, you know, pulling me out. For a minute there, I thought I was a goner.' She relived the brief moment when she'd closed her eyes, and woken up with a jerk to find herself on the wrong side of the road with the car about to go on to the pavement and mow down a dozen people sleeping there. She'd desperately swung the wheel around, missing them by inches. Then she'd seen the headlight of the oncoming motorcycle, and had panicked completely, letting go of the wheel. Perhaps that was the most sensible thing she could have done—the car had hit a lamppost, and she'd fallen forward, hitting her head hard, in spite of the seatbelt. Then, of course, she'd passed out.

'No worries.' He gave her a brief smile; it was difficult not to admire her independent 'I can take care of myself' attitude. Any other woman would have been leaning on his arm and screaming for her mamma.

'So what's your name again?'

'Jai.'

'Just Jai?'

'Jaiveer Singh,' he said, grimacing a little. 'Parents were *Sholay* fans.'

Nikita laughed. 'Found it difficult to choose, did they? *Jai bhi tum, aur Veeru bhi tum?*'

'If I was a girl, they'd have probably called me Dhanno,' he said bending down to pick up her laptop bag. 'My elder sisters are called Basanti and Radha. Come on, let's get you home.'

'Seriously?' Nikita asked, her eyes widening. He laughed and shook his head. 'Only one sister and she's called Pooja.'

'Hmmm. Oh, I'm Nikita, by the way. Nikita Dewan.'

'I know,' he said. 'Your name's up in big letters on your door.' Jai's flat was on the same floor as Nikita's, and her nameplate was difficult to miss.

Nikita winced. The nameplate with hideously large handcrafted letters had been a gift from her mother. She'd found it embarrassing, but hadn't had the guts to take it off the door, just in case her mother visited her unexpectedly.

'Can I bum a ride back to the complex?' she asked.

'I'll get a cab,' he said. 'You could wait in the reception area.'

'What about your bike?'

'You're in no shape to be on a bike,' Jai said. 'I'll come back and fetch it later.'

'Nonsense, I'm perfectly OK.'

Jai shrugged and brought the bike around. He also had the details of the garage the car had been towed to. A car full of middle-aged Gujarati businessmen had helped him get Nikita to the hospital and have the car taken care of. But once they'd done their bit they'd gone on to the party they'd been on their way to, leaving Jai to wait for Nikita in the hospital.

Once on the pillion of Jai's bike Nikita began to feel rather faint, and by the time he pulled up in front of their apartment building in Prabhadevi, she could barely stay upright.

'I told you the bike was a bad idea,' he muttered, grabbing her arm as she almost keeled over. 'Is there anyone I can call? You shouldn't be on your own.'

Nikita sat down on the absent watchman's chair and stuck her head between her knees and took a couple of deep breaths.

'My cousin,' she said. 'He lives nearby—in Carlton Towers.'

Jai raised his eyebrows. 'Swanky,' he said. Carlton Towers was within walking distance, but with its own gym and clubhouse with attached swimming pool, it was in a completely different league from their own stolid and unashamedly middle-class apartment building.

Nikita ignored him, took out her cell phone and dialled a number. She didn't get through, instead she heard a smug-sounding recorded message in Putonghua.

'I think he's in China,' she said frowning. 'Maybe I should let it be, the doc's given me enough painkillers to send me to sleep. I'll call someone over in the morning.'

Jai shrugged. He badly wanted his dinner now, and wasn't in the mood to argue.

'I still think you should have someone with you,' he said. 'But it's your funeral. Come on, let's get you to your flat.'

Nikita stood up a little shakily, and followed him into the tiny stairwell of Shiv-Shakti Cooperative Housing Society. She was feeling too sick to talk, and all she wanted to do was curl up in bed and go to sleep. Partly it was the pain in her arm, but partly it was the shock settling in. She'd had a lucky escape—a few inches here or there, and she could have either been dead, or in jail for culpable homicide.

Shiv-Shakti didn't have a lift, and by the time Jai had hauled Nikita up four floors, he was wishing he'd abandoned her on the road after the accident. She was in no shape to be climbing stairs, but she kept refusing his help, even when she was clearly on the verge of fainting again. When he finally ignored her protests and took her by the good arm to part-drag, part-carry her up the stairs, she was most unappreciative.

'Is it the pain or do you have a naturally sweet disposition?' he asked sarcastically, after she'd snapped at him for the fourth or fifth time.

'Sorry,' she muttered under her breath. They were both silent as they climbed the last flight of stairs to the fourth floor. Under the light of the single bulb she looked so pale and wan that Jai's conscience pricked him.

'You sure there's no one else you can call?' he asked. Nikita shook her head. 'I'll figure something out tomorrow,' she said, as Jai opened her door for her. 'Right now I just want to take a couple of painkillers and go to sleep. Thanks for everything.'

Jai scribbled something on a piece of paper and handed it to her. 'That's my mobile number,' he said. 'Call me if you need anything. I'll check in on you in the morning.'

'I'll be OK,' Nikita said, but she took the scrap of paper before she closed the door. There were five flats on each floor, and Jai's flat was diagonally opposite Nikita's. It struck him as he unlocked his own door that he didn't even know if the other three flats were occupied or not.

Jai spent a largely sleepless night. He hadn't been hurt at all—in fact, there hadn't been much direct danger, but those few seconds with the car headlights bearing down on him had been unnerving. So had the sickening crunch with which the car hit the lamppost, and he'd been petrified when he opened the door on the driver's side and found Nikita slumped unconscious over the wheel.

A pretty, tired-looking woman in her early thirties opened the door when he rang Nikita's doorbell the next morning.

'You must be Jai,' she said, smiling at him. Jai noticed that her teeth were very even and perfectly white. At the same time he noticed the diamond solitaires in her ears, and the rock on her finger. She was otherwise very simply dressed in a loose cotton shirt and jeans, but the few pieces of jewellery she wore probably cost more than a medium-sized car.

'That's right,' he said warily. 'I, uhh, just dropped by to ask how Nikita was—I won't come in.'

'She's doing a lot better,' the woman said, stepping back and opening the door wider with a welcoming gesture. 'You must come in, I wanted to thank you, and Nikita would like to see you too, I'm sure. I'm Shilpa, by the way, my husband is Nikita's cousin.'

The Carlton Towers one. That explained the diamonds. Jai had done a short stint trying to learn the jewellery business—he'd hated it, but he still subconsciously assessed the value of any piece he saw.

Nikita had come into the room. 'Hi Jai,' she said, cheerfully enough, but her face was very pale.

'You don't look OK,' he said bluntly. She shook her head. 'I can hardly move this arm,' she said. 'Shilpa's taking me to the doctor.'

'You should have called her last night,' Jai said, and Nikita shrugged. She'd called Shilpa as an absolute last resort, her arm was hurting really badly, and she had no idea who else to reach out to. It had actually been quite a revelation. Three years in Mumbai and she didn't have a single friend to call for help, and she'd had to fall back on her cousin's wife. Not that Shilpa was bad—it was Anuj she couldn't stand with his newly developed airs and graces. Shilpa was the real thing, genuinely upper-class, and with no airs and graces to speak of, but Nikita and she had very little in common. Right now, however, all Nikita needed was someone who could get her to the doctor. It didn't matter if Shilpa liked the Beatles and old Bollywood movies—she could jive to 'I am a Disco Dancer' and watch Chota Bheem in her spare time for all Nikita cared.

'The garage called,' Jai was saying, and Nikita made a desperate attempt to focus.

'How bad is it?' she asked with trepidation.

'The guy said it'd cost around thirty-three thousand to get the car back on the road.' Nikita closed her eyes in despair. 'Won't your insurance cover it?' Jai asked.

'God knows,' she said. 'I hope it does, but there's usually something that they decide not to pay for.'

She hesitated a little. There wasn't much she could do about the car in her current state, and none of the ambitious, workaholic people she hung out with would take the day off to run around getting her insurance papers sorted out. Jai on the other hand... Ranjana, Nikita's cook and all-round help, had told her that Jai didn't work, he was just taking care of his brother-in-law's flat.

'Jai, would you know who could help me with getting the car fixed?' she asked, putting on her best damsel-in-distress face. She very rarely used it, but desperate times called for desperate measures, and so far the combination of large-eyed helplessness and a sexy pout had never failed her. Jai unfortunately seemed immune to it.

'I'll leave the garage number with you, they seemed pretty competent,' he said, getting to his feet. 'See you around then, take care of yourself.'

'Anuj's driver is free until Anuj gets back from China,' Shilpa said, coming back into the room as Jai shut the door behind him. 'He'll get your car fixed. Shall we leave then? The doctor asked us to be there by eleven.'

Nikita nodded. The last painkiller she'd taken was beginning to take effect, and her arm didn't hurt quite so badly. Jai's sudden exit was troubling her though. She thought back to their conversation, maybe he didn't like the thought of being conned into becoming an errand boy. Or maybe he just found her scary. Ever since a disgruntled ex-boyfriend had told her that half the men in college avoided her because of her sharp tongue, she'd tried to keep it under control. Even so, she knew that she put off a certain type of man; it was just that Jai hadn't seemed the type.

'I wonder why Jai doesn't have a job,' she said to Shilpa. 'He seems intelligent enough.'

'Maybe he's trying to break into Bollywood,' Shilpa said. 'Are you ready to leave?'

'I need my BlackBerry,' Nikita said abruptly. ' It is in my bedroom, maybe on the bedside table. If it isn't there, it'll be on my bookshelf.'

Bollywood, that was a thought. Of course Jai *was* very good-looking. Lean face with a strong jaw and the most amazingly sculpted cheekbones; cloudy black eyes under eyebrows that swept up at the corners, and a fabulously sexy mouth. He was tall as well, and broad-shouldered with narrow hips. Nikita had only seen him in well-worn jeans and ancient T-shirts, but she would have bet a month's salary that the body under the ratty clothes was to die for. Still, there was something in the way he held himself that made her rule out Bollywood almost immediately. He seemed quite unconscious of his appearance, and he didn't make the slightest attempt to flaunt it. And the automatic swagger that came with wanting to be in the public eye was missing. If anything, he gave the impression of being a very private person.

'It's not on the bookshelf, could it be in your wardrobe?' Shilpa was calling out, and Nikita reluctantly dragged her mind off Jai.

'What... Oh, the BlackBerry. It's in my bag, sorry,' she said, not sounding sorry at all. Shilpa sighed as they finally left. She had taken the day off from work to look after Nikita, and so far it had been a singularly unrewarding experience. 'Ungrateful bitch' was the phrase that sprang readily to mind. She'd never liked Anuj's cousin much—Nikita was shallow, selfish and crazily ambitious, and to top it off, her mother had been abysmally rude to Shilpa on several occasions. On the positive side, Nikita was very independent, and this was the first time she'd ever asked Shilpa to do anything for her. Hopefully it would also be the last.

'It's a hairline fracture,' the doctor pronounced cheerfully after two rounds of examination and several X-rays. 'No cast, we'll put your arm in a sling, and it'll heal in a few weeks.'

Nikita looked at him in horror. 'Can't I use the arm at all? I need to get back to work.'

'Unless you're a traffic policeman, you should be able to manage with one arm for a couple of weeks,' the doctor said.

'Ha ha,' Nikita said sourly. 'Can I drive?'

'Absolutely not.'

'You can use Anuj's car and driver till he's back,' Shilpa said once they were on their way home. 'Have you told your mom about the accident?'

Nikita looked at her as if she'd suddenly grown purple horns. 'Of course not! She'd probably come haring down to look after me, and she'd drive my maid up the wall until she quits, and where would I be then?'

That was something Shilpa could sympathize with. Anuj's and Nikita's mothers were sisters, and while Anuj's mom was a holy terror in her own right, she was an absolute lamb compared to Nikita's. Even then, Shilpa tried to keep her as far away from the household help as possible.

In 405, Shiv-Shakti Cooperative Housing Society, Jai was staring blindly into his laptop screen. The words just seemed to have stopped flowing, and he was worried, genuinely worried for the first time since he'd left home to try and write a book. Mumbai was an expensive city, and the small stock of money he'd brought with him was depleting rapidly. Luckily he was living rent free, but there were still groceries to be bought and the electricity bill to be paid, and the Internet subscription. He'd already cancelled the cable TV subscription, and he didn't use the AC or the electric geyser.

The doorbell rang, and he got up to open the door. It was Ranjana, the cook; for a brief moment, he'd thought it might be Nikita.

'Morning saab,' Ranjana said as she scurried in. She was dark, wiry and seemingly tireless, and had been working for him ever since he'd moved into the apartment four months ago.

'I need to talk to you,' Jai said and Ranjana stopped in her tracks at the unfamiliar note in his voice.

'I don't need you to work for me anymore,' he said, the words coming out with difficulty. 'It's the twenty-second, I'll pay you for the full month, but you can stop coming here from tomorrow.' He couldn't meet her eyes—she had two children, a college-going daughter and a son who was still in school, and her husband had died in an industrial accident several years ago.

'Who'll cook and clean for you then?' she asked, and there was something in her steady voice that made him look up and straight at her.

'I'll manage on my own,' he said. 'I can't afford your salary any longer.'

'I'll keep coming till the end of the month,' she said, picking up the broom and beginning to sweep the kitchen floor. 'If you're paying me till then, there's no point wasting the money.'

'If you find anything in the meantime...' he said, and she shrugged.

'I'll tell you if I do,' she said. 'But I have the time to take on another job, the people in 203 have moved out, so right now I'm working only for you and Nikita didi.'

Feeling unbearably guilty, Jai said, 'If you're short of cash, you can keep working here until you get something, things aren't that bad with me.'

Ranjana gave a brief mirthless smile. 'There's no point,' she said. 'I'll manage, don't you worry about me. What we should worry about is teaching you cooking—you can't even boil an egg. And the last time you tried to cook yourself some Maggi noodles, you burnt the pot, I had to soak it overnight to clean it. And...'

The intercom rang at that point, saving Jai from any further reminiscences.

'Is Ranjana there?' Nikita demanded when Jai answered. 'I need to speak to her.'

Sorely tempted to tell her to say 'please', Jai beckoned to Ranjana and handed her the phone.

'*Haan, Nikita didi*', Ranjana said. '*Boliye.*' She listened for a while.

'OK... Have you told the watchman?... OK. I'll try to find someone, but no driver would want a temporary job... Ten thousand, I think... Yes, of course... Yes, I'll see you in the evening then.'

'Nikita didi wants a driver till her arm gets better,' Ranjana said, putting the phone back on the hook. 'But who would want a job for only a month?'

Jai gazed at her, suddenly struck by the germ of an idea. When Ranjana left, he waited for a few minutes and went across to Nikita's flat.

'I hear you need a driver,' he said without preamble, and Nikita's brows arched up. 'Yes, do you know of one?' she asked. 'I've interviewed a few, but they weren't much good. The first guy looked positively scary, like a serial killer; I didn't want to take any chances. And the next one had really terrible body odour—he stank from halfway across the room. If I was stuck in the car with him, I'd have to wear a clothes peg on my nose. And the third guy was perfect, but he couldn't drive.'

Jai allowed himself a brief smile. 'Maybe the first one just had a slight attitude problem,' he suggested.

'He looked like he had a wanting-people-dead problem' she said with a shudder. 'He could walk into the sets of a Hannibal the Cannibal movie, and they'd hire him on the spot. It's my own fault—I've gone and told everyone that I need the driver only for a month or two, and they're sending me the pick of the loser's list. Should have just hired someone and sacked him after a month.'

'Would you hire me?' Jai asked. 'I need a job, and a temporary one is just fine.'

Nikita began to laugh.

'You?' she said. 'Joking, right?'

Jai shook his head, wondering if this had been such a good idea after all. He really didn't like Nikita, in spite of that frisson of attraction that seemed to run through him every time he met her. She was rude, loud, inconsiderate and she talked too much.

Nikita stopped laughing. 'But you could do anything,' she said sounding genuinely puzzled. 'Why be a driver? You're a graduate, aren't you?'

'MSc, Physics,' he said, and passed a hand over his face. 'Look, I need a job that gives me a fair amount of spare time. And there aren't too many of those available.'

'Spare time for what?'

'I'm writing a book,' he said. 'And I'm not on the best of terms with my parents, which is why I came away to Mumbai to work on it. I can't afford to live here anymore unless I start working.'

Nikita frowned. When she'd looked at Jai properly after she had recovered from the accident, her first opinion had been confirmed—he *was* incredibly hot with his floppy hair and intense black eyes. She'd even toyed with the idea of starting a mild flirtation with him, but now he was beginning to sound distinctly weird.

'A book on what?'

Jai hesitated. He really didn't want to tell her, something told him she'd sneer at the idea of a book about his grandfather's days as a freedom fighter during the 1940s. If his own parents didn't understand what was driving him to write it, he couldn't expect a random spiky-haired woman with attitude to get it.

'Semi-historical fiction,' he said finally.

'Semi-fiction, or semi-historical?' she asked, and clearly not terribly interested, went on without waiting for an answer. 'Are you really, truly serious about wanting the job?' she asked. He nodded, trying not to show her how much it mattered. Ten thousand could be stretched a long, long way, and hopefully by then he'd have found something else to do.

'And you can drive?' she asked. He nodded again.

Nikita surveyed him silently. Shit, why was it that the really hot men turned out to have no money? There he was, looking good enough to eat, and instead of buying her diamonds and whisking her away for a holiday in Paris, he was applying to become her driver. What a complete waste.

'You can have the job,' she said finally, hoping she wasn't making a big, big mistake. Being closeted in a tiny car with him in Mumbai traffic might be a bit much for her self-control. Oh well, she'd cross that bridge when she came to it.

'Only a month, mind,' she said. 'My arm should be OK by then, and I don't really earn enough to be able to afford a driver.'

Struck by a thought, he asked, 'Why aren't you taking cabs then instead of wasting the money?'

She gave him a horrified look. 'Cabs stink! I'd rather crawl to work.'

2

Jai was idly flipping through a newspaper Nikita had left in the car—his newspaper subscription was yet another thing that had fallen victim to his latest austerity drive—and an ad made him stop short. Wayne Studios, one of Hollywood's most successful movie-churning machines, was expanding into Bollywood, and they were running a contest to decide on the story for their first film.

'The Great Indian Love Story'. Cheesy, but the prize was what caught the eye—five lakhs for the winning story. Jai's hands automatically clenched together. Nikita's arm was healing fast, and the ten thousand rupees she'd paid him had already been stretched to incredible limits—it wouldn't last him more than a month longer. And no more jobs with oodles of spare time had appeared on the horizon. He'd considered taking up another driver's job, but if he was honest with himself, he hated the hours of waiting in the car and in parking lots. Perhaps it wouldn't be so bad in winter, but in summer it was terrible. And while Nikita had been OK to work for, sitting next to him in the passenger seat and treating him more like a friend than an employee, he couldn't expect that from everyone.

Feeling like he was selling out, he pulled his ancient laptop towards him and opening a new Word document, began to type. It wasn't like he had any real chance of winning, he thought defensively. This was just a wild shot, he would get back to his real work as soon as he'd put together something halfway decent and sent it off...

'Prabhadevi sounds a little stodgy,' Nikita was saying to the nerdy looking man walking by her side. She was still a few feet away, but her clear, rather strident voice cut through the noise in the parking lot like a chainsaw through plywood. 'But it's a nice enough area to live in.'

'That's odd, I always thought it sounded rather cool, like the name of a dancer or something.'

'That's Prabhudeva, not Prabhadevi,' Nikita said, amused. 'Jai, we need to drop Vinay to his hotel.'

Jai nodded briefly. Nikita had chosen to sit in the back with Vinay—she did that sometimes, when she wanted to impress someone. Jai did his best not let it bother him, but the fact that she did it only when she was in a serious man-catcher mode hadn't escaped him. Vinay smelt strongly of some expensive male aftershave that made Jai want to puke. What had the bloody man done, poured the entire bottle over himself? And what did Nikita see in him anyway? He looked like a boiled lobster, his pale eyes nearly popping out of his head. Thankfully he was staying in the ITC Grand Central, and it took only ten minutes to get there from Nikita's Lower Parel office.

'Prospective candidate for your hand in marriage?' he asked, after Vinay had gotten off. Nikita shrugged. 'Could be,' she said. 'Stop the car Jai, I want to sit in front. Sitting in the rear seat makes me feel sick.'

He obediently pulled to the side while she made the shift. 'He's a partner in the firm,' she said. 'Joined a few days ago.' Which answered part of the question at least.

'Would you actually want to marry someone like that?' he asked. Nikita yawned and stretched. 'Not sure,' she said. '*Abhi shaadi tak baat nahin pahunchi*, I've just talked to him a few times.'

Jai stayed silent. Nikita was an amazingly mixed-up piece of work—genuinely amusing and generous a lot of the time, bitchy and money-grabbing for the rest. She made no secret of the fact that she was looking out for a rich husband—poor Vinay was just another possible amongst many.

Nikita's phone rang just as he was about to switch the topic to something that didn't get him quite so hot under the collar.

'Hi Shilpa,' she said, her voice much nicer than usual. She still didn't admire Shilpa's taste in movies and music, but a little corner of her self-centred brain was actually grateful to her.

Shilpa grimaced. She didn't like calling in favours, but she was absolutely desperate.

'Nikita, that cook of yours, Ranjana, you told me that she's got some free time, didn't you?'

'Yes, now that Jai's sacked her,' Nikita said cheerfully, ignoring Jai's frown. 'She only works for me.'

'Can you give me her mobile number? I'm stuck without a maid yet again. I've got this elderly temp woman to come in, but she's so fat she can hardly move, and she reeks of mustard oil.'

'What happened to that woman you hired? The one who spoke English and all?'

'Sacked her,' Shilpa said tersely.

'Why?' Nikita didn't really want to know, but Shilpa had sounded so cagey, she couldn't help needling her a bit.

'Because she started writing love letters to Anuj,' Shilpa said, groaning as Nikita gave a little shout of laughter. 'Shut up, Nikita. And don't you dare pull Anuj's leg about it, he's dreadfully embarrassed about the whole thing.'

'Knocked him off his high horse a little, has it?' Nikita asked, still giggling helplessly. 'Oh, but this is priceless. What did the letters say?'

'There was only one,' Shilpa admitted, beginning to laugh as well. 'She cornered him early in the morning and gave it to him. I don't remember the whole thing, but it ended with *"main sampoorn aapki hoon"*.'

'All his…' Nikita said, sounding very serious now. 'Ooh, sexxxxy. Shilpa you have com-pet-tion.'

'Serious competition,' Shilpa said lightly. 'Can I have Ranjana's number then?'

'I'll message it to you,' Nikita said, and rang off. 'You'll never guess what happened,' she said gleefully to Jai. 'Anuj's maid fell for him and started writing him love letters.'

'What's so funny about that?' Jai asked.

Nikita stared. 'Have you seen Anuj?' she demanded. 'He's ever so pish-posh—Ferragamo ties and Zegna suits—I can imagine his face when the maid gave him the letter. And I've seen her, she could speak English and stuff, but she's fat and at least five years older than him.'

'Classist,' Jai remarked, 'Not to mention weightiest, and, oh ageist.' Nikita scoffed, 'Yeah, right, like you'd be thrilled if the woman had made a pass at you.'

'I'm a driver now, I'm fair game,' he said, grinning at how completely that shut Nikita up. She was paying him a salary, but she didn't think of him as one of the working classes yet.

In Carlton Towers, Shilpa slumped down on the sofa, completely exhausted. She hadn't gone to work, and she could picture the backlog that was building up—a heap of CVs slowly piling up on her desk, teetering over and then swamping her nice airy little glass cabin. Being a hotshot HR executive was glamorous enough on the good days, but on the bad ones it was murder. And when you tried clubbing the hotshot executive career with being a mom, you were just begging for trouble. Specifically when you were married to a man who travelled on work all the time.

Actually scratch that last one out. When Anuj wasn't travelling, the maids fell in love with him and she had to sack them; and right now, she felt like she needed a maid a lot more than she needed a husband. Groaning, she rolled over on the sofa and stared at the ceiling. The thought of quitting her job was so tempting that she had to physically restrain herself from getting up and calling her boss to put in her papers. The trouble was that they were living far beyond their means. The loan they'd taken to buy their flat was massive, of sub-Himalayan proportions. The idea had been to pay it back from Anuj's bonuses, but then the recession had hit and his bonus for the last two years had been practically nonexistent. Or not nonexistent exactly, there was enough money left post taxes to pay for about a hundred square feet of the 2,600-square-foot-flat. So the servants' bathroom was probably now all theirs or maybe even the kitchen balcony. For the rest, well, unless the economy un-recessed itself double quick, they'd be paying EMIs till they were eighty.

'Can you read me a story?' her nanny-less seven-year-old asked, wandering into the room wearing his best pair of jeans and an inside-out Ben10 T-shirt. He'd changed all on his own after getting back from school. For a few seconds Shilpa contemplated asking him to wear the T-shirt the right way round, but she didn't have the energy for the inevitable argument that would follow. Anyway it probably looked better inside out, from what she could remember, the design was pretty horrific.

'I'm tired, Suraj,' she said. 'Why don't you get a book and sit next to me and read, hmm?'

'I learnt a Marathi poem today,' he announced proudly.
Superman, superman, superman
Varti chaddi, ajun pant.

'It says Superman wears his underwear outside his trousers!'

Shilpa groaned. 'I don't think that's what your teacher meant when she said you needed to work harder on your Marathi,' she said, but Suraj had lost interest in the conversation. 'Can I have some juice?'

'Yes, OK,' she said, and was about to add 'Ask Lalita to pour it for you,' when she remembered that she'd sacked Lalita. The doorbell rang while she was debating whether to get up and pour him the juice, or let him do it himself and risk the kitchen floor being flooded with Real Activ Orange Carrot. Then again, it was rich in antioxidants; it might actually do the floor some good.

'Open the door, will you, Suraj,' she called out, and heard his little feet patter across the hall obediently.

The door was heavy, and it took Suraj a few seconds to drag it open. He gave the dark, sari-clad woman standing outside a cheerful grin. Ranjana smiled down at him. 'Is your mother at home?' she asked.

'Yes, I am,' Shilpa said coming to stand behind Suraj. 'You're Ranjana aren't you? Come in.' Hoping she didn't sound too desperate, she explained the situation she was in—no cook, no nanny, just a cleaner who came in once a day and grudgingly pushed a mop around the house.

Ranjana had come a little further into the flat, and was looking around with frank awe on her face. 'So will you be able to take on the cooking?' Shilpa asked eagerly. 'Nikita told me you've got some free time.'

Ranjana pulled her gaze away from the elaborate chandelier and gave Shilpa an embarrassed look. 'I'll think about it and let you know,' she said. OK, so that was a bummer. If she was going to 'think', she probably wouldn't take the job.

'Is there a problem?' Shilpa asked. Ranjana shook her head.

'Then?'

Ranjana made an awkward wriggling gesture.

'You're probably used to very "hi-funda" cooking,' she said. 'I can only do basic stuff, dal—roti—subzi. I don't know how to do all that pasta and Chinese kind of stuff.'

'That doesn't matter, we eat simple. Dal roti is good.' Anuj would have had a hissy fit if he'd heard her, but then again he'd throw a much larger fit if he had to eat Dominos pizzas and Subway salads for the next three weeks or more.

'And I don't know how to use the kind of oven you have,' Ranjana said, clearly bent on making a clean breast of her shortcomings. Shilpa gave the state-of-the-art oven a look of unadulterated hatred. Her swish interior decorator had insisted on it, and so far, it had caused nothing but trouble. 'I'll show you how to operate the burners,' she told Ranjana. 'Don't bother about the rest.'

'OK,' Ranjana said. She'd started looking a lot more comfortable, and she positively beamed when Shilpa quoted a salary that was 30 per cent higher than what Nikita paid her. Shilpa knew what she was doing—quote too high and it was likely that Ranjana would smell a rat, too low and she might not join. Twelve years as a compensation and benefits expert had to come in handy sometime.

'And if you know a girl who can help look after my son, that would help too,' Shilpa said. 'I had to tell the ayah to leave, and I need someone urgently. I've been working from home the last few days, but I'll have to get back to work from Monday. Even someone temporary would do while I search for a new nanny.'

'If it's temporary, my daughter might be able to come around,' Ranjana said. 'She was doing her BCom, but she's taking a year off to help me out.' There wasn't enough money to pay Madhuri's fees for her last year of college, but Ranjana didn't want to say that.

Shilpa almost flung her arms around Ranjana in relief. 'That would be perfect,' she said.

After Ranjana had left, Shilpa did a solemn little jig in the middle of the living room. 'You're weird,' Suraj said, a bemused look on his serious little face. Shilpa stopped mid-pirouette to grab him and dance him around the room. 'You sound just like your Dad,' she said, hugging the little boy. 'Don't worry, I haven't lost my marbles, I'm just so happy this mess is getting sorted out.'

'There's a dead, dusty dragonfly in the kitchen,' Suraj said, politely freeing himself from her arms. 'Is it supposed to be there, or can we put it in the rubbish bin?'

3

It was the middle of summer, and the humidity had reached dizzying peaks. Nikita grimaced as she stepped out of her office. Brought up in the north, she could handle dust storms and the temperature touching 50 Celsius, but the sweltering heat of Mumbai was something else altogether.

'It's like a bloody Turkish bath outside,' she gasped when Jai brought the car out of the basement parking lot a minute later. 'What took you so long? I couldn't get through to your cell after I first called you.'

'Bad signal in the basement,' Jai said tersely. Nikita could be a complete spoilt brat at times. 'Where to?'

'Bandra-Kurla complex. Don't take the sea-link, someone told me the traffic's awful at Worli seaface.'

One of the other drivers had just told Jai that Tulsi Pipe Road was even worse, but Jai had learnt not to argue with Nikita. If they took a road she recommended and got stuck in a jam for an hour it was fine, but if he insisted on taking another road, she nagged and fretted if they were held up even for five minutes.

'My wrist's almost OK,' Nikita announced a few minutes later. Jai took his eyes of the road for an instant to glance at her.

'When do you want me to leave?' he asked.

'Oh, I don't know,' Nikita said. 'It's kind of nice being driven around, I don't have to struggle to find parking space and I can get work done on the way. But I still can't afford your salary on a regular basis. Do you think you'd be able to work for me part-time?'

'Drive you to office and walk back?' Jai asked. 'Or cycle down and pick you up after meetings?'

Nikita made a little moue of annoyance. 'We'd have to work out the details. Maybe you could work for me two days a week or something, the days I have meetings and need to drive all over town.'

Jai's mobile decided to interrupt the conversation at that point, belting out a heavy metal number at top volume without any warning whatsoever.

'Is it ringing, or is it about to grow legs and attack us?' Nikita asked, staring at the phone in horrified fascination.

'Ringing,' Jai said, a smile twitching at his lips. 'Sorry, some of my friends were fooling around yesterday—they must have changed the ring tone. Will you be a sweetheart and put it on speaker?'

Nikita shrugged and complied.

'Hi, this is Harsh Pradhan from Wayne Studios,' a male voice said. 'Could I speak to Ms Nikita Dewan please?'

Jai muttered a curse under his breath and grabbed the phone, taking it off the speaker. At the same time, he swung the wheel around to bring the car to a halt by the side of the road.

'I'm sorry, she isn't available right now,' he said, and Nikita gasped in astonishment. He leaned away from her, fending her off with one arm as she tried to take the phone from him. 'I can take a message if you like.'

'Her story's been shortlisted as one of the three finalists

of the 'Great Indian Love Story' contest,' Harsh Pradhan said briskly. 'Ask her to call me back.'

'I will,' Jai said, just before Pradhan cut the call. He took a deep breath and stared at the phone hardly registering Nikita's exasperated voice as she demanded to know what the call had been about.

'I need your help,' he said cutting her off neatly in mid-tirade.

Nikita gawked at him, and he explained about the Wayne Studios contest. And that he'd submitted an entry in Nikita's name.

'But why?' she asked in bewilderment. 'If you win, wouldn't this be a big break for you?'

'Not the kind of break I want,' Jai said. 'I want to be taken seriously as an author, and right now, all I want to focus on is the book I'm doing on my granddad.'

'Why enter the contest then?' Nikita asked reasonably, and Jai winced. 'There's a five-lakh prize,' he said. 'Given my money situation right now, winning the contest would just about save my life.'

Money considerations, Nikita could understand—and five lakhs seemed a big enough sum to let go of some of the scruples.

'What d'you want me to do for you?' she asked. 'Now that you've entered the story in my name.'

Jai restarted the car, carefully manoeuvring it back on to the road.

'You'll need to call this guy back for one,' he said. 'Find out what they're planning next. Pretend that you wrote the story, and play it by ear after that. If it wins the contest, we'll have some figuring out to do, if it doesn't, we won't need to worry.'

Nikita called Pradhan from her own mobile; there was a formal award ceremony planned that Friday which she was expected to attend. 'I'll be there,' she told him, hoping she sounded excited enough. 'And Harsh, perhaps you should call me at this number from now on. My old number is being used by a friend.'

'Yes, of course,' Harsh said. 'I'll email you details of the venue and dress code.'

'What email id have you given them?' she asked Jai, her eyebrows raised, and Jai finally had the grace to look a little embarrassed. 'I set up a Gmail one in your name,' he admitted. 'I'll give you the password.'

'We need to talk,' Nikita said drily as she got out of the car. 'This meeting will take a couple of hours, and I'm done for the day after that.'

'Message me ten minutes before you're ready to leave,' Jai said. 'I'll find a place to park, and a café to hang out in till you're done.'

'Why don't you wait in the car?' Nikita asked. 'It's a pain, having to message you at the fag end of every meeting.'

'Have you ever stepped outside during the day?' Jai asked patiently. 'It's almost 40 degrees in the shade. I can't keep the AC running, and if I spend two hours sitting inside the car without it, I'll smell like a BMC garbage heap by the time you're back.'

Nikita leaned in and sniffed the nape of his neck. 'You smell of pretty expensive cologne to me,' she said. 'Jai, you sure you're not doing some kind of undercover operation, right? How did you afford the cologne if you don't have money to eat?'

'My aunt gave it to me for my birthday,' Jai said, preparing to move off. 'Don't forget to message me.'

Aunt indeed. Not for the first time, Nikita wondered if Jai was seeing someone. A well-off someone probably—that would explain a lot of the things that puzzled her about Jai, like his well-worn but originally expensive jeans and his designer cologne. But then he did seem genuinely short of money... It was all very confusing.

⁓

Halfway across town, Shilpa was giving the young man in front of her a weary look. He was a competent HR professional, but his organizing skills when it came to planning the team's annual offsite convention were proving to be abysmally poor.

'Avinash, you need to mail out an itinerary to the team,' she said. 'You can't take a bunch of people into the middle of nowhere without giving them an idea of what to expect.'

'But the whole point is that it's to be a surprise!' Avinash said, his Adam's apple bobbing up and down vigorously. 'Giving them a taste of the unexpected—and the activities are out of this world. There's river-crossing, and we're doing white-water rafting, most people don't even know you can do that so near Mumbai. And...'

'Yes, I saw the list,' Shilpa said, interrupting him. 'Around half of them involve getting soaked from head to toe; you need to tell people so that they can pack the right gear. Half the team is female for one thing.'

'Why do the women always get special treatment?' Avinash muttered under his breath, and Shilpa saw red. Normally she would have been patient with him, but right now she was in no mood to put up with rubbish.

'There are reasons,' she said crisply. 'For one, men don't need to worry about needing to wear a padded bra and a dark

T-shirt if they're wading into a river. Or about getting wet when they have a period. Or about…'

'Yes, right, I get it,' Avinash said, backing out of her cabin hastily. 'I'll send out an email.'

'I hate my job,' Shilpa said loudly once Avinash had left. Her laptop pinged with yet another meeting reminder, and she clicked it off in exasperation. Suraj would be home from school by now, she thought, picking up the phone to call him.

'Madhuri, is Suraj home?' she asked when the new nanny picked up the phone. Ranjana's daughter had made herself indispensable in the few days she'd worked for Shilpa.

'He's gone across to Vivaan's flat to play,' Madhuri said in Hindi, her voice low and musical. 'Should I call him home?'

'No, don't,' Shilpa said, but she felt dreadfully disappointed all the same. Talking to Suraj on the phone was one of the high points of her day, but it seemed that Suraj was already outgrowing their daily ritual. Her mobile rang as she put the phone down.

'Hi Rakhi,' she said dispiritedly. Rakhi's daughter, Saira, and Suraj were in the same class at school, and cordially detested each other. Despite their frequently expressed views on the subject, they'd been forced to form a two-child car pool, with Shilpa and Rakhi's cars taking turns dropping and picking them up. Sometimes Shilpa wondered whether the good they were doing for the environment was worth running the risk of her son turning into a confirmed misogynist, but she hadn't yet dared to suggest doing away with the car pool.

'Hey Shilpa,' Rakhi said, dragging the words out for just a little bit longer than necessary. 'What's up? Are you at work?'

For a second, Shilpa was tempted to tell Rakhi that she'd stepped out of office for a minute to hire a gigolo for the evening, but she bit the words back. Rakhi's sense of humour was rather conventional, and the car pool was important.

'Yes, I'm at work,' she said, her voice artificially bright. 'What's happening with you?'

'Listen, this class picnic that we're planning, the teacher just told me that you've volunteered as well.'

'I believe I have,' Shilpa said. She'd gone to school to pick up Suraj, and bumped into his class teacher, who had efficiently conned her into volunteering. And her working-mother guilt syndrome hadn't let her wriggle out of it subsequently.

'Well, so we need to meet, don't we? To plan for it? I thought we could do a lunch with the other two mothers who're in this with us.'

'The picnic's in September,' Shilpa said in disbelief. It was three bloody months off, for God's sake. Rakhi didn't have a job or not a real one at any rate—she claimed to be a dress designer, but so far all that Shilpa had seen her designing was the Humpty Dumpty costume for her daughter's school play.

'Well, there's hardly any time left then, is there,' Rakhi said reprovingly. 'We need to make bookings and hire a bus… And we'll have to organize the menu depending on the location, like if it's a beach, we should have light snacks that we can carry easily, but if it's a farmhouse or something like that…'

'Um, I have a meeting to get to in ten minutes,' Shilpa said as her laptop pinged again. 'I'll call you when I'm on my way home, OK?'

'Yes, of course,' Rakhi said, immediately contrite. 'You must be busy. So anyway, I'll do the initial research, and we can meet after that. Oh, and I forgot to tell you, the Sports Day photographs were up on the bulletin board in school, so I've ordered the ones with Suraj in them for you.'

'Thanks a million,' Shilpa said in relief. She'd been wondering when she'd find the time to get to the school and pick out the photos of Suraj narrowly missing a bronze in the egg-and-spoon race. Immediately she felt dreadfully guilty about her uncharitable thoughts about Rakhi earlier.

'So I'll call you on my way home then. And let's meet up at my place this weekend, shall we? With families.' She put the phone down wishing she hadn't issued the invitation. There were a dozen chores she needed to get through, Madhuri was taking the weekend off, and—most importantly—she didn't really like Rakhi.

'I'm growing into a misanthrope,' she announced when Nikita called two minutes later. 'I've called some neighbours over for lunch on Sunday, and I wish I hadn't.'

There was a little pause, and Nikita said firmly, 'Un-invite them.'

'I can't.'

'Tell them you had another engagement you forgot about. With the TV, watching James Bond re-runs.'

'Can't,' Shilpa said, though a little hint of wistfulness had crept into her voice.

'Well OK, then don't crib about it,' Nikita said with characteristic brutality. To everyone's surprise, including their own, Nikita and Shilpa had managed to become fairly good friends over the last two months. There was something about Nikita's unashamedly single-minded devotion to her own interests that appealed to Shilpa. As for Nikita, she'd started out being grateful to her cousin's wife for helping her after the accident, but she'd found herself liking Shilpa more and more as she got to know her better.

'You're like an onion,' she told Shilpa abruptly.

Shilpa frowned. 'I smell?'

'No, idiot, I mean you have layers,' Nikita gestured madly before realizing that Shilpa couldn't see her. 'I mean when I first met you I thought you were a a typical conventional 'good girl', very insipid. Then I figured you're pretty quirky inside though you try to hide it. And it's cute the way you tie yourself into knots trying to keep everyone happy. Like these ghastly people you've invited. I *know* you'll spend half a day slaving over your space-age oven cooking for them, and you'll be wiped out by the end of the day, and you'll fall asleep at 8 o'clock, and poor Anuj will be left wishing he hadn't spurned the maid, at least he'd have got some action...'

'Yes, OK, OK,' Shilpa said hastily, before Nikita could launch into one of her theories about Shilpa's sex life. 'Did you want something in particular, or were you just calling to insult me in general?'

'Ooh, you'll never guess what happened,' Nikita said, suddenly remembering why she'd called. She got herself a little mixed up explaining the Wayne Studios contest, and why Jai didn't want to go, but Shilpa finally got the gist of what she was saying.

'They're holding an event to announce the winners next Friday,' Nikita said. 'Need some advice on what to wear.' Nikita had conventional tastes as far as office-wear went, but her party clothes ranged from slightly over-the-top to frankly bizarre.

They spent ten minutes discussing the relative merits of saris and dresses, before Shilpa exclaimed in horror, 'I'm supposed to be on a call with our Singapore office. Nikita, you wretch, you made me forget about it completely—I'll ring off now. Give Jai my love, and I hope he wins.'

Nikita grinned as she put the phone down. The whole 'Great Indian Love Story' thing had appealed to her sense of humour, and at the very least she'd get a free dinner out of it, and meet a couple of Bollywood stars.

'I told Shilpa about the contest,' Nikita said to Jai when he came across to give her a copy of the story. She'd flatly refused to read it on the computer, and he'd had to put it on a USB drive and get it printed out at the corner Xerox shop.

'I don't think it'll win,' Jai warned. 'It's not a typical Bollywood plot.'

'That's OK, I told her you wrote the story,' Nikita said, and burst out laughing at the look of horror on Jai's face. 'Chill, she's family. Anyone who knows me won't believe I wrote it anyway. The longest thing I've ever written was an essay on cows when I was in middle school. And I copied most of that from the guy sitting next to me.'

4

Even Nikita was impressed by the scale of the Wayne Studios event. It was held at the Westin Hotel in Goregaon, and Harsh had told her that the guest list had over 200 invitees. And not just any invitees, some pretty well-known directors and producers were going to be there. Wayne Studios had announced that the lead pair in the movie would be unknowns, chosen to fit the winning story, but the director and scriptwriter were going to be big names. It was a deft move, and according to a few blogs Nikita had read on the subject, the movie industry was abuzz with the 'Holywoodization' of Bollywood. The Wayne name and the unusual way of selecting a story and cast made for excellent PR. Also, it saved Wayne Studios from having to pay astronomical amounts for temperamental superstars who could potentially derail their carefully planned launch. Unfortunately, this also meant that there weren't as many stars at the event as there could have been, and Nikita was having a good moan about it as they left for Goregaon.

Jai, who'd listened to this a dozen times already, said patiently, 'But you wouldn't have got to meet them anyway. They're always surrounded by PR people and bodyguards.'

Acknowledging the truth of this, Nikita moved on to her next grouse. She'd been to the Westin once before, and though she'd loved it, she thought that it could do with being uprooted and set up a lot closer to town. Within walking distance of Prabhadevi, preferably. Failing which, in her opinion, Wayne Studios could have held the event somewhere in Parel or even in Nariman Point.

'Why Goregaon?' she demanded for about the fifteenth time as they drove over the Bandra-Worli sea-link. 'They might as well have held it in Ahmedabad—at least we could have flown there.'

'It's in Goregaon because the entire film industry except for Lata Mangeshkar lives on that side of the town,' Jai retorted. 'Stop cribbing, it's a pretty good hotel, and the food's good.'

'There has to be someone other than Lataji who lives in town,' Nikita said, frowning as Jai took a turn onto the Western Express Highway. 'What about Shammi Kapoor?'

'Died last year,' Jai said.

'Rajesh Khanna?'

'Ditto.'

'Salman Khan,' Nikita said triumphantly.

'Lives in Bandra—that counts as a suburb.'

'For someone who doesn't want to be associated with films, you know an awful lot,' Nikita grumbled. 'Wait, I've got it—Deepika Padukone doesn't live in the suburbs, she lives near our place in one of those swanky new buildings.'

'OK, I'll give you Deepika Padukone,' Jai conceded. 'But everyone else lives in the suburbs.'

Nikita shot him a quick glance. He was wearing a dark suit that looked expensive; she'd tried to look at the label, but he'd dodged away. There was some mystery here, and the more he avoided her questions, the more curious she became.

'Do you watch films a lot?' she asked, and he shook his head. 'Can't afford to. I read the newspaper supplements you leave behind in the car, and I get a fair idea of what's happening in Bollywood.'

'It's odd, not being hooked on to movies,' she said. 'Do your folks watch them?'

Jai shrugged. 'My mom only watches movies starring Amitabh Bachchan. Dad's less picky, but he doesn't like new movies much either.'

Unable to resist the opening, Nikita asked, 'What does your dad do?'

'Has a couple of jewellery shops,' Jai said laconically, and Nikita got the impression he wasn't fooled by her 'innocent' line of questioning. 'What about yours?'

'Died when I was fifteen,' Nikita said. Then to avoid the usual expressions of sympathy she received when she told people, she went on. 'He was a bank clerk, nothing very swanky. Both he and my mom were nuts about Bollywood though.'

'And you as well?' Jai asked. 'I mean, do you like films?'

'Love them,' Nikita said firmly, and for a second, Jai contemplated asking her out for a movie. Better sense prevailed, and he didn't say anything for a while.

They were a little early for the event. The doors to the main ball room were shut, and Nikita had a momentary panic attack when she saw the number of expensively dressed people standing around the bar in the waiting area.

'Looks like a holding pen for cattle,' Jai muttered. 'Keep 'em drunk, keep 'em happy.' Nikita shot him a quick look. She'd been a bit wary about Jai accompanying her, though she could hardly have refused. Partly this was due to a fear that if the story actually won, he would be unable to restrain himself. She had nightmare visions of Jai leaping on to the stage and grabbing an Oscar-ish statuette from her hands and hissing 'That's mine!'

But she'd also been worried about his looking out of place. In spite of his undeniable good looks, Jai had a raffish, devil-may-care air about him, and she'd never seen him wearing anything other than ancient jeans and black rock-band T-shirts. She'd been deeply relieved to find that he actually possessed a suit—and looked good in it. She self-consciously pulled the hem of her black dress down a little. Shilpa had helped her select the dress, but at the last moment, Nikita had changed her black pumps for a pair of blood-red patent-leather heels, and now she wasn't sure that the switch had been a good idea.

'Do the shoes look sluttish?' she muttered to Jai, and he gave them an appraising look. 'Frankly, yes,' he said, and Nikita longed to hit him. 'I saw the same...' she started to say, and Jai threw up his hands. 'Look, you asked me, I told you,' he said. 'Don't ask if you don't want to know.'

Nikita was still composing a suitably cutting response when a slim, slightly effeminate man came across and said, 'Nikita? I'm Harsh Pradhan, the India marketing director for Wayne Studios.'

'So glad to meet you,' Nikita said, shaking his damp hand, and wondering if he was gay. He was definitely looking at Jai more interestedly than he was at her, and she smoothly stepped sideways, excluding Jai from the conversation and ensuring that she had all of Harsh's attention.

'I didn't expect this to be quite so grand,' she said, gesturing around her.

'It's actually pretty low-key,' Harsh said. 'We'll be following this up with auditions for the lead pair, and that will be big. Come on, let me introduce you to Gareth and

Naveen. Gareth's come down from the US to set up Wayne's India operations, and Naveen owns the PR company that's handling the launch.'

Gareth was red-faced, overweight and balding. Naveen Kabra, on the other hand, looked interesting. He had a thin, intelligent face, close-cropped hair and a lopsided, slightly cynical smile. He wasn't very tall, but given that his income probably ran into several crores a year, Nikita felt that the lack of height was something she could overlook, along with the receding hairline. Careful not to offend Gareth, she made sure that Naveen received the full blast of her charm.

Abandoned among the canapés, Jai looked on as Nikita flirted and laughed. 'Getting on well, aren't they?' asked a voice behind him, and he turned around to look into the unnaturally blue eyes of a curvy girl standing right next to him.

'They're contacts,' she said impatiently as he continued to stare into her eyes. Jai recovered his composure. 'Why d'you wear them?' he retorted. 'They're hideous.'

The girl grinned, and putting up a hand swiftly took the lenses out. 'There,' she said, holding her palm out to Jai and beaming up at him. 'Does that meet with your approval?'

Jai leaned closer to look at the two little blue discs in her palm, and caught a whiff of her perfume; after an hour in a car reeking of Nikita's industrial strength application of Miss Dior, the light, citrusy smell was simultaneously refreshing and tantalizing.

'Friend or girlfriend?' the girl asked nodding towards Nikita.

'Oh neither,' Jai said. 'I'm her driver.'

The girl laughed, and Jai smiled down at her. 'I'm serious,' he said.

She put her head to one side. 'Really?' she asked, and he took out his wallet and showed her the ID card that Nikita's office had given him. It said Employee's Personal Driver in a large, ugly font, and it had his picture on it as well. The girl scrutinized it carefully and handed it back.

'Wow,' she said. 'Either you take your practical jokes seriously or you're really her driver. I'm Saloni by the way.'

'I'm Jai,' he replied, wondering why she wasn't backing away from him now that she knew he wasn't part of the glitzy movie industry world. 'Umm, do you work with Wayne Studios?'

She shook her head vigorously. 'Hoping to,' she said. 'I'm a dentist…no, seriously, I really am,' she said as Jai raised his eyebrows. 'And I've done some part-time modelling. I met Naveen at an event a couple of months back, and he called me last week saying that I'd be perfect for the role of the heroine's elder sister, she's supposed to be tall and curvy and a cardiac surgeon…' she broke off as she saw the expression on Jai's face.

'What did I…oh my God,' her hand flew up to her mouth. 'The winning story hasn't been announced yet, has it? I never realized… Naveen didn't tell me it was confidential, but unless all three stories have curvy cardiac surgeons in them…'

'I doubt it,' Jai said, involuntarily breaking into a smile. *His* story did, though, and the sense of relief was amazing. Five lakhs… That would see him through the three months he needed to complete his book and he'd have money to spare.

'Don't tell me, the toothpick in the red shoes is one of the authors,' Saloni was saying, gesturing towards Nikita. Her face was a comical 'O' of horror. 'Is it her story that's won?'

'I haven't read her story,' Jai said. It was technically correct, he hadn't read anything Nikita had written other than the signature on his pay cheque. Toothpick. Nikita *was* whip-thin of course, but till now it hadn't struck him as an unattractive feature, he'd always liked slim women. Saloni's lush curves were an exciting contrast.

'Well, you're not going to tell her anything,' Saloni said firmly, grabbing Jai's arm and steering him towards the bar. 'Actually you're not telling anyone anything until the winner is announced. I'm officially kidnapping you.'

When the doors to the banquet hall opened, Nikita looked around for Jai, but he'd vanished. A little piqued, she followed Naveen on to the elaborate stage. The other two contestants were seated already—one man and one woman. The man was so stereotypically the long-haired, unshaven khadi-wearing and jhola-carrying writer type that he looked like a caricature. The woman was in her forties, plump and motherly, and seemed to be enjoying herself thoroughly.

'I've already got three movie offers because I was shortlisted for this,' she whispered to Nikita after they were introduced. 'I don't have a hope in hell of winning, but this is excellent fun.'

'What do you do?' Nikita asked, expecting her to say housewife or school-teacher. 'I'm a microbiologist,' the lady said, and Nikita felt her jaw drop. 'I know,' the woman said ruefully. 'I look like Lalita Pawar, only less glamorous.'

She clapped enthusiastically when Nikita won—even the *jhola-dhaari* man congratulated her warmly. 'These people are so nice,' she said wonderingly to Naveen later on. 'I can't imagine anyone in the corporate world being so sporting.' Naveen laughed. 'They're amateurs,' he said lightly. 'The film world is a dozen times more cut-throat than anything you've seen before.'

'I'm counting on you to help me manage,' she said, turning her best little-girl-lost-in-the-woods gaze on him. 'Of course,' he said, but there was a slightly cynical note in his voice as he picked up her hand to kiss it lightly. 'Congratulations once again, and I'll see you around. Here's Harsh, I guess he wants to discuss some hideously practical stuff like your contract.'

Escaping from Harsh a good twenty minutes later, Nikita spotted Jai standing with a remarkably pretty girl at one end of the hall. He raised his glass in a salute when she caught his eyes. 'Strictly non-alcoholic,' he said, his eyes dancing as she came within earshot. 'I need to be sober for the drive back.'

'Well I don't,' the girl stated firmly as she swigged back a Bacardi Breezer—not the first one either from the looks of her. 'Where do you guys live?'

'Prabhadevi,' Nikita replied, and the girl grimaced. 'Completely opposite direction,' she said. 'I'm in Borivali. Pity, I could have bummed a ride back.'

'I'll drop you,' Naveen said, materializing by their side and twitching the bottle out of her hands. 'That's enough Saloni, I can't have you throwing up all over my car.'

'It's the opposite direction from where you live as well,' Saloni informed him, though she let herself be dragged off. 'Unless you're planning to go home via Nasik. See you Jai,' she turned back and gave him a rather tipsy wave. 'Was fun kidnapping you.'

Jai waved back, and asked Nikita 'Should we leave as well?'

'Sure,' she said, a strong hint of acid in her tone. 'It's your party.' She was greatly tempted to ask who the girl was, but she bit the question back. Wouldn't do, being too curious.

'I have good news and bad news,' she announced once they got into the car. 'Which do you want to hear first?'

'Bad first,' Jai said.

'So, it'll take them two months at least to give us the money. They need to get a contract drawn up, agreed with their US office, and so on—it's an awfully long process. And if I'm claiming it for you, well I'm in a pretty high tax bracket—you'll end up getting a lot less than five lakhs.'

Jai stayed silent for almost a minute. He'd assumed hazily that the money would come to them in a couple of days, a week at the most. 'Can't you ask them to hurry things up a bit?' he asked, his voice sounding desperate even to himself.

'I'll do my best,' Nikita promised. 'But Jai, the tax angle is important, too, isn't it? I was thinking maybe we should go and speak to Naveen and tell him that the money needs to come to you.'

Jai shook his head. 'It'll only make matters worse,' he said. And in any case, he was in a pretty high tax bracket himself. He wasn't claiming his share of the income from the family business, but he knew his sister was filing his tax returns for him. 'What's the good news then?' he asked, trying to sound unaffected by the bad.

'They really, really like the story. And they want you... I mean me, I guess...to collaborate with them on the script as well and there's more money in that, perhaps even a share of the film's profits.'

'Say no to that part of it,' Jai said abruptly, and Nikita turned to stare at him. 'We won't be able to keep the charade up,' he explained. 'And I'm quite happy with the five lakhs or OK, with whatever per cent of the five lakhs I end up with.'

They drove in silence for a while, and then Nikita piped up, 'Where were you when the awards were being announced? I couldn't spot you anywhere.'

'I was at the back of the hall with Saloni,' Jai said. 'She made a bit of a blooper—let out the name of the winner by mistake, and she wanted to be sure I didn't say anything.'

Nikita looked thoughtful, and for a second Jai wondered if she was jealous. When she spoke, however, the thought was instantly dispelled.

'Naveen seemed to know her pretty well,' she said, 'though he didn't talk to her during the party at all.'

'She said they met socially,' Jai said. 'Are you lining Naveen up as a prospect as well? He seemed loaded.' The second the words were out of his mouth, he wished them unsaid; Nikita wasn't answerable to him, and his voice had sounded judgemental even to his own ears. Thankfully, Nikita was either too drunk or too thick-skinned to notice.

'Maybe,' she said, and stretched dreamily. Naveen had seemed the answer to her prayers—rich, almost-handsome and with just enough of a *haraami* attitude to make him interesting. She gave Jai a disparaging look—in spite of his striking looks, he had turned out to be a bit of a disappointment. Too intense, too serious and no money at all. Still, other women appeared to find him attractive.

'Did you take Saloni's number?' she asked, prodding Jai in the arm. 'She took quite a liking to you, you're probably just the thing to distract her from Naveen.'

'Bait, that's all I'm good for,' Jai muttered, but he laughed when Nikita put an arm around him and squeezed, luckily he had stopped at a signal, and they didn't crash into the divider. Nikita was unashamed of the way she was—'I am *toh* like this only' seemed to be her guiding principle in life. Well, at least she was honest, Jai thought wryly, watching her as she trawled through radio stations till she found one playing 'Sheela ki jawaani'. Saloni's infectious giggle was already fading from his memory, and the fading scent of Miss Dior mixed with cigarette smoke didn't seem that repelling after all.

The signal changed, and Jai put the car into gear. 'I'm not playing the gigolo for you,' he said. 'If you want to get Naveen, you'll have to do it without my help.'

'I'll have a shot, but he's probably way out of my league anyway,' Nikita yawned and kicked off the red shoes, pulling her legs up to sit cross-legged on the passenger seat. 'Dammit, when am I going to meet the perfect guy?'

'You remind me of my cousin,' Jai said after a pause. 'She was describing the ideal man to her mom—tall, handsome, good sense of humour, rich, caring, blah blah.'

'So?' Nikita asked.

'So, my aunt's from Lucknow, right, very polite, all *ji* and *aap*, even with her own kids. She hears her daughter out, and then she says, "*Bete, maan lijiye duniya mein koi aisa aadmi ho ya itifaaq se aapki us se mulaqat ho bhi jaaye...*"'

'And?' Nikita asked suspiciously, not liking the way the story was going.

'And then my aunt hesitates, and asks—still very, very politely—"*Bete, bhala woh aap se shaadi kyon karega?*"'

Nikita punched him in the arm hard and Jai said 'Owww, sorry, it just popped into my mind.'

'Next time something like that pops into your mind, you'd better un-pop it pretty quick unless you want your pretty face rearranged for you,' Nikita said, but she was smiling. '*Chal*, let's stop at Dadar station and have some *anda-bhurji* before we go home—that fancy food didn't really fill me up, I'm starving.'

5

'There's a puja for the new office this weekend,' Anuj said. 'Most wives are attending, so it might be a good idea for you and Suraj to come along.'

'I was planning to meet the party organizers to finalize details for Suraj's birthday party,' Shilpa said absently, then 'Hang on, you didn't tell me you were moving into a new office. Where is it?'

'BKC,' Anuj said. 'We can't afford the rent for the Worli office apparently, and the retail bank's expanded big-time. Some of the new guys are hot-desking because we don't have enough space. Bloody idiots, they lose money for the bank as fast as we make it. We tried to work an arrangement out for the corporate and investment bank to stay in Worli, and move only retail, but that got shot down by the Singapore office. Apparently…'

Shilpa cut in, in any case she hadn't heard anything beyond the first few words. 'Bandra-Kurla?' she said in dismay. 'How're we going to manage Suraj's carpool then?' Their current arrangement was for Anuj's car and driver to drop him at work, come back and pick up Suraj and Saira and take them to school. Suraj's swanky South Mumbai school had been promising for more than a year to extend their bus route to include Prabhadevi, but it hadn't happened yet.

Shilpa herself usually took a cab to work. The Bandra-Kurla complex hosted some of the swankiest office buildings in the city, and for Anuj, the shift probably meant a better workplace. Unfortunately, it was also in completely the opposite direction to south Mumbai, and too far away for the car to be back in time to pick Suraj up.

'I thought the bus thing was about to get sorted out,' Anuj said. 'At least that's what you and Rakhi were discussing the last time we met.' He wandered to the dining table where Madhuri had laid out dinner and started lifting the covers to inspect the dishes.

'Madhuri!' he said, and the girl appeared in a hurry from the kitchen, wiping her hands on her kameez. '*Haan*, bhaiyya?' she said.

'I've told your mother not to cook baingan—I'm allergic to it,' he said. 'Will you remind her when she's here tomorrow?'

'Bhabhi likes it,' the girl said. 'And mummy's made two other subzis—see, there's gobi and the other dish has beans.'

'Right,' Anuj said, giving Madhuri a quick smile. It was the same smile that had made her predecessor go weak at the knees, but Madhuri's knees were made of sterner stuff. 'I don't much like either, but at least they're edible.'

'Bhabhi likes…' the girl began, but Shilpa gave her a quick nod of dismissal. Anuj had been travelling when Ranjana and Madhuri had started working for her, and they now both displayed a single-minded allegiance to her that was embarrassing at times. Though at present, Shilpa was feeling almost as irritated with Anuj for fussing about his food as she was about his not telling her that his office was shifting.

'The bus route won't change till the next session,' she said. 'That's another seven months away. What am I supposed to do till then?'

'Maybe Rakhi can...' Anuj began, but Shilpa had had enough. 'No, maybe *you* can do something,' she said fiercely. 'Considering you do absolutely nothing around the house, or for Suraj, and considering you're responsible for this mess in the first place!'

'I'll get a second car, and a driver,' Anuj said soothingly.

'How?' she demanded. 'Take another loan for the car? We're up to our ears in debt already! We haven't been able to have a second child because I can't take a break from my career, I hardly get any time to spend with Suraj—all because you had to satisfy your ego by buying this huge, big, bloody, I don't know... *phallic symbol* of a house!'

Anuj suppressed a sigh. Nowadays conversations always seemed to come back to the topic of babies. Shilpa's biological clock was ticking so loudly you could set your watch by it. And if she had another child, she wanted to take a couple of years off work. And she was on edge all the time, a washed out version of her former ebullient self.

'We took the decision to buy the house together,' he said wearily. 'No one expected the recession to hit—it seemed to make sense to stretch a little and buy the best house we could afford.'

'Well the point I'm making is that we *can't* afford it,' Shilpa said. 'Forget it, I'll figure out what needs to be done.'

Anuj nodded. That was typical as well. With the amount of travelling he had to do, it was a wonder he was able to find his way back to his own home, let alone do anything to help run it. But whenever he did volunteer to help, Shilpa shot his suggestions down with the precision of an encounter specialist. Absent-mindedly, he helped himself to a generous heap of baingan. It took a few mouthfuls before the gloopy texture permeated into his consciousness, and he grimaced.

'I thought you were allergic to baingan,' Suraj said. He'd walked into the room halfway through the conversation, and had been listening interestedly. 'What'll happen to you now? Will your face swell up and become patchy?' Suraj was an avid watcher of Discovery Channel. He probably knew more about allergies than the average GP.

'I'm not allergic that way,' Anuj muttered. Honestly, kids nowadays were utter ghouls. Whatever happened to being respectful and sympathetic towards your parents?

'Your dad means he doesn't like the taste,' Shilpa said drily. 'And, no, before you ask, you aren't allergic to anything, so you need to eat whatever's on the table.'

'The tablemats too?' Suraj asked, and Anuj looked up to catch Shilpa's eyes. Both of them burst into reluctant laughter, and Anuj said, 'Just the food, Suraj.'

Shilpa sat down to eat as well. Truce had been declared for now, but she knew they would return to the discussion some other time. She glanced at Anuj, the years had been kind to him, and he still looked as good as he had the day she first met him. On their first date he'd told her that she looked like Julia Roberts, and she'd been flattered. She'd thought he looked like a young Shashi Kapoor, but she'd kept the thought to herself, not wanting to sound over-eager. When she told him later, he'd given her a lazy grin and slipped an arm around her as he murmured, 'What a copycat compliment that is. And why Shashi Kapoor? Why not Pierce Brosnan or Tom Cruise, or…'

'Or Anthony Hopkins,' she said and he'd begun to laugh. He'd proposed to her the same day, and within a few months they'd been married.

Shilpa smiled grimly at the memory. They'd been head over ears in love in those days, hardly able to keep their hands off each other. Who would have known that in just ten years they'd be squabbling over baingan and home loan EMIs. There was a mirror on the wall behind Anuj, and she gave herself a quick look. She hadn't let herself go, not really—she exercised regularly, and she was only a couple of kilos heavier than when they first met. A couple of weeks away from work would probably banish the dark circles under her eyes, and brighten her perennially washed-out complexion. Some make-up would help, too, if she had the time to apply it. It was her eyes that had changed the most, she realized. At twenty-two, they had sparkled with life, now they looked as tired and faded as the eyes of a sixty-year-old woman.

Anuj had picked up a magazine and was idly leafing through it. 'Who's the guy in the hood?' Suraj asked interestedly, leaning across to peer at it.

'Some actor—looks like Darth Vader, doesn't he?' Anuj said exactly at the same instant his son said 'Looks like a Dementor.'

He gave a wry grin, and Shilpa laughed, saying, 'Generation gap.'

'I love you,' Anuj said softly when Suraj went to the kitchen to raid the fridge for dessert. Shilpa looked up, her eyes momentarily swimming with tears. 'I love you too,' she said softly, as he gripped her hand over the table.

'Fererro Rocher or rasgullas?' Suraj demanded, coming back into the room, and they dropped each other's hands quickly. A full-fledged reconciliation would have to wait for bedtime, that is, if neither of them fell asleep out of sheer exhaustion first. Nikita hadn't been far off when she said that they looked as if their sex life was nonexistent. Well, not nonexistent exactly, the few embers left did a good job of flaring up when the time was right. It was just that, lately, the time hadn't been right very often.

～

'What if I pay Jai's full salary?' Shilpa asked. 'In return for using your car to drop the kids to school every morning. Does that work for you?'

Nikita thought it over.

'Yes, it does,' she said finally. 'But I don't know how Jai's going to feel about it.' The solution had occurred to Shilpa after Anuj had fallen asleep the night before—for once the time *had* been right, and they'd done a good job of making up. There was Nikita with a car she didn't use much, and a driver she couldn't afford—it was an opportunity not to be missed. All that was left was to broach the topic with Jai.

Jai thought it was an excellent idea, probably the best he'd ever heard. He had exactly 2,382 rupees left, and the prospect of having to stop writing and find a proper job was looming threateningly over his head. He, however, knew Nikita too well, to let his relief show.

'What d'you think I am, a bloody code-share flight?' he demanded. 'How's this ever going to work? What if both of you need to be driven somewhere at the same time? And how am I going to get any time to write?'

'It's just an hour in the morning,' Shilpa said hastily. 'You take the kids to school, come back and then you drive Nikita to office. My friend picks the children up in the afternoons.' Hooray for the car pool. Shilpa still hadn't gotten around to discussing the class picnic arrangements with Rakhi, but she felt more positively disposed towards her than she had in months.

The positive feeling vanished pretty quickly though, after she spoke to Rakhi. For some reason, Rakhi was disposed to be very pernickety about the whole thing.

'I don't knooww...' she said, stretching the words out slowly in the irritating way she had. 'A young guy, and you say he's a writer... He just sounds a little unreliable to me.'

'He'll only be driving the car,' Shilpa said tightly. 'Madhuri will be taking care of the children, the way she does now.'

She wished she hadn't said anything about Jai—all Rakhi really needed to know was that they had a new driver, but Shilpa had been worried about how Rakhi would treat Jai; she was the kind of woman who could be horribly condescending with the help. Madhuri detested her, and Shilpa could understand why.

'Maybe I could speak to Anuj's cousin,' Rakhi said finally. 'She's employed this Jai, hasn't she?'

Shilpa didn't see how she could refuse, but her gut told her that introducing Nikita to Rakhi was a very, very bad idea. The reality was even worse than her expectations. Nikita bristled like an angry cat at the thought of being 'interviewed' by a perfect stranger, and Shilpa had to almost physically drag her to Carlton Towers to meet Rakhi.

'Nikita should I drop you?' Jai asked when Nikita told him grumpily that she needed to go to Carlton Towers in the evening after work. Nikita shook her head. 'I'll walk,' she said. There was something about Shilpa's apartment complex that she found intimidating, and having Jai with her would only make it worse. Logically, she knew that Anuj and Shilpa were a lot older than her and, therefore, could afford a better flat—in practice though, it seemed a replay of her growing up years, watching her mother scrimp and save while her cousins across the road had a much more comfortable life.

Carlton Towers was an imposing structure—forty-five storeys high, it dwarfed the buildings around it. The three buildings were connected by walkways at every tenth floor, and there were impressive vertical gardens on the walls next to each (walkway, each of them around three floors high. Vertical gardens were the latest thing in space-starved Mumbai, but only the swankiest buildings could afford them, Carlton Towers had them in addition to three artificial lawns on the first floor and a kid's play area. 'Show-offs,' Nikita muttered under her breath as she looked at the swathes of green going up the walls.

'Yes madam?' The security guard at the main gate was looking at her suspiciously—perhaps he'd had bad experiences with skinny women who walked around mumbling to themselves.

'Tower A, 1601,' Nikita said. 'Shilpa and Anuj Malhotra.'

'Purpose of visit?' the guard asked, still looking suspicious.

'Arson and grievous bodily harm,' Nikita said, carefully writing it down in the register he thrust at her. 'Anuj is my cousin.' She gave the man a brilliant smile and sauntered past him, feeling only slightly guilty about poking fun at him.

'Some security your building has,' she told Shilpa. 'All show and no go. Where do we need to meet the Grand Inquisitor?'

'Rakhi's pretty OK actually,' Shilpa said soothingly as they walked across the lawn on the first floor. 'And her husband's a sweetheart—he works in the same bank as Anuj, but he's in the retail division, and we got to know them only when they rented a flat here.'

'Bet I'll hate him,' was Nikita's succinct reply, and Shilpa smiled. 'No one hates Sandeep,' she said. 'Look there he is, the thin chap walking out of the club- house.'

'Looks like a weed,' Nikita muttered, but she smiled nicely enough when Shilpa introduced them. Sandeep was in his late thirties, around the same age as Anuj, but while Anuj was the embodiment of an aggressive and very successful corporate banker, Sandeep was mild-looking and could have passed off as a college professor. Calling him a weed was a typical Nikita-ish piece of exaggeration, in his quiet way, Sandeep was actually not bad-looking.

'Where's Rakhi?' Shilpa asked, and Sandeep gestured towards the clubhouse. 'Waiting for you in the restaurant,' he said. 'I have a two-hour meeting, so I need to go into work—it's going to be a nightmare when the office moves to BKC. Oh, and this whole driver thing, as far as I'm concerned, it's OK—I trust your judgement. It's just that Rakhi gets a little concerned about such things because we have a daughter...' his voice trailed off, and Shilpa nodded understandingly. Sandeep was the gold standard as far as henpecked husbands went—to imagine him standing up to Rakhi was like imagining Manmohan Singh outshouting Mamata Banerjee.

'Why doesn't she drop the kid to school herself, then?' Nikita asked when Sandeep was out of earshot. 'If she's so concerned and all.'

'No clue,' Shilpa said briefly as she opened the door to the clubhouse. Rakhi was sitting alone at one end of the restaurant, she waved when she caught sight of them.

'This is Nikita,' Shilpa said, as Rakhi stood up and gave her a very mwah-mwah kind of air-kiss. Her perfume was light and flowery, and she was wearing a very impractical looking pair of white Capri trousers with a long chiffon top and blingy flip-flops. Very much the woman of leisure, Shilpa thought, biting back a smile as she compared her with Nikita.

'Hi Nikita,' Rakhi said, smiling stiffly as she took in

Nikita's sharp features and rather edgy style of dressing. Nikita had been in a rebellious mood when she woke up, and after a day spent crammed into a business suit, her rebellion had found expression in a pair of ripped jeans with a biker-chick T-shirt. Rakhi's smile faded away as Nikita gave her a far more obvious once-over and took an immediate and very evident dislike to her.

'Umm, Rakhi,' she said musingly. 'I've always wondered why someone would call their daughter that. Did you already have a brother, or were your parents hoping for a son, and you turned up instead?'

Rakhi flushed. 'I have a younger brother,' she said, and pointedly changed the subject. 'I actually had a few questions to ask about this Jai person,' she said. 'Shilpa's all praises for him, but she says she doesn't really know him well—he's a friend of yours apparently?'

Her tone was a veiled insult, but Nikita was the wrong person to say it to.

'I don't see why I should answer questions about Jai,' she said bluntly. 'You're not employing him, Shilpa is.'

'I'll be sending my daughter to school with him every day,' Rakhi said. 'I think I'm entitled to ask a few questions.'

Nikita turned to Shilpa. 'Did she ask for character references for your current driver?' she asked, and Shilpa frowned at her. 'Nikita...' she said warningly, but Rakhi had had enough. 'I'll see you around, Shilpa,' she said as she got to her feet. 'Perhaps Sandeep's right, I should just trust your instincts on this one, though I must say, I'm still not comfortable with the arrangement.'

'Nikita, you can't say stuff like that,' Shilpa said once Rakhi was safely out of the clubhouse. 'She was offended.' Nikita shrugged. 'Didn't like her.'

Shilpa groaned. 'Nikita, you don't need to like her for heaven's sake! You'll probably never even meet her again.'

'She's awful,' Nikita said. 'And Sandeep is a wimp. Give me a hundred bucks, and I'll start a fund to buy him a 'Born to be Bullied' T-shirt.'

'She's a bit overbearing with him,' Shilpa admitted. 'But OK otherwise.'

'That's like saying Phoolan Devi was a bit aggressive,' Nikita muttered, but she didn't push the topic, and Jai started on the new job the next Monday.

'There's no parking outside the school, and the traffic's usually crazy in the morning,' Shilpa said as she bundled the kids in. 'You'll have to take a left off Peddar Road into the school lane, and just stop for a minute so that Madhuri can get the kids out. Suraj, no bothering Jai Uncle, okay?'

'They can call me Jai,' he said, grimacing a little at the 'uncle'.

'Yes, OK, as long as *you* don't start calling me aunty,' Shilpa said. 'You're young, but not that young. What do you want Madhuri to call you?'

'I'll call him Jai bhaiyya,' Madhuri said hastily—Shilpa was being unusually snappy. The whole aunty rant had been triggered by a young security guard who was unfamilar with Carlton Towers and had used the dreaded 'A' word instead of saying ma'am in a fake accent like everyone else. It had been a hectic morning, and being called aunty by a man who was not even ten years younger than her had been the final straw 'Right then, all sorted,' Shilpa said. 'Off you go. Bye Suraj, bye Saira.'

The children waved to her as Jai drove towards the gate. Too late, Shilpa realized that Nikita's car didn't have seat belts in the rear seat, but then the school buses wouldn't have seat belts either. Well, that was Incredible India for you—it wouldn't occur to even the most paranoid parent to ask the school to put seat belts in the buses.

'You'll have to tell me the way,' Jai said to Suraj and Saira, and they giggled happily. For once the two of them were on chatting terms, and Madhuri didn't need to play referee while they tried to kill each other.

'Jai bhaiyya, next left please,' she said softly as they reached the end of Peddar Road. She had a nice voice, Jai thought as he cast a quick glance at her in the rear-view mirror. He hadn't really looked at her when she got into the car, but the voice was beguiling—musical with a husky undertone. She wasn't much to look at, he decided, though she was fairer-skinned than average, and had neat little features.

There was no way Jai could have known, but Madhuri was an acknowledged beauty in the chawl that she lived in. This was partly because of her rippling, waist-length hair. When she was at work her hair was always pulled into a tight plait with only a few curly tendrils escaping to frame her piquant little face. But when she was at home, she often stood on the balcony with her Rapunzel-like tresses hanging loose, pretending to ignore the whistles and lovelorn looks of the local Romeos. And then there was that come-hither look in her long-lashed brown eyes. She bestowed it on very few, but when she did, the unfortunate young man was lost. At the ripe old age of eighteen, Madhuri had already broken several hearts because she was as fickle as she was alluring. If she'd wanted to, she could have made Jai notice her, but she didn't want to, having the natural mistrust of a working-class girl for a sahib who was voluntarily doing a menial job.

There was utter chaos in front of the school—parents, maids and kids milling around, and dozens of buses and cars lining up to deposit kids at the main gate. The burly security guard in charge of controlling traffic was being harangued by an anorexic woman with blonde streaks in her hair, he looked like he was inches away from breaking down and bawling into his hankie. 'Is it always like this?' Jai asked, frankly appalled. Nikita had told him that Suraj went to a very high-end school—the picture in front of him resembled a high-end madhouse more than anything else.

Madhuri gave him a quick smile. 'It's usually worse,' she said in Hindi. 'Two of the older classes are out on an educational trip, so there's less of a crowd today. Come on Suraj, Saira.' Efficiently she gathered up the school bags, water bottles and folders on the rear seat of the car, and ushered the kids out. The driver behind Jai started honking hysterically in the few seconds it took her to hand the kids over to the ayah at the gate, and Jai was forced to take the car a little ahead.

'Sorry,' he said as Madhuri slid into the passenger seat, a little out of breath from hurrying to catch up with the car. 'The lady behind me was going crazy, I thought she'd burst a blood vessel if I didn't move.'

Madhuri twisted around in her seat to look at the woman. 'Ahh, that's Aryan's mom,' she said. 'Aryan is in Suraj's class.' There were rumours that Aryan's father was having an affair with a woman at work, and that his mother was slowly turning into an alcoholic, but Madhuri didn't feel the need to mention either fact. The drive back was mostly silent—Jai tried to make a couple of polite remarks, to which Madhuri gave monosyllabic answers, and after a while he gave up. Madhuri was not used to talking to men outside her immediate family. All her flirtations so far had been conducted through sighs and looks, and she was seized with an almost paralyzing awkwardness now that the children weren't around.

'So how was Day 1?' Nikita asked, as Jai drove her to office later in the day. Jai shrugged. 'Bearable,' he said. 'Though the drive back with the maid was a bit of a pain.'

'Hmmm,' Nikita said. 'Listen, I know I keep coming back to this over and over again, but are you sure you don't want me to tell Naveen the truth about the story? Because they're sending me the contract this week.'

Jai shook his head. 'I'm sure,' he said and there was a short pause, after which Nikita said in a voice that sounded uncertain for the first time since Jai had met her, 'I don't understand you at all.'

'Don't worry about it,' he said curtly. 'I'm not important enough. Has Naveen been in touch?'

Nikita nodded. 'He called a couple of times, and we're meeting up for lunch next week.' Was it her imagination, or did Jai sound a little bitter, maybe even jealous? The thought of him being jealous did strange things to her insides. She'd removed Jai from her list of 'eligibles' the second she's found out he had no money and no prospects, but the initial flare of attraction had never quite gone away.

Jai was cursing himself for having asked about Naveen. It was none of his business who she went out with, and how often they called, and being dog-in-the-manger-ish about a girl who hadn't shown the slightest bit of interest in him wasn't his style. Mentally, he made a note to call Saloni soon, at least she'd take his mind off Nikita.

As it turned out, Saloni ended up calling him first. 'Where've you been?' she demanded. 'I've been waiting and waiting for you to get in touch, but you didn't bother. *Kya hua*, you already have a girlfriend or something?'

Wow, was that direct or what. 'No girlfriend,' he said. 'But I wasn't sure if you...'

'Rubbish,' she said. 'Of course you were sure. I spent a whole evening throwing myself at your head, and that was even before I'd had anything to drink. *Chal, aaj shaam ko free hai*? Want to go for a movie or something?'

'Yes, OK,' Jai said. He was used to women sending out 'I am available' signals when he was around, but they were usually a lot more subtle, specially the attractive ones. Saloni seemed to read his mind. 'Sorry, am I being too pushy?' she asked. 'I can ring off, and we can pretend I never called. Then later when you've made up your mind, you can be all macho and ask me out for a date.'

Jai laughed. 'Let's just go out today,' he said. 'I don't have a car, but I can come and pick you up in a taxi.'

'No worries, I'm with Naveen, he'll drop me,' she said. 'Or he'll lend me his car. Where do you live?'

'Prabhadevi,' he said, and just because she'd told him she was with Naveen, 'I'm really looking forward to seeing you.' It was true, he thought as he put the phone down a few minutes later. There was something very pleasant and wholesome about Saloni, and the fact that she so obviously liked him was secretly flattering as well.

He found himself liking her even more when she landed up at his doorstep carrying a little stack of homemade aloo parathas and pickle. She was dressed in a flowing printed cotton skirt and a form-fitting navy T-shirt that outlined her curves and made her look more appetizing than the food.

'I guessed you might not have a fridge,' she announced, depositing the parathas on the coffee table that served him as writing desk and dining table rolled into one. 'But these will keep till tomorrow—you can have them for breakfast.'

Jai felt like kissing her; after Ranjana had stopped working from him, he got/ate about one square meal a week. The rest of the time, he survived on bread, eggs and maggi noodles, with raw carrots and cucumbers thrown in for balance.

'Pretty nice place,' Saloni was saying, looking around her. 'How come you live here if you're a driver? I thought you'd stay in a chawl or something.'

'Belongs to my brother-in-law,' Jai said. 'And the living room is all there is—the bedrooms have his stuff stored in them, and they're locked.' Too late, he realized that talking about bedrooms when he was alone with a singularly pretty girl could be misconstrued, and he quickly added, 'I mean, the place isn't mine or anything, I wouldn't even be able to afford the rent of a flat like this...'

Saloni gave him a mischievous smile, and Jai had the feeling she knew exactly why he was floundering. 'Don't worry, I'm not after you for your money,' she said, little dimples appearing in her cheeks. 'Are you ready to leave? We'll be late for the movie.'

The movie was terrible, so bad that they walked out halfway through.

'It went downhill right from the national anthem,' Saloni said once they were out. 'It's only in Maharashtra that they play the anthem before movies, did you know that? I love the one they show in Big Cinemas, the silent national anthem with the little kids. Gets me crying every time.'

'Well I'm glad they didn't show that then,' Jai said frankly. 'I wouldn't know what to do if you started bawling in the cinema hall. Probably burst into tears myself. The movie was torture enough for one day.'

'I met the director's wife at Naveen's place once,' Saloni said. 'She was very snooty, and the way she talked about this movie, I thought it would be the biggest thing after *Sholay*. Maybe she hadn't seen it herself."

'If he forced her to, she can divorce him for mental cruelty,' Jai said, looking at his watch. 'What do you want to do now? Dinner? It's almost 8.30.'

The Palladium Mall next to PVR had eating places where a single meal would cost more than a month's salary. Hoping Saloni wouldn't choose one of them, Jai patted his pocket to make sure he was carrying his debit card. The money from Wayne Brothers hadn't come in, and his account balance was dangerously low, if she chose a fancy restaurant, he'd have to survive on *vada pav* for the rest of the month.

'I thought we could go to the McDonald's in High Street Phoenix,' Saloni said, and then misreading the expression on his face, she added hastily, 'Or we could eat elsewhere if you want, I'm OK with anything.'

'Are you saying this because you know I'm hard up?' he asked.

'Partly,' she said, and smiled suddenly. 'And partly because I'm hard up as well. We'll go Dutch, right? That's the least I can do, considering I've practically forced you to go out with me.'

Jai nodded, but he was comparing her with Nikita and thinking how different the two women were. And then he was annoyed with himself. It wasn't like Nikita was some kind of platinum standard among women—tin standard would be more like it, or maybe lead, whichever was the cheaper metal. There was no reason to be thinking of her, and to prove to himself that he wasn't, he put an arm around Saloni and led her towards the escalator.

'McDonald's it is,' he said. 'But I promise you that when I do get some more money, I'll take you out to some place really nice.'

'KFC?' Saloni asked, and they simultaneously burst into laughter.

⁓

'Jai Uncle's hugging a girl, eeurgh,' Suraj announced as he caught sight of Jai from his vantage point on the first floor. He was waiting outside the Hamley's toy store with Saira as their mothers retrieved multiple shopping bags from the baggage counter. Saira looked across quickly. 'She's pretty,' she said. 'Looks like a Barbie doll. Look, Mom, doesn't she?'

Rakhi and Shilpa turned automatically. Saloni wasn't skinny enough to qualify for Barbie status, but both women had to agree—she did look rather pretty. Immediately, Rakhi's mouth pursed up in disapproval, but Shilpa smiled indulgently. 'They've probably just started dating,' she said.

'Taking a girl to McDonald's is hardly a date,' Rakhi sniffed.

'That's all Anuj could afford when *we* started dating,' Shilpa said with a laugh. 'But it's good to see Jai has a social life, he's always seemed a bit of a recluse, and he's so good-looking, I always wondered...'

Rakhi's brows shot up. 'You actually notice what your driver looks like?' she said, and Shilpa lost her temper.

'I need to be able to tell him from the doodhwala, right?' she said sweetly, and Rakhi flushed red. She'd been guilty of mistaking a very well-off, but rather scruffily dressed, neighbour of theirs for the milkman, and was halfway through telling him off for the milk coming late twice that month before a horrified security guard corrected her.

'Well, anyway, we can't go to McDonald's now that he's there with that woman,' she said to cover her mortification at being reminded of one of the most embarrassing moments of her life. What had made it worse was the fact that the man she'd mistaken for the doodhwala was hugely amused, and had spread the story all around the building, even now whenever he saw her, he bowed deferentially and asked her if the milk was coming on time, and should he speak to his buffaloes about the quality?

'Can we go to California Pizza Kitchen?' Suraj demanded at the same moment that Saira said, 'Oh, but can't we go say hello to Jai Uncle? I wanted him to show me the videos on his phone.'

Rakhi stiffened immediately. 'What videos?' she asked.

'Some song stuff,' Suraj said dismissively. 'Pizzas? Please?'

'Yes, of course,' Shilpa said, ushering them into the restaurant, with a wary eye on Rakhi. Rakhi was extremely protective of Saira—in her eyes, anything male was a potential rapist or child molester, but even to herself, Shilpa had to admit that this video thing didn't sound good.

'What kind of song videos does Jai Uncle show you, Suraj?' she asked once they had settled down at a table.

'He doesn't show us any videos,' Suraj said. 'Saira grabbed his phone the other day and started playing with it, though he told her to give it back. It's the same model as Lalita didi used to have, it comes with some Bollywood stuff pre-loaded on it.'

Rakhi relaxed visibly, and Shilpa thanked her stars that Suraj was a tech-savvy kid. He had his nose buried in the menu now, as he debated the relative merits of pepperoni and roast chicken.

'You have an ink stain on your nose,' she told him. Suraj frowned. 'Really?' he asked, sounding so much like Anuj that Shipa smiled involuntarily. 'Can I have your phone?'

He took the phone, flipping the camera setting to show his face on the screen and inspected it carefully to determine the exact position of the stain before he scrubbed it off with a tissue. 'You could have used a mirror,' Rakhi suggested. Suraj looked at her as if she was slightly abnormal. 'The mirrors are in the bathroom,' he said patiently, in the tones that Einstein would have used if he was asked to explain the General Theory of Relativity to George Bush Jr. 'The phone's right *here*.'

'So it is,' Shilpa agreed. 'Can we order now?'

6

'So would it be correct to assume that women are essentially more complicated than men are?' Naveen asked, smiling slightly.

'Yes, absolutely,' Nikita said, her voice sugary sweet. 'Just the way humans are essentially more complicated than chimpanzees.'

Naveen grinned. They had met up for lunch at a café ostensibly to discuss Nikita's contract, but so far he'd been entertaining himself by asking Nikita a set of seemingly pointless questions, right from the colours she liked to her favourite shoe stores to her views on feminism. Apparently it had to do with getting to know her better, and Nikita was playing along. She wasn't yet sure if she liked Naveen, but she was fascinated by him. And as she'd told Shilpa, he was seriously loaded, which made him even more interesting.

'Right, next question,' he said. 'It's little off-track, but bear with me, I'm trying to get at something here. When you walk into your house, how d'you feel?'

'Flat, not house,'

'Yes, well OK, flat. Or no, when you walk into your apartment building, what do you feel?'

'Into my apartment building? I feel thankful that God made me a bossy bitch, so that I could bully the building society into repainting the lobby.'

This time Naveen laughed right out. 'Well put,' he said. 'I assume Naina's character isn't autobiographical then?' Nikita stopped herself from asking him who the hell Naina was in the nick of the time—right, heroine of the story—she couldn't afford to slip up on that one. She racked her brains to link the question to the story, but she couldn't for the life of her remember anything about the heroine's feelings for her flat or house or hovel or wherever the damn woman lived.

Naveen was watching her between narrowed eyes. 'You haven't read the story through have you?' he asked abruptly, and Nikita's face went red.

'Of course I have, I wrote it!' she blustered, but even as she said the words she knew she wasn't fooling him.

'Jis school mein tum padhe ho...'

'Aap uske headmaster reh chuke ho,' she completed. In a way, it was a relief—she really couldn't handle the lying any more. Some Bond girl, she'd have made; 007 would have had to seal her mouth with duct tape if he wanted to keep MI6's secrets safe. Hmm, interesting fantasy that—Daniel Craig and the Duct Tape Dalliance. Perhaps Jai could use it as the base for his next movie plot.

Naveen was looking at her with eyebrows raised, and Nikita reluctantly dragged her mind out of the gutter, and away from Daniel Craig.

'Jai wrote it,' she said. 'He's a friend of mine, kind of.'

'Kind of?' Naveen asked, determinedly keeping his eyebrows raised.

'He's a neighbour. As in, he's looking after the flat opposite mine for his brother-in-law. And he was my driver for a little bit.'

This time, Naveen had to struggle to lower his eyebrows. Raising them for effect was all very well, but if he wasn't careful, they'd get stuck in his hair.

'Your driver,' he said, keeping his voice studiedly neutral.

'Sort of,' Nikita said uncomfortably.

'So this 'sort of' driver—is he presentable?'

'You mean looks-wise? Yes, he's pretty OK. And he speaks well –he's been to a good school and everything.'

'Then why…' Naveen stood up, uncoiling his lean body from his chair like a snake while Nikita watched him nervously. 'WHY didn't he submit the story in his own name?'

'He… ummm…he's a bit of a highbrow…' Nikita admitted. 'He's writing some very grim and serious novel about the Independence movement, and he thought this was a little ummmm…'

'Beneath him,' Naveen said. 'One of those. Well, this is a fine mess, isn't it?'

Nikita shrugged. She'd been worried about signing a legal contract, but it hadn't come to that stage yet, and to be honest, she didn't care. Naveen took a few turns around the room.

'Look, here's the thing,' he said. 'We've already announced the winner, and sent out press releases. If this Jai guy doesn't want to be associated with the film, you can continue to be his 'front'—if he changes his mind, we'll have to figure out what we need to do.'

Jai was very sure he wasn't going to change his mind when Naveen spoke to him. 'This doesn't fit in with the kind of writing I want to do,' he said, his brown eyes meeting Naveen's frankly. 'No offence meant—I had a good time writing the story, but I'd much rather Nikita continue being the official author than me.'

'Your call,' Naveen said shrugging. 'I'm curious about this book you're working on though. Got a publisher?'

Jai shook his head. 'I'll probably self-publish,' he admitted. 'I did approach a few big-name publishers, but they weren't keen. I doubt they even read the sample chapters I sent them.'

'Mail me a couple of chapters,' Naveen said. 'I'd like to take a look.'

Jai was about to demur, but Nikita caught his eye, and he nodded. 'I'll send them across,' he said, not believing for a moment that Naveen would read beyond the first two lines.

'Drink?' Naveen was asking. Jai shook his head and said 'I should be leaving,' just at the same moment that Nikita nodded enthusiastically and said 'I'd love one!' There was an awkward pause. Naveen hadn't wanted to meet Jai in office, and they were at his flat in Bandra—Nikita and Jai had driven down together from Prabhadevi. Jai hadn't wanted to come in the first place, and he was feeling as out of place in the swanky bachelor pad as a vegetarian in Karim's Kebab Korner. Nikita on the other hand was enjoying herself thoroughly—by the looks of it, she wouldn't mind if Jai made himself scarce.

'Try a cocktail,' Naveen said to Jai. 'I'm not an expert, but I can put together something that's drinkable.'

'I'd prefer a beer,' Jai said stolidly, and he went to stand by the floor to ceiling windows that made up an entire side of the room. Naveen's flat was on Carter Road, and overlooked the sea—the view was amazing.

Nikita opted for a cocktail. She took a sip and said knowledgeably, 'This is a mint julep, right? You should try it Jai, it's amazing.'

Jai leaned across and sniffed at the glass. 'It smells like Pudin Hara,' he said, and Nikita elbowed him viciously, almost spilling the drink. 'What?' he asked, moving hastily out of range. 'It genuinely does.'

'That's the most honest description of a cocktail I've ever heard,' Naveen said amused. The more he saw of Jai the more he liked him; he was a refreshing change from the self-centred and overly ambitious young men he was used to.

'I'm serious about wanting to read your book,' Naveen said as Nikita and Jai got ready to leave twenty minutes later. 'Here's my card—my email id is on it. Send the book to me, and we'll talk later.'

'You didn't even thank Naveen!' Nikita burst out when they were safely out of earshot. 'He's really going out of his way to help you, and you're treating him like you're the one doing him a favour!'

'I'm not asking him to help me,' Jai pointed out. 'And he was being unnecessarily nosy about why I left home.'

'You think people are being nosy if they ask you your name,' Nikita said. 'Or if they look at you too long. Or if they...'

'Right, right, I get it,' Jai said. 'I'll prance up to Naveen and give him a hug and a smooch next time I meet him.'

'Do that with Harsh instead,' Nikita advised rudely. 'He's gay—he'll *really* appreciate it.'

In spite of his misgivings, Jai did end up mailing the first few chapters of his book to Naveen. Partly because Nikita would have nagged him to death if he hadn't, and partly because *very* deep down, he did want an independent opinion on it. A lot of his self-confidence had leached away in the last few months, and he'd started wondering whether he was being stupid, dedicating more than a year of his life to writing a book that no one might actually want to read. Sending it to Naveen was a kind of test, if he said outright it was rubbish, well, at least he'd know. He didn't think he'd stop writing the book, whatever Naveen's opinion, but he'd definitely start thinking seriously about getting a job. A proper one, not ferrying gold-digging women and hyperactive children around town.

He frowned as he drove Nikita's car into Carlton Towers the next day. Shilpa had spoken to him about the whole video incident with Saira, and it had rankled, even though she was obviously on his side. That was the problem, trying to do a job of this sort. Nikita and Shilpa both did their best to make him feel comfortable, but he couldn't get away from the fact that he was a hired servant.

When he parked the car in his normal spot to wait for Madhuri and the children, he was too preoccupied to notice a security guard gesturing at him; he turned only when the man walked up to the car and knocked on the glass. *Khidki neeche karo*, the man said, and Jai rolled down the window frowning. 'What's the matter?' he asked.

The man wouldn't meet his eyes. '*Gaadi yahaan nahin lagaa sakte*,' he said.

Jai raised his eyebrows. '*Kyon*? I always park it here.'

'*Allowed nahin hai*.'

'I'm here to pick up the children,' Jai said. 'Where am I supposed to park then?'

'*Woh sab nahin pataa*,' the guard said. His tone was truculent, almost as if he was trying to pick a fight. 'The car doesn't belong to this building, it doesn't have a parking sticker. If a society member allows you, you can park in their spot.'

'This is the visitor's parking slot, isn't it?'

'You're not a visitor,' the man said. 'Taxi pick-up point is at the main gate.'

'We'll figure it out later, after I've spoken to Anuj Sir,' Jai said, and the man thumped the bonnet of the car. '*Sunai nahin detaa kya? Aage le, chal!*'

'Right,' Jai said, finally losing his temper. He opened the door in one swift movement and got out. '*Ghar mein tameez nahin sikhaaya kya?*' he asked silkily, standing so close to the man that he instinctively shrank back. Clearly he hadn't expected Jai to get out of the car.

'*Rule hai toh…*' he started to stammer—he was a short, skinny man, and Jai was towering over him.

'What's wrong?' Rakhi asked as she came out of the building with Saira and Suraj.

The guard plunged into a garbled explanation—cars weren't allowed to be parked here, it was a rule, and the security supervisor had said that there could be no exceptions Jai would have to go and wait near the main gate, or in the basement parking in Anuj's parking slot.

'Nonsense,' Rakhi said, cutting the guard off mid-tirade. 'The children will not walk to the main gate or anywhere else—Jai will wait for them here as he always does. Tell the security supervisor to speak to me if there's a problem. Let's go, Jai, the children are already late for school.'

The guard was still muttering to himself, but something about Rakhi's imperious expression made him shut up. He gave Jai a rather malevolent look before he went back into the lobby.

Rakhi got into the rear seat with the kids; in her mind Jai was just a rather over-educated driver, and sitting next to him hadn't even occurred to her. In a way, Jai found her attitude easier to deal with than Shilpa's. Shilpa was sometimes so paranoid about being politically correct that she made him uncomfortable.

'Hasn't Madhuri come into work today?' Jai asked as he pulled out of the main gate on to the road.

'She has, I needed to meet Saira's class teacher, so I decided to drop the kids off today,' Rakhi said. 'I won't take more than fifteen minutes in the school, so I'll hitch a ride back with you.' In the event, she took almost half an hour, and Jai was late to pick Nikita up.

'I knew she'd delay you,' Nikita grumbled as she got into the car. 'Why did you have to wait for her? She could have taken a cab back, or Sandeep-the-wimp could have sent his car to fetch her.'

'She saved me from beating up a security guard,' Jai told her. 'The least I could do was drop her back home.'

Nikita was silent for a few seconds after he told her what had happened. 'Would you have actually hit the man?' she asked. Jai thought for a while. 'I'm not sure,' he said at last. 'He really got to me. I guess what he was saying was reasonable enough, but it was the way he said it...'

He broke off, wishing he hadn't started talking about the incident. He was ashamed of the few seconds of pure rage that had overcome him while he was talking to the guard—if Rakhi hadn't come out of the building just then, it was quite likely that he'd have punched him in the face. And telling Nikita, well, she wasn't a terribly sensitive person at the best of times, she might decide to bring the topic up at some completely inappropriate time.

Nikita surprised him however. 'You could stop working for Shilpa,' she suggested, just when the pause grew long enough for Jai to assume that she'd lost interest in the conversation.

'I need the money,' Jai reminded her.

'I could pay your salary,' Nikita said. 'I got a raise last week, forgot to tell you. And there's some new salary structuring policy that our HR department has come out with—I can show a driver's salary as a tax-deductible expense. Or if you want to take a break for a bit and concentrate on your writing, I'll give you an advance against the 5 lakhs that's coming in from Wayne Brothers.'

'That's very generous,' Jai said, unsure what had prompted the offer, but was very touched all the same. 'It's OK though, it's not so bad that I need to quit.'

Nikita shrugged. 'Let me know if you change your mind,' she said. 'You see, it's different working for me, we're friends—Shilpa and Anuj, well, they're nice people, but they're in a totally different league from us...'

'And I'm a glorified servant as far as they're concerned,' Jai finished for her. 'I know, and I'm OK with it. If it gets too bad, I might take you up on your offer to advance me some of the 5 lakhs.'

'Three lakhs, 30 thousand,' Nikita said. 'You forgot the tax!'

'Why would they be so fussed up about Jai?' Shilpa asked, quite honestly puzzled. The drivers in the building had apparently put up a little petition—if they weren't allowed to use the visitor's parking slots, or the residents' lift, neither should Jai.

'I can actually see their point,' Anuj said, frowning as he put the intercom down after a long conversation with the security supervisor.

Shilpa's eyebrows shot up in disbelief. 'Are you serious?' she asked. 'The reason we have two separate lifts is because the male staff used to harass the maids, not because of any discriminatory rubbish.'

Anuj gave her the are-you-for-real look that never failed to get her goat. 'The lifts are segregated because of the 'discriminatory rubbish',' he said patiently. 'The maids have been allowed to use the residents' lift because they *were* being harassed.'

'Well whatever the reason, I'm not asking Jai to use the servants' lift,' Shilpa said hotly. 'It's insulting. And maybe he could park the car in your parking slot, and Madhuri could get the kids there, but it seems a rather pointless exercise—Jai's here for hardly ten minutes in the morning.'

'Whatever you think is best,' Anuj said. He was losing interest in the conversation; he'd met Jai a couple of times, but Shilpa was the one who'd hired him, and Anuj really couldn't see the point of all the fuss. His phone beeped, and he picked it up to look at his messages.

'All the best for the pitch tomorrow,' said one, and he smiled automatically. The sender was a woman who'd joined the bank a few weeks ago. She'd made her interest in Anuj very clear—he didn't reciprocate it at all, but he found the attention flattering. And Diya at least remembered that he had an important client meeting tomorrow; he'd mentioned it to Shilpa at least thrice, but it seemed to have slipped her mind completely.

'Aren't you getting ready for dinner?' he asked, as Shilpa picked up a magazine and started leafing through it, her brows still puckered up in worry. They had a dinner to attend at Anuj's boss's home at 9.00, and it was already past 8.30.

'I got ready some time ago,' Shilpa said. 'I'll do my make-up just before we leave—I end up smudging it all over my face otherwise.'

'Is that what you're wearing?' Anuj asked, frowning at her sleeveless khaki shirt and high-waist jeans.

'Something wrong with it?'

'It's very casual', he said, missing the tightness in Shilpa's tone. Unconsciously, he was comparing her with Diya, and wondering why Shilpa looked so worn-out and harried all the time.

'The dinner isn't formal, is it?' Shilpa said. 'I'm not planning to change, if you're embarrassed to be seen with me, I can stay at home. I'd welcome some time to myself in any case.'

'Don't be silly,' Anuj said, as he finally realized that he'd upset her. 'It's just that some of the other wives dress up like they're auditioning for the next Mrs World crown, so I thought you might …'

'Might want to tart up a little?' Shilpa asked dryly. The importance Anuj assigned to outward appearances was one of his least attractive traits. Most of the 'other wives' didn't work, they spent hours in the gym and at beauty parlours trying to looking thinner and younger, and their conversation drove Shilpa nuts. Perhaps dressing up a little wouldn't have been such a bad idea after all, but she'd be damned if she'd back down now. A couple of good pieces of jewellery and slightly heavier make-up than usual were the maximum concession she was prepared to make.

'Oh that's lovely,' Anuj's boss's trophy wife gushed over the antique silver cuff-bracelet Shilpa wore on one wrist. 'Designer?'

'No, I picked it up at an exhibition of works by indigenous artisans,' Shilpa said, smiling sweetly back at Payal. In spite of Payal's American accent, her vocabulary didn't have many words of more than two syllables—Anuj's boss hadn't married her for her brains. She was looking a little puzzled now, probably wondering if indigenous artisans were artists who suffered from chronic indigestion. Over her shoulder, Shilpa caught Rakhi's eye with a relieved smile. For all her other irritating qualities, Rakhi was no fool. And she was dressed even more casually than Shilpa was; she was extremely conscious of her rather lush backside, and stuck to kurtis and jeans whenever she could.

'Oh, do you know Rachana?' Payal asked, rather with the air of someone saying 'Oh, have you actually *met* the Abominable Snowman?'

'We're neighbours,' Shilpa said, adding in an undertone, 'And her name's Rakhi.'

'Yes, of course, that's what I meant. Neighbours, of course, you're both in Carlton Towers, right? Such a *sweet* place, I mean if one wants to live in that area of course.' Clearly Payal couldn't see any reason for such weird preferences when there were flats in Cuffe Parade and Nepean Sea Road available for only a few more crores. 'Her husband's in the *retail bank*,' Payal whispered. 'Not normally one of our set, you know, but he did some small project for Rish, and Rish absolutely *insisted* on inviting him, you know how he is, so informal and friendly with everyone.'

Rishiraj Patel was about as informal and friendly as the average Ganges ghadial, but contradicting Payal was out of the question. Both Shilpa and Rakhi submitted to being reintroduced at great length and were finally left to 'get to know each other better', as Payal wafted off in an expensive cloud of Chanel No 5 to terrorize her next set of guests.

'I need a drink,' Rakhi said firmly, grabbing Shilpa's glass of wine and taking a big swig. 'What's wrong with the retail bank anyway?'

'It's not, umm the swanky part of the bank, I think,' Shilpa said guardedly. The retail division normally lost the bank a quarter or a third of the money the corporate bank made each year, and the corporate bankers understandably weren't too thrilled about it. Rakhi tossed her head. 'Trust Sandeep to be working there then,' she said. 'I've asked him a dozen times why he doesn't change roles, but there's always some complicated reason or the other. People ten years younger than him are raking in money, and here we are, still living in a rented flat and driving a five-year-old car.'

'I don't think it's very easy to shift,' Shilpa said, wondering whether it would have been safer to stick with Payal after all. Rakhi seemed to be all set to launch into a full-fledged Sandeep-is-such-a-wimp-I-deserve-better rant. Luckily before she could really get going, the hapless Sandeep wandered up in person, looking ridiculously pleased to see Shilpa. 'I'm sticking with you,' he announced. 'I've been polite to everyone I needed to, and now I plan to have a couple of drinks in peace.' He beamed happily at both women, and Shilpa gave a little inward groan of despair. Sometimes she wondered whether Sandeep deserved Rakhi after all, he was such a chump.

'Shouldn't you be networking?' she asked. Anuj would throttle her with his bare hands if she mentioned it, but Shilpa knew that there was a real chance of the bank shutting down its retail division if it made more losses again. And if that happened, Sandeep's best chance of survival would be to move to the corporate bank. He should be using this opportunity to network like crazy.

'She's right,' Rakhi said. She was too well-bred to start attacking Sandeep in the middle of a party, but she was mentally pawing the ground in fury. 'Look at Vipul, he's been speaking to everyone he can.'

Sandeep made a face. 'Vipul would talk to a hijra if he thought it would get him a larger year-end bonus.'

From Rakhi's expression, it was evident that she could see no harm in Vipul's nondiscriminatory attitude either towards hijras, or towards people who could increase his bonus. She didn't say anything, but Sandeep got the hint anyway. Sighing, he ambled away towards the corner where Anuj and Rishi were animatedly discussing the latest licence scam. Rakhi's eyes narrowed as she watched him hover uncomfortably around the edges of the group.

'The building guys have been making a fuss about Jai getting the car up to the lobby level,' Shilpa said, more to take Rakhi's attention away from Sandeep than anything else.

'Saira told me that one of the 'big guards' has been bothering Madhuri,' Rakhi said absently, her eyes still on Sandeep. 'That's probably the reason behind all this.'

'She would have told me!' Shilpa protested. 'And why would they give Jai a hard time, it's completely unrelated!'

'She'd have to walk across the basement to get to the car if it's parked in your parking lot,' Rakhi said. 'More opportunity for the security guy to try and speak to her there. And if it's the security supervisor who's running after her, none of the guards would dare to say anything to him. He's probably feeling threatened by Jai as well; Madhuri's started talking to him quite a bit, there might be something going on there.'

'I think Jai has a girlfriend,' Shilpa said. 'The girl we saw him with in High Street Phoenix. Rakhi shrugged. 'I'm just guessing,' she said. 'He could just be flirting with Madhuri—I doubt he'd get serious about a servant girl. You might want to figure out what's happening there. This is why I employ older women, there's far less trouble.'

Madhuri strenuously denied flirting with 'Jai bhaiya' when Shilpa hinted at it. She did admit, however, that the security supervisor had been bothering her.

'I don't think you should get involved,' was all Anuj would say when Shilpa tried to discuss this with him. Ranjana, to Shilpa's surprise, was furious with her own daughter when she heard about the whole fracas. 'I gave her a few slaps when she came home this Saturday,' she told Shilpa defiantly. 'She should be working hard and saving money for her wedding, not decking herself up and attracting all kinds of riff-raff.' And when Shilpa tried to remonstrate with her for being unfair and unnecessarily harsh, all she would say was, 'It's different for people like us. She doesn't have a father, anything could happen to her if she isn't careful.'

Madhuri herself became tearful when Shilpa offered to lodge a formal complaint with the building society about the security supervisor. 'He'll bother me even more, didi, just let it be. I'll apologize to Jai bhaiyya.' Which was neither here, nor there. Shilpa finally spoke to the building secretary about Jai, and he agreed to both let him use the residents' lift and park by the lobby when he came to pick up the kids. As far as the security supervisor went, she contented herself with giving him a hard glare whenever she saw him.

7

'My mother wants to visit next month,' Anuj said. 'Radha Mausi might come down as well, but she'll stay with Nikita.'

'OK,' Shilpa said, heaving a huge sigh in her head. Anuj's mother's visits had a Russian roulette-like quality to them—sometimes everything would go off well, and at other times all hell would break loose, the servants would quit, and Suraj would turn into a spoilt, wilful version of his normal self.

'Is it convenient for her to be here now?' Anuj asked, and Shilpa looked up in surprise. 'We can't ask her not to come,' she said. 'And it's been a long time since her last visit.'

'I guess,' Anuj said, but he looked rather unhappy.

Nikita, on the other hand, was thrilled to have her mother and aunt visit—for the first time, Shilpa realized how lonely Nikita probably was. 'Do you get along with your mom?' Shilpa asked. Somehow, she remembered that particular relationship being a little stormy.

Nikita laughed. 'We fight a lot,' she admitted. 'Mom thinks I should be married by now, preferably to one of the Tatas or Birlas. And I want her to come and live with me, but she refuses to leave Chandigarh.'

Nikita's father had been a manager in a public sector bank when he died of a heart attack at the age of thirty-five. His wife was given a job in the same bank on compassionate grounds, however, since she was only a Home Science graduate, the job was a clerical one, and she bitterly resented having to report to someone who had been junior to her husband. She was also fiercely proud, refusing all offers of help from her relatively well-off older sister. Over the years, her struggle to give her daughter a good education while maintaining a respectable standard of living had made her bitter and resentful of the world in general.

Mrs Malhotra and Mrs Dewan travelled down from Chandigarh together—they'd elected to take the train rather than fly, Mrs Dewan to save money, and Anuj's mother because she loved trains. They made a striking pair. In her early sixties, Mrs Malhotra was still very good-looking in a flashy kind of way. Nikita's mother was younger, but lines of discontent had hardened her face—it was difficult to imagine that she had originally been the better-looking of the two.

Nikita went to the station with Jai to pick up her aunt and mother. Anuj was travelling yet again, and Shilpa had a meeting she couldn't shift.

'*Kitna sundar ladka hai!*' Mrs Malhotra said, as Jai helped a porter load their multiple suitcases on to a wooden trolley. '*Yeh driver ka kaam kyun kar rahe ho beta? Graduate ho naa?*'

Jai had already blushed scarlet at the comment on his looks—the earnest query about his occupation and educational qualifications almost finished him off. He mumbled something inarticulately, and Nikita took pity on him.

'*Arre, chalo naa, maasiji,*' she said. 'I'll explain about Jai once we get home. I'm taking both of you to my place first so that you can freshen up, and Shilpa will pick you up once her meeting is over.'

'I don't know why Shilpa needs to work,' Nikita's mother said waspishly. 'Anuj is doing very well, isn't he?'

'*Haan*,' Mrs Malhotra said absently, her eyes still fixed on Jai as he strode ahead with the porter, a heavy bag that hadn't fit on the trolley slung over one muscular shoulder.

'Such a nice body too,' she said appreciatively. '*Bete, tum modelling-wodelling kyun nahin karte?*'

This was too much for Nikita; she stopped in the middle of the platform and doubled up with laughter while Jai and her mother both glared at her. Her aunt was unfazed. 'I'm just suggesting it,' she said. 'I bet it's no fun working for you and Anuj, you must be driving the poor boy completely *paagal*.'

'Sushma didi, you're creating a scene as usual,' Nikita's mother hissed. 'Can we at least get to Nikita's flat before you start talking—there are people staring at us.'

'*Dekhne do*,' Mrs Malhotra said, but she changed the topic, much to Jai's relief.

'She's quite something, your aunt,' he told Nikita later when they were making a second trip to the car to haul the last of Mrs Dewan's ten-ton suitcases up four flights of stairs.

'*Cheeni nahin hai*,' Mrs Malhotra announced as Nikita dragged the suitcase in. 'Don't you take sugar in your tea?'

'I drink green tea,' Nikita said. She had remembered to buy a carton of milk, but she hadn't even realized she was out of sugar. 'Can you manage without sugar this one time? I'll order it from Krishna Stores along with anything else you need this afternoon.' Her aunt looked as horrified as if she'd suggested they drink rat poison. Jai grinned and said, 'Hang on, I think I've got some sugar. I'll be back in a minute.'

'What a nice boy,' Mrs Malhotra sighed, once Jai dropped the sugar off and left. 'You should marry someone like him, Nikita. You make enough money for two, and you'd have a much better life than if you married some fat, rich man like your mother wants you to.'

'She didn't say he needs to be fat,' Nikita said, casting a nervous look at the bathroom door; her mother had gone in for a bath leaving her sugarless tea to cool on the dining table, but she had very sharp ears.

'All rich men are fat,' Sushma Malhotra stated with the air of someone repeating an incontrovertible fact. 'At least the ones who're left after the film stars and society women have had their pick definitely are.'

'What about Anuj?' Nikita couldn't resist asking. 'He's quite nice-looking isn't he? And he's rich, at least by my standards.'

'He married a girl from a rich family,' Mrs Malhotra pointed out with unerring logic. 'And anyway, he's not such a great catch. Just like his father he is.'

What part of Anuj's resemblance to his father had caused this drop in market value, Mrs Malhotra didn't elaborate upon. Instead she dipped a biscuit into her sugary tea and ate it with evident enjoyment.

'Your children would be good-looking too,' she said, once the biscuit was done, and in answer to an inquiring look from Nikita, she continued, 'If you married Jai.'

'Mom will be out in a minute,' Nikita said apprehensively. The thought of her precious daughter marrying an indigent driver, however good-looking, would send Mrs Dewan into a paroxysm of rage, and Nikita didn't feel up to refereeing a yelling match between her mother and aunt. Luckily, Mrs Malhotra took the hint and subsided.

Shilpa rang the doorbell half an hour later. Mrs Malhotra got to her feet. 'So nice to see you beta,' she said, sweeping Shilpa into a comfortable hug. 'Meeting over?'

'Yes,' Shilpa said. 'I'm sorry I couldn't come to the station to meet you. Namaste Radha Maasi.'

'Namaste,' Nikita's mom said, not very warmly. She'd taken a dislike to Shilpa the day she met her, on the rather flimsy grounds that Shilpa had 'ignored' her during her wedding reception. There had been over six hundred guests at the reception, and Shilpa hardly had any time to speak to her own parents, but that wasn't sufficient excuse as far as Mrs Dewan was concerned.

'So, are we ready to leave?' Mrs Malhotra asked brightly. 'I can't wait to see Suraj.'

'Yes, why would you want to hang around with boring old us when you've got your son's hi-fi house to go to,' Mrs Dewan said.

'Mom...' Nikita muttered casting an agonized look at Shilpa's stiff expression, but Mrs Malhotra had twenty-six more years of experience in handling her sister than Nikita did.

'You're right, if all I wanted to do was listen to you grumble, we could have both stayed back in Chandigarh,' she said airily. 'I'll come and pick you up tomorrow morning so that we can go to the Siddhivinayak mandir together. Try to be a little more cheerful. *Nikita beta, mummyji ke liye thoda ice cream mangaa lena.*'

'*Kyon, us se mera dimaag thanda ho jayega?*' Mrs Dewan asked, but she smiled reluctantly.

'She's had a tough life,' Mrs Malhotra said to Shilpa in explanatory tones as they went down the stairs. 'Now, how far is your building from here?'

'Won't take more than ten minutes,' Shilpa said. She was still rather miffed at the way Nikita's mother had behaved, and it was difficult to stop thinking about it. Hi-fi house indeed.

Jai brought the car around, giving Mrs Malhotra a wary look as she got in.

'You should get your own car,' Anuj's mother told Nikita Shilpa. 'You work hard, and you're doing so well, you deserve a car of your own.' Unlike most mothers-in-law, Mrs Malhotra was an ardent supporter of Shilpa's career. She could be embarrassing with her show of solidarity on occasion—like when she'd told a roomful of hairy-chested ultra-macho Punjabi cousins that Shilpa earned more than all of them put together. Still, on the whole, it was comforting to have her approval. Shilpa had female colleagues whose in-laws thought that working mothers were only a step above child molesters and serial killers.

'The EMIs for the flat are huge, I don't want to spend money unnecessarily,' Shilpa murmured in an attempt to prevent Jai from overhearing. Pretty futile, really, given that he was less than a foot away. Even more futile when her mother-in-law replied at the top of her voice, 'The flat is pretty huge too. I don't know why you need such a big place when it's just the three of you. But I suppose that's Anuj's doing, even when he was a kid, he'd insist on buying the biggest and flashiest toys in the store.'

Jai smothered a smile. He was beginning to like Anuj's mom in spite of her disastrous frankness.

'Should I tip him?' Mrs Malhotra asked Shilpa in worried tones after Jai hefted her bags into the living room. Although slightly classier looking than Mrs Dewan's luggage, the bags still weighed a ton. 'I don't want to offend him, but he's been so helpful that I want to give him something.'

'He might get upset,' Shilpa said. 'He's not really a driver, he's doing this more as a favour to us because he's got the time....' That was the latest excuse Shilpa had thought of to explain Jai's presence in their lives.

'I'll knit him a sweater,' Mrs Malhotra decided. 'Nice navy blue I think.'

'Mummyji, I don't know if he'll need a sweater in this weather, it's quite warm in Mumbai.'

'Nonsense, it was chilly when I got out of the train. And he's from Rajasthan he told me, it gets very cold there. Jai beta,' she raised her voice a little. 'Shirt size 42 or 44?'

'Forty-two', Jai said, hugely amused. He'd heard pretty much every word of the conversation—at one point he'd been tempted to intervene and say he didn't mind being tipped. But a sweater sounded so much better than a tip, assuming auntyji got it done before summer.

'*Chalo, toh kal I'll buy the wool,*' Mrs Malhotra said. 'You can help me choose the colour. Sleeveless I think, it doesn't get very cold in Mumbai.' She said the last words with the air of someone stating a not very commonly known fact, and behind her back, Shilpa rolled her eyes in mock despair.

8

'Eager to get home?' Diya asked, and Anuj smiled. 'I'm missing my son,' he admitted. 'And my wife, of course.' After saying this, he wondered why he'd phrased it that way, tagging on the 'of course' implied that he was saying he missed Shilpa only because he felt it was expected of him. The only excuse he could find for himself was that he was too tired to think about what he was saying. The team's annual offsite business meet in Goa had come after weeks of extended travel and he was sick of living out of a suitcase.

'Not missing the maid?' Rishi said jocularly. The story of the maid falling for Anuj had done the rounds in office, and Anuj had been the butt of Shiney Ahuja inspired jokes for a few weeks now.

Anuj grimaced. 'Not this one,' he said. 'Very traditional type, wears her sari in the "bumfloss" style.' Rishi raised his eyebrows, and Anuj said. 'Free end tucked firmly between her... er... her legs.' Rishi's sense of humour had never evolved beyond the locker-room level, and he guffawed delightedly. For a second, Anuj thought of how Shilpa would have reacted to the remark. Then Diya started to laugh as well, and he conveniently erased the image from his mind.

'You've made a hit there,' Rishi said in an undertone as Diya excused herself to go to the restroom, her hips swaying as she walked towards the exit. 'Lucky bastard.'

Anuj pretended to be surprised, though he'd have had to be as blind as a bat to miss it. Short of getting an 'I'm available' sign tattooed on her forehead, Diya had done everything possible to get the message across.

'I'm a family man,' he said, trying to gauge Rishi's actual views, and the atmosphere was pretty relaxed, but Rishi was still his boss.

'Arrey, the family's in Mumbai, you're in Goa, what's the problem? Not saying that you have to actually do anything, but go out, take her to a few bars, live life a little.'

'Only if you come along,' Anuj said, quick to pick up on the slight note of envy. Rishi was reported to have been quite a player in his younger days, and at thirty-nine he was definitely not over the hill yet. And if Anuj was reading him right, Rishi had a bit of a thing for Diya as well.

'Happy to,' Rishi said, and Anuj breathed a little sigh of relief. His boss-radar had never failed him yet. When Diya came back, he gave her a swift smile and said, 'Rishi's offered to take us on a pub crawl. You game?'

'Of course,' Diya said, trying to hide her disappointment. She was only twenty-seven, and Rishi looked positively old to her. She'd expected him to go tamely off to bed and leave her alone with Anuj, but here he was suggesting pub crawls. Next he'd want to go to a disco or take up roller skating—why couldn't people ever act their age? She looked up and saw Anuj frowning at her. Unknowingly she'd allowed her face to show what she was thinking—well, maybe not the bit about roller skating, but it was pretty clear she didn't want Rishi to come along.

Anuj's phone rang right then, providing a welcome distraction.

'Got a minute?' Shilpa asked, and Anuj's frown deepened. Once, Shilpa would have purred sexily into the phone, now she sounded as brisk and matter-of-fact as a doctor's receptionist.

'Yes, of course.'

Shilpa came directly to the point. 'Your mom's a bit upset that you haven't spoken to her since she got to Mumbai.' 'Bit upset' was an understatement—Mrs Malhotra was threatening to pack her bags and move into Nikita's flat if her son didn't call her pronto.

'I'm in the middle of a discussion,' Anuj hissed, moving away from the rest of the group.

'Come off it,' Shilpa said sceptically. 'It's past ten, you must be drinking yourself silly and laughing at your boss's idiotic jokes.' That was the problem with Shilpa, Anuj thought. His colleagues who were married to housewives got away with pretending that their lives were one long, high-pressure round of meetings and PowerPoint presentations. Shilpa had been in the corporate world for almost as long as he had, and she was supremely unimpressed by any work-related cribbing.

'I still can't get away to chat with my mom for three hours about her latest kitty party scandals,' he protested. 'I'll be seeing her in two days in any case.'

Men, they could be utterly thick-headed at times. 'She's come all this way to visit us,' Shilpa explained patiently. 'Ideally you should have been here when she arrived, and since you weren't, the least you can do is call her and speak to her.'

'Yes, OK,' Anuj said. Diya was casting languishing looks in his direction, and he could feel his pulse race in response. 'You want me to speak to her now?'

'She's gone to bed, tomorrow will do.' There was a brief pause, then Anuj asked, 'How's Suraj doing?'

'Pretending to be asleep, but I know he's awake and obsessing about his birthday party,' Shilpa said with a sigh. 'He wants a haunted-house theme. He's keeping it a closely guarded secret—I only hope he allows us to talk to the party organizer about it.'

Anuj laughed, unconsciously angling away from Diya. Suraj was the most important person in his life, and he found he was suddenly missing him hugely. 'Give him a big hug from me,' he said. 'I guess it's too late to talk to him now?'

'Much too late,' Shilpa said firmly. 'If you do want to talk to someone, you can speak to your mother.'

Anuj shuddered. He hadn't been taken in by Shilpa's diplomatic 'she's a bit upset'. He had known his mother for thirty-six long years—when she was in a temper she generally started off with reminding him of various unflattering incidents from his early youth. And, in chronological order, starting with how he had ungratefully tried to strangle himself with the umbilical cord just before he was born. Far better to wait till the next morning when she'd calmed down.

'No thanks. I'll call her first thing tomorrow.'

'Right then, you can go back to flirting with Deepa or Diya or whatever her name is.'

Anuj flinched. 'I wasn't...' he began, but his voice sounded so guilty even to his own ears that he stopped mid-sentence.

'No, of course you weren't,' Shilpa said soothingly. 'I'll see you on Wednesday then.' Anuj glared at the phone as she rang off. The worst thing was that she seemed as unconcerned as if he was sitting in a corner reciting the Gayatri Mantra to himself, it didn't even occur to her that Diya might pose a real threat to their marriage.

'All OK?' Diya asked when Anuj rejoined her at the bar. He nodded, and struck by a mad impulse to prove that he wasn't a henpecked wimp, he picked up her hand and raised it to his lips. 'Can I have the honour of this dance?' he asked with exaggerated formality, then without waiting for an answer, he stood up and pulled her into his arms.

~

In Mumbai, Nikita was ringing the bell of Jai's flat, jiggling from one foot to another impatiently as she waited for him to open the door. What was he *doing*?

'Were you asleep?' she asked as the door finally opened. 'I've been ringing the bell for *hours*.'

'I heard, I was in the bathroom,' he said. He had a weird expression on his face, and he was blocking the door almost completely. Nikita craned her neck to try and look in. 'Budge up, I can't get past you,' she complained.

Jai didn't move. 'The room's in a bit of a mess.'

'Can't be worse than mine,' she said impatiently. 'Achha, can I come in? I need some help.'

The agonized look on Jai's face intensified. 'Uhh, this isn't a very good time,' he said. Nikita frowned at him. His expression reminded her of someone—Anuj, she thought, a sudden light bulb going off in her head. He must have been around sixteen then—she'd gone to his house to drop off a cake her mother had baked for her aunt, and he'd taken it from her at the door and not let her in. Deeply offended, she had refused to speak to him for the next three months. Years later, Anuj told her that he'd smuggled his girlfriend into the house while his parents were away at the cinema. His baby cousin standing on the doorstep and hollering for him had been the worst possible dampener.

'You have a girl in there?' Nikita asked Jai, speaking without thinking. His expression darkened, and he hesitated, clearly about to tell her that it was none of her damn business. Wishing she had had the sense to keep her mouth shut and go away, Nikita started to apologize, but was forestalled by an amused female voice.

'He does, actually,' Saloni said, coming to stand next to Jai. She'd had time to rearrange her clothes and finger-comb her hair while Jai was chivalrously keeping Nikita out of the flat. Her make-up was still smudged, but what the heck. It was about time she met Nikita, Jai insisted that Nikita was awful, but he still spent a huge amount of time with her even when he was not driving her around.

'Oh hi,' Nikita said, a little taken aback. Saloni was wearing an inside-out pink shirt over grey cut-offs, and her wavy hair was tumbling over her shoulders in a Madhuri-Dixit-in-*Dil* kind of way. Actually, Saloni looked a lot like Madhuri Dixit too. Nikita had watched *Dil* as a wide-eyed four-year-old, and Madhuri had become her gold standard for female beauty; even now, Saloni's resemblance to the *dhak-dhak* girl was giving her an instant inferiority complex.

Jai was mentally banging his head on the wall. Women, who could predict what they'd do next? 'You said you needed my help,' he prompted Nikita, who was looking uncertainly at Saloni.

'Oh yes,' Nikita said, shuddering eloquently as she remembered. 'A rat's gone and drowned itself in my best bucket.'

'Committed suicide, did it?' Saloni still sounded amused, but her eyes were snapping fire. 'Can't the doorman or someone help out?'

'There's no doorman,' Jai said mildly. 'This isn't the Hyatt Regency. I'll be along in a minute.'

For a second, Saloni wondered whether storming out would be a good idea, Nikita had interrupted them at a particularly critical point, and she was feeling as frustrated as it was possible for a woman to feel. Then, as Jai went back in to put on his shoes, she remembered with a jolt that Nikita was his employer. Technically, even if he was off duty, she was within her rights to expect him to help dispose of rat corpses.

'Umm, your shirt's inside out,' Nikita whispered, and Saloni looked down. 'Thanks,' she whispered back, suddenly liking Nikita a lot more. She could easily have pointed it out while Jai was around and embarrassed both of them, this showed that in spite of her corporate-bitch looks, there was some basic female fellow-feeling in her.

'What do you want to do with it?' Jai asked after solemnly surveying the rat in its watery grave. 'Chuck the whole thing away,' Nikita said firmly.

'What a lot of fuss about nothing,' Nikita's mother said in disgust. 'Bring the bucket back, Jai, we can wash it out.'

'Ughh, no way,' Nikita said. 'Throw the bucket away, I don't ever want to see it again.'

'Bring it back.' A hint of steel had crept into Mrs Dewan's voice.

'Mom, it's my bucket, I'll do what I want with it.'

'Is that any way to...' Mrs Dewan's voice was rising, and Jai intervened hastily. 'The car wash boy's been asking for a new bucket, should I give it to him? After I've got rid of the rat?'

Both women glared at him, and he shrugged. 'Or not,' he said. 'I'll get rid of the rat and leave the bucket outside your door.' It was late, Saloni would probably not let him near her after this, and he was getting a bit sick of holding the half-full bucket with its dead inhabitant.

'Give it to the car wash boy,' Nikita said ungraciously, and Jai raised his eyebrows. 'Please,' she added. 'And thanks. And sorry.'

As Jai went out, he heard Nikita's mother say, 'Why are you apologizing to him? He's just a *maamooli* driver, isn't he?'

'Mom!'

Saloni raised her eyebrows as Jai shut the door and came on to the landing. 'Charming pair,' she remarked, all her old antipathy towards Nikita coming back in a rush. 'You need a hand with that?'

Jai shook his head. Damn Nikita. Saloni looked all worked up and hassled. He got rid of the rat, chucked the bucket into a corner of Nikita's parking space, and went back up the stairs.

'Give me a second while I wash my hands,' he said to Saloni. She hadn't put on her shoes, or re-tied her hair, he noted. That had to be a good sign, but he didn't know her well enough yet to be sure. He was bent over the sink, lathering his hands with soap when he felt her arms encircle his waist. OK, that was definitely a good sign. Jai had a fair amount of experience with women and he knew that saying he was sorry right now would be a bad move. He pretended to ignore the hands sliding up his chest, and turned on the tap. Saloni slid her hands over his, rinsing the lather off very, very slowly. He could feel her breasts pressed up against his back, and her soft breath on his neck.

'Towel,' he said, jerking his head towards the clothes line, and she moved away to fetch it. When she came back, he ignored the towel, taking her by the shoulders instead, and putting his mouth on hers in a hard, scorching hot kiss. She melted into his arms, clasping him around the neck and kissing him back blindly. He broke the kiss after several minutes to pick her up and carry her into the living room. But even as he snapped the light off and deposited her on the mattress that served as his bed, he found he was thinking of Nikita, and as Saloni pulled him down on top of her, he imagined Nikita in her place, Nikita's hands unbuttoning his shirt, and Nikita's voice moaning softly into his ear.

Back in Goa, Anuj was trying to get away from Diya, who was pursuing him single-mindedly. 'I really like you,' she was saying, putting a confident hand on his thigh. 'I like you, too,' Anuj said, in the tone he used with Suraj's more annoying friends. He had switched from single malt to Diet Coke an hour ago, and he was feeling very sober, and wishing he hadn't led Diya on. It was always like this—he'd find a woman attractive, but the second she started acting too interested, he got put off. Maybe it was his subconscious mind forcing him to stay faithful to his wife, he thought.

'So, do you want to do something about it?' Diya was saying, and his attention snapped back as the hand returned to his thigh, a little higher this time. Something about what? The economic crisis? Global warming? Nuclear arms proliferation?

The hand inched a little closer to his groin, and he looked down. Oh, about that. For a second, he was actually tempted. Like Mount Everest, she was there, and he was a long way from home. Nerdy and bespectacled all through high school and college, it was only when he was in B-school that Anuj had discovered that a certain section of the female sex found him irresistible. For the next five years until he met Shilpa, he had happily made up for lost time by sleeping with every woman who was willing and not positively hideous. Back then, he'd have jumped at the thought of a one-night stand with Diya.

'I'm married,' he said, giving the straying hand an avuncular pat and returning it once more to its owner.

Diya shrugged. 'So were my last two boyfriends.'

OK, tough one to counter. They were cheating bastards? He respected her too much? In theory, Anuj abhorred unfaithful husbands, in practice, he was often tempted to be one himself. The only thing that held him back was the knowledge that if Shilpa ever found out, she would take Suraj and walk out of their marriage without a backward glance.

'I happen to love my wife,' he said, getting to his feet. 'Good night, Diya.'

Rishi and the rest of the gang had gone back to their rooms ages ago, the pub crawl hadn't happened after all, and they'd spent the evening propping up the hotel bar. Anuj felt a little cheap as he walked across the lawns towards the main part of the hotel. He'd encouraged Diya shamelessly, and chickened out when she'd responded. If he'd been a woman, he'd have been branded a tease. Luckily, men didn't have to deal with labels of that sort.

9

'Are Chicago wings pork?' Saira asked, worriedly peering at the Dominos menu card.

'Only if you believe in flying pigs,' Suraj came back at her, and Shilpa had to stifle a smile. Anuj had just come home, and was making peace with his mother; Shilpa and Suraj were in Rakhi's flat to give them some space. The kids had managed to convince Rakhi that ordering pizza was a far, far better idea than eating bhindi sabzi and rotis (Yeeeurgh!), but they were now squabbling over the order.

'Here, I'll order for you.' Rakhi took the menu away, blithely ignoring the smouldering looks from both children. 'One plain margarita, and one cheese-crust with barbeque chicken, all right?'

'We want Coke,' they chorused. Rakhi frowned, she'd already dialled the pizza company. 'No Coke,' she mimed at them, and they turned to Shilpa to protest.

'Sorry, we go with what Rakhi says,' she said, raising her hands laughingly. 'Oh, and I can hear my phone ringing, give me a minute, I think I left it in the other room.'

It was Eknath, Anuj's driver. 'Bhabhi, I need some time off,' he said, and Shilpa's heart sank into her flip-flops. 'I've been trying to call Anuj Sahib, but he's not picking up his phone.'

No wonder, his mother would have probably hit him on the head with it if Anuj tried to answer the phone while she was talking to him. 'Why, Eknath, what's happened?'

His father was critically ill apparently, and he needed to go back to his village. Shilpa made all the correct noises, offering him money if he needed it, and wishing his father a speedy recovery. After he got off the phone though, she buried her head in her hands and groaned.

'Toothache?' Sandeep had come into the room, obviously just back from work. Shilpa shook her head. 'Anuj's driver is going on leave. And he'll be back only after a month, and Anuj's mother's here, she needs the car almost every day, and there's the car pool, and...'

'Relax,' Sandeep said, smiling at her, and not for the first time, Shilpa thought what a genuinely nice man he was. He was of average intelligence, and not a brilliant conversationalist by any standards, but he was comfortable to be with, and she liked him far better than the ambitious, backstabbing bankers who were Anuj's friends.

'I know,' she sighed. 'I'm overreacting as usual, but this has been a bloody awful week. The only thing left is for Madhuri to quit, and then I'm officially screwed.'

'How's work?' he asked, and Shilpa shrugged. 'Good, I guess. I've been offered a promotion, my boss is moving to Singapore, and they want me to take his job.'

Sandeep's face lit up. 'Wow, that's amazing news. Congratulations!'

Shilpa gave a little sigh. 'It means a lot more travel, and with Anuj being away so much, I'm not sure it's best for Suraj. I haven't even told Anuj yet.'

'Oh,' he said, his face falling. 'Can you decline the role?'

Shilpa gave a wry smile. 'And end up reporting to someone at the same level as me? Technically yes, but I know I'll end up taking it. Oh well, something will work out. How're things with you? Work going well?'

Sandeep's brow furrowed and she felt a prickle of unease. 'Not too great.' he said.

'Boss being a pain?'

'She's losing it,' Sandeep said despondently. 'Women bosses—my last boss was a woman too, and she was mercurial, blowing her top over something one minute, and being unnaturally nice the next. This one's even worse, she's older of course, but she's so temperamental it isn't funny.'

'It's the difference between PMS and menopause,' Shilpa said. 'Cheer up, things will get better.'

Sandeep hesitated. 'Actually that's not all of it,' he said. 'I need to come and speak to you some time.'

'We can talk now,' Shilpa said, but Sandeep shook his head. 'I don't want to worry Rakhi. I'll call you and come over, maybe to your office. Come on, let's go see what the kids are doing.

'I want a basketball hoop on the wall like Suraj has,' Saira was saying to Rakhi, her arms akimbo. 'Why can't we have one?'

'Because this is a rented flat, and we can't drill holes in the wall,' Rakhi said brusquely, but she shot a look at Sandeep that was loaded with resentment.

'Can we move into a flat like Suraj's then?' Saira was a persistent little person. Shilpa could imagine her twenty years later asking a hapless boss, 'Why can't I have a raise... Oh so I'll be paid more than you so?... I don't see a problem?...Yes, a 50 per cent hike, and with retrospective effect please...'

'So can we?' Saira was saying. 'Buy a big flat like Suraj's?'

'Maybe someday,' Sandeep said. 'When I have the money.'

'But if you work in the same bank as Anuj Uncle does, how come you don't make as much money? Suraj has much nicer things than I do.'

Sandeep's face went white, and Shilpa involuntarily looked at Rakhi, expecting her to reprimand her daughter. Rakhi stayed silent though, and her expression suggested that she thought her daughter was asking a very valid question. Shilpa felt a sudden surge of anger sweep over her.

'I don't think you're old enough to be asking your father how much he earns,' she said, her voice like ice. Suraj looked up, and immediately removed himself to a safe distance—his mother lost her temper very rarely, but when she did, it was prudent to keep out of her way. 'Actually I don't think it's a question you ever have the right to ask. He's working hard to give you the best life that he can, and that's all you can expect of him.' From the corner of her eye, she could see that Rakhi was about to say something, and she continued smoothly, 'But since you do want to compare your family with Suraj's, the reason we have a bigger house is because both Suraj's dad and I work.' Saira was looking at her with eyes wide open, not used to such blunt talk.

Shilpa gave her a quick smile. 'It's like that Lego house Suraj was building. It got done faster when both of you were working on it, right?' Wow, how was that for a metaphor—completely apt and something that the kid could understand without wracking her brain. Her anger was ebbing fast, though she still thought that Rakhi could do with a few home truths.

'It got done faster, but Saira put a totally disgusting set of pink windows on one side,' Suraj said, sidling back now that his mom emerged from her scary Ice Queen mode.

'Well, that's the kind of stuff you need to live with if you're working together,' Shilpa said. Then before her mouthy son could retort and completely spoil her perfect simile, she said 'Oh, I wonder where the pizza guy is?'

'If he comes later than 30 minutes, we get the pizza free, right?'

The doorbell rang at that second, dispelling any hope of free pizzas.

'The guard should have called us on the intercom before letting the delivery boy into the building,' Rakhi said, frowning. She'd decided not to get into an undignified argument with Shilpa, but some of the remarks she'd made had stung.

'Bloody awful woman,' Shilpa said, collapsing on the bed once she got home. Anuj raised an eyebrow. 'My mom?'

'Yes of course,' Shilpa rolled her eyes. 'No, idiot, I meant Rakhi. She gives Sandeep such a terrible time, runs him down in front of the kid…'

'No one's forcing him to put up with it,' Anuj said, shrugging. 'If it bothers him, he should do something, tell his wife to shut it or he'll stop paying the bills.'

Shilpa winced—Anuj could be totally crass at times. 'I do hope you don't say things like that at work,' she said. 'Being politically correct is the in thing. By the way, how are things with your mom, has she forgiven you yet?'

'Kind of,' Anuj said. 'She went on a bit about how I've changed, and I'm getting too busy, no time for family, but then she got talking about Suraj and calmed down.' Shilpa's phone beeped and he leaned across to pick it up.

'You and Sandeep seem to have formed quite a mutual fan club,' he said, sounding amused. 'He's asking if he can come across to your office tomorrow morning and meet you. Should I be worried?'

'I hate you reading my messages,' Shilpa said angrily. 'I don't read yours, do I?'

Anuj grinned and handed the phone across. 'I'm so sorry,' he said, his tone mocking. 'I thought we had no secrets from each other, no skeletons in our cupboards…'

'No messages from pretty young things from office,' Shilpa said sweetly. She'd never looked at Anuj's phone, but his expression when certain messages came in was a dead giveaway. Ha, she'd been right, he was looking guilty as hell.

'I think I'll go and spend some time with your mom,' she said, getting to her feet. Anuj was the kind of person who would go crazy wondering which message she'd read and when, and she wanted to let him stew in his own juice for a bit. 'She must be bored with nothing to do.'

'She's knitting something,' Anuj said sulkily. 'I hope it's for you, and not for me; I haven't yet worn the sweater she made for me the last time she was here.'

'It's for Jai,' Shilpa said, enjoying the flabbergasted look on Anuj's face. 'Your mom's really taken a shine to him. If you're not careful, she'll disown you and adopt him instead.'

༄

Shilpa was on the phone when Sandeep was ushered into her cabin the next morning.

'Give me a minute,' she said apologetically, holding one hand over the receiver. 'Monthly review calls with my teams in the other cities, it's a bloody pain, takes up most of my day.'

'No worries, I'll wait.' Sandeep looked around Shilpa's cabin. There was a picture of Suraj on her desk, and another on the wall, but none of Anuj. Should one read something into that, Sandeep wondered. Rakhi had vented at length on how

Shilpa spent hardly any time with Suraj and even less with Anuj. Disloyally, Sandeep had wondered if that was why Anuj and Suraj seemed so much happier than him and Saira. But then, Shilpa, unlike Rakhi, was not the nagging kind.

Shilpa had finished the last segment of her orange, and was gazing at the pips and the peel abstractedly as she jotted down the figures her Bengaluru team was reading out to her. Damn, there was orange juice all over her fingers now, even on the touch pad of her laptop. She scrubbed at it with a bit of tissue, and then tried to put the peel and pips into the tissue and wad it all up. It didn't work—the tissue was damp, and split open, the pips falling out. Better try something else.

Carefully she folded the orange pips up in the peel and sellotaped the little bundle together and put it in the corner of her desk. Glancing up, she noticed Sandeep smiling slightly and she flushed. 'We're not supposed to eat at our desks really,' she said, as she put the phone down. 'So I'll need to go and throw this in the wet waste bin in the pantry, and I don't feel like walking all the way right now. And I don't want the pips staring me in the face either…'

'So sellotaping it shut makes a lot of sense,' Sandeep said, nodding gravely. 'It's a good idea actually, you could sell it to 3M as their next big marketing innovation.'

'Hmmm, and use the money to buy myself a proper rubbish bin,' Shilpa said. 'You wanted to talk to me about something, Sandeep?' Not that she wanted to hurry him up, but she still had to speak to her Kolkata team, and they were the most excitable of the bunch; their review sessions typically lasted over an hour and had at least one impassioned speech on labour relations, with quotes from Lenin and Karl Marx thrown in for good measure.

'They've given me three months to find another job,' Sandeep said abruptly. Shilpa stared at him in dismay.

'But I thought things were going better!' she exclaimed. 'Rakhi said...'

'I haven't told Rakhi.' Sandeep passed a tired hand over his face. 'She doesn't understand how things work in the corporate world, and well, anyway she doesn't think I'm successful enough. She'd have gone completely ballistic if she'd known there was any risk of my getting sacked.'

He held up a hand as Shilpa opened her mouth to burst into indignant speech.

'Don't blame Rakhi,' he said. 'There's a lot of stuff that you don't know about—I've not always been the most ideal husband. And right now, I don't want her to know about this, I just want to try and find a job before the three months are up. You're in HR, can you help?'

'I'll try,' Shilpa said, her voice troubled. 'Send me your CV, and I'll speak to a few headhunters, and people I know in HR in other companies. But the market's bad right now. I can't guarantee that you'll get the kind of job you want.'

Sandeep gave her a brief smile. 'I'll take anything, if it helps me pay the rent and keep the house going,' he said. 'We haven't saved much money.'

'Are you OK with moving out of Mumbai?'

Sandeep hesitated. 'If I have to,' he said. 'But if I do manage to get something here, I'd like to stay in Mumbai.'

10

'So who's the girl who drops Anoushka to school?' Madhuri asked as she put Suraj's breakfast in front of him. 'The Chinese-looking one?'

'Her name's Jenny,' Suraj replied. 'She talks funny too, has a Chinese accent.'

Appalled, Shilpa swooped down on Madhuri and Suraj. 'She's *Indian*. She's from one of the northeast states!'

'Which one?' Suraj asked interestedly.

Ah, good question. Not Assam, but which one was it then? Mizoram? Nagaland? Sikkim? Was Sikkim even a part of India? Wishing she'd paid more attention to her geography teacher in school, Shilpa snapped back, 'I haven't asked her. But don't say she looks Chinese. That's really rude!'

Suraj frowned. 'Why, aren't Chinese people nice-looking?'

'Hmm, I always rather liked Michelle Yeoh,' Anuj said wickedly. 'And Lucy Liu isn't bad either. No, Suraj, I don't think Chinese people are bad-looking at all.'

'Stop it,' Shilpa said. 'And Madhuri, don't encourage Suraj to gossip, please.'

'Sorry, didi,' Madhuri said, but she quite obviously thought that Shilpa was barking mad. If someone looked Chinese, why not say they did?

'Rishi's asking if we can join him for dinner at his club tonight,' Anuj said looking up from his phone. 'Payal and he are hosting a few people. There's this hotshot private equity guy who's just relocated from the States, and Rishi thought it would be a good idea to meet him.'

'Who else is coming?' Shilpa asked. 'It's a weekday, and I don't like staying out late, Suraj refuses to go to bed on time if I'm not around.'

'One of Rishi's B-school classmates who's with Reliance,' Anuj replied. 'Some guy from a PR firm. And I think Darius and Shaheen were supposed to be there as well, but they have a Navjot to attend.'

Shilpa curled her lip. 'So Rishi invited you instead.' 'You', not 'us', Anuj noted. 'Shilpa, Rishi's my boss, it's difficult to say no. And it's a good opportunity to…'

'To network. I know.' Shilpa sighed. She couldn't blame Anuj, he probably wanted to be there as little as she did. 'All right, let's go. Suraj should be OK with Madhuri.' With Eknath on leave Jai was roped into driving Shilpa to the club—Anuj was hitching a ride with Rishi, presumably to network for a few precious minutes more.

'I'm late,' Shilpa fretted as she got into the car. This time she'd wanted to make more of an effort; she suspected that Anuj was a little upset with her cavalier approach to the compulsory socializing his job entailed. After finding out that Sandeep had lost his job she was more appreciative of Anuj's desire to get ahead. Perhaps he'd turned a little materialistic and show-offy, but it beat being unemployed any day.

'It'll take around forty-five minutes to get to the club,' Jai said. 'There's a massive traffic jam on Peddar Road.'

'Just my luck,' Shilpa moaned. She'd land up late, and the evening would get off to a bad start. The 'other wives' she was always being compared to, would have spent the evening getting dolled up, and would probably already be waiting for their husbands. She pulled out a mirror and surveyed her face. She'd planned to wash her hair in the morning, but Suraj had misplaced an all-important science notebook, and by the time she'd found it for him, it was too late. Her clothes thankfully were OK—she'd worn one of her more expensive black shirts over formal black trousers, and a simple pearl pendant on a platinum chain. Her unwashed hair looked lank and greasy though, and after trying for a few minutes to coax some bounce into it she gave up and pinned it into a French knot.

When the car came to a halt at the next signal, she took a tube of lipstick out of her purse and slathered some over her lips. 'Bugger, this is the wrong shade,' she said in dismay, looking at her face in the mirror and trying to scrub the bright pink lipstick off with a tissue. 'Now I look like a retired bar girl. Why do all the tubes have to look the same I really don't know…'

Jai looked into the rear view mirror and smiled involuntarily, 'It isn't that bad,' he said. 'Makes you look less washed out.'

Shilpa grimaced. 'If that's supposed to boost my confidence it didn't work,' she said. 'You might as well be honest and tell me that I'm a hideous old hag.'

'You're a hideous old hag,' Jai said obediently, and Shilpa swatted him on the shoulder. 'Idiot,' she said. She'd finally got over her stiff 'politically correct' manner with Jai, and treated him as if he was a younger brother or cousin, and Jai was far more comfortable with her as well.

As it turned out, Shilpa wasn't that late after all—Rishi and Payal were there and so was Anuj, but no one else had arrived.

'What's the name of the private equity guy?' Shilpa asked. She knew the other people who were expected, but Anuj and Rishi were engrossed in conversation near the bar, and neither had mentioned the name.

'Vikram, I think,' Payal said vaguely. 'Or Vikas. I've never met him. He had some meetings in the suburbs that's why he's late. He's driving down all the way from BKC.' She made it sound as if he was driving in from Outer Mongolia, and Shilpa smiled involuntarily. At the same moment, Rishi called out, 'Ah, there he is, the whiz kid himself. Meet Anuj, he's the most important man in my team, I'd be lost without him.'

Shilpa turned. The man who'd just walked in was tall. He had his back to her, but there was something very familiar about the set of his shoulders. Her heart thudded loudly in her chest as she waited for him to turn. Anuj was holding his hand out. 'Pleased to meet you, Vikrant,' he said, and then Shilpa knew. She sank back into her chair, tightly clenching her fists, and wishing that there was some way she could be invisible.

'Come and meet the lovely ladies,' Rishi was saying, and one tiny part of Shilpa's brain registered that he sounded like a patronizing old fart. He was bringing Vikrant across to where she and Payal were sitting. Shilpa kept her face averted for as long as she could, but when Vikrant came to stand next to her, she stood up to face him.

'Hi Vikrant,' she said, looking straight into his incredulous eyes.

There were a few seconds of silence, and then he held out a hand, not breaking eye contact even for an instant.

'Hi Shilpa,' he said quietly. 'It's been a while.' It certainly had. Eleven years and two months to be precise. He hadn't changed much—he looked older of course, which was hardly surprising, but the warm melted-chocolate eyes and perfectly sculpted features were just the way she remembered them. His hair still curled untidily over his forehead, and the gesture he used to push it back was the same. His shoulders were broader though, and his body had lost its hesitant, boyish grace. He'd always been athletic; now he looked harder somehow, and stronger, as if he spent his evenings at the gym rather than kicking a ball around on the football field.

'Do you know each other?' Rishi asked, and Shilpa was tempted to snap at him.

'We've met,' Vikrant said. 'I did my engineering summer training in a manufacturing firm, Shilpa was in their HR team and she was on my interview panel.' He gave her a quick smile that didn't quite reach his eyes. 'It was a wonder she recruited me.'

'I'm sure you were brilliant, wasn't he, Shilpa?' Rishi clearly had an axe to grind as far as Vikrant was concerned, he was never so nice otherwise. It felt weird, being in a group where Vikrant was clearly the most powerful person. When she'd met him for the first time, he was nineteen—very bright, almost in the genius category, but just a college kid all the same. He'd been strikingly good-looking even then, so good-looking that she'd hardly been able to tear her eyes away from his face during that short, ten-minute interview.

'He was very talented,' she said, smiling at Rishi though it was torture trying to keep her composure. And she couldn't help remembering the various talents Vikrant had, not all of them academic.

The other couple Rishi had invited came into the club, and the conversation turned general. Shilpa stayed as quiet as she could, trying not to draw attention to herself. Rishi was telling her about a strategy book he had read recently when Vikrant turned to Anuj.

'You were saying something about property rates, do you know where the market's at now?'

Anuj nodded, and began telling Vikrant about their flat in Carlton Towers, and how much the value of the flat had appreciated since they had bought it two years ago.

'Is it a good investment even now?' Vikrant asked.

'Yeeees,' Anuj said. 'Property prices are still rising. But home loan rates have gone through the roof, so...'

Vikrant shrugged. 'I wasn't planning to take out a mortgage, so that doesn't bother me much. I'm selling one of my Manhattan properties and I'll reinvest the money here.'

Selling one of his Manhattan properties. Buying a flat worth 8 crores without a loan. Shilpa felt an absurd impulse to giggle. Vikrant had come a long, long way from not being able to afford meals at the Udupi restaurant outside the office.

'But darling, you should look at buying something this side of town,' Payal said. 'Central Mumbai is nice, but it doesn't...' Rishi caught her eye and she subsided. Anuj grinned. 'Central Mumbai isn't as swanky,' he said. 'Full of terrible upstarts and social climbers.' Shilpa and Rishi both laughed, though Payal looked embarrassed.

'You grew up in South Mumbai didn't you?' Vikrant asked turning to Shilpa. She flushed, hoping he wouldn't say anything more and betray exactly how much he knew about her... Navy Nagar, she said. 'It's not the same as living on Marine Drive or Nepean Sea Road.'

'Hmmm. Well, I'll ask my broker to include Carlton Towers in the list of buildings to view.' Vikrant smiled at Payal. 'I'm sure south Mumbai is great, but I want an apartment complex which has a swimming pool.'

He'd been a state-level swimming champion in school. It was weird how she could suddenly remember all kinds of things about Vikrant. For years she'd blocked him completely out of her mind, probably because of the overwhelming sense of guilt at how she'd treated him

Her phone rang, and she fished it out of her bag. Anuj frowned, and Rishi said jokily, 'Our high-flying HR executive—someone's career's probably hanging in balance while Shilpa sips her low-calorie orange juice.'

God, he was so annoying. For a second, Shilpa wanted to tip her juice over his head and see if that wiped the smug grin off his face. 'It's from home,' she said. 'Suraj probably wants something. Excuse me, I'll be back in a minute.'

Except that it wasn't Suraj, it was Madhuri, calling to report that Suraj had locked himself in the TV room. '*Darwaza nahin khol raha hai*,' she said despairingly. She had been knocking on the door and pleading with him for almost forty-five minutes.

'Did you two have an argument about anything?'

'I told him to stop watching TV and have his dinner at 8 o'clock,' Madhuri said defensively. 'Just like you told me to. Then he ran in and slammed the door and locked it before I could do anything.'

Shilpa didn't know whether to laugh or cry. This was what being a mother did to you. Here she was, meeting an ex-lover twelve years after their tempestuous relationship had broken up, a lover she'd never told her husband about, and her number one priority was trying to figure out why her son had put himself under voluntary room-arrest.

'Tell Suraj to pick up the extension in the TV room,' she said. Two minutes later, Suraj came onto the line.

'I can't open the door,' he said blithely. The TV was blaring in the background, it sounded like Tom and Jerry.

'You've latched it,' Madhuri said. 'You aren't even trying to unlatch it!'

'I *have* unlatched it, so there! The door thingummy that locks on its own isn't opening!'

Shilpa sighed. 'I'll come back home,' she said. The door could be unlocked from the outside, but the key was inside her wardrobe and the wardrobe key was in her purse.

'I'll need to leave,' she said, going back to their table. Anuj looked up and frowned. 'Something serious?'

'Suraj's got locked into the TV room,' she said, and as he half rose up, 'You stay here, I'll handle it.'

Anuj nodded, though he still looked worried, and Shilpa felt a sudden surge of affection towards him. This dinner was important, but he was evidently prepared to walk out with her if she needed him to. She cast a quick glance around the table. Payal looked a little disapproving; she had strong views on bringing up children and on the amount of time a mother should devote to them. Rishi and the other couple were quite obviously amused. Vikrant's expression was inscrutable.

'I'll see you around then,' Shilpa said awkwardly, not able to meet Vikrant's eyes. Quite probably he thought she was making an excuse to get away from him. For a second, she remembered the look of utter devastation on his face when she'd seen him last, and a fresh wave of guilt swept over her. 'Bye Vikrant, it was nice meeting you again.'

'Good meeting you too,' he said, his voice formal and completely matter-of-fact. It was so matter-of-fact that as she walked away, Shilpa began to wonder if she was overreacting. He'd been only nineteen, of course he'd been devastated, but he'd had almost twelve years to get over it. And probably dozens of women to help him get over it as well—he could be looking at her right now and thinking, 'My God, what a lucky escape!'

'Shilpa,' Vikrant called out, and she turned. 'OK if I take your number from Anuj? It would be good to catch up some time.'

She nodded, unable to speak, because for a few seconds something had flickered in his eyes—something dark and a little twisted. Then she turned away, and hurried out of the club, her heart beating twice as fast as normal.

11

Sandeep gave Rakhi a harassed look. 'Let's not do the bookings right now,' he said. Rakhi had brought home a bunch of travel brochures—Spain, Italy, Greece—and there soon wouldn't be money even to go to Matheran.

'The rates will go up,' Rakhi said. 'And it would be nice to go to Spain with the Sethis, they're confirming their bookings this week.'

'I'm not sure I want to go with them,' he said. Sonia Sethi was an incredibly stuck-up woman. Her two biggest achievements in life were having been born to a rich father, and then marrying a rich husband. Rakhi thought she was the ultimate in style and sophistication, and did everything she could to encourage the friendship between their daughters.

She exhaled with a little puff of annoyance. '*I* would like to go with them,' she said with emphasis. 'And so would Saira.'

Something seemed to snap within Sandeep. 'We can't afford it,' he said baldly. 'You might as well know. I've lost my job, and I haven't been able to find another one. I have only a month and a half left of my notice period.'

Rakhi stared at him as if she didn't recognize him anymore. 'You've lost your job,' she said after a bit in an almost unrecognizable voice. 'When did this happen?'

'It's been almost two months since they told me,' he said. His senses felt dull in preparation for the inevitable onslaught of fury from Rakhi, but not having to pretend any longer was a relief. 'Shilpa's put me in touch with every headhunter she knows, but all of them say the job market's terrible, there's nothing suitable for me. So that's that. Sorry to be such a disappointment.'

'Shilpa knows.' It was a statement, and still in that unrecognizable tone.

'She promised not to talk about it,' he said. 'And she's the only person I know who's in HR outside my company.'

'Why didn't you tell me earlier?'

'I was hoping I'd find something,' he said.

'So you told Shilpa and you didn't tell me.'

Sandeep suddenly lost his temper, perhaps for the first time since they got married. 'How the hell does that matter? I've lost my job, have you got that simple fact into your thick skull? There isn't going to be any money coming in from next month onwards. We won't have money to pay the maids and the drivers, and I definitely can't afford the rent of this flat. We'll have to move. And we might not be able to afford Saira's school fees either.'

Rakhi paled. 'But we have savings,' she said. 'Can't we stay on here till you find another job.'

'We can,' Sandeep said. 'And then if I don't find a job, we won't have money for food.'

'But Sandeep...'

Sandeep wasn't in a mood to talk, and he got to his feet in a hasty movement. 'I'm going for a walk,' he said. 'You can think this out and decide if you still want to stay with me, or if you'd prefer going back to your parents.'

Rakhi stared at him. 'But of course I'll stay with you,' she said, tears slowly welling into her eyes. 'Why do you want me to go?'

'For the last ten years, you've constantly cribbed about my not earning enough,' Sandeep said. 'Now that I'm not going to be earning anything at all, sticking around might not be worth your while. Think it over and let me know.'

He was out of the flat before Rakhi could say a word, and she was left gazing at the closed front door.

༄

'This is physically, mentally and Bruce Lee impossible,' Suraj said in disgust. He was trying to lick his elbow in response to a dare from Saira.

'That makes no sense at all,' Saira said with immense scorn. 'Who's Bruce Lee anyway?'

'He's a Martian artist,' Suraj said confidently.

'Martial arts…ummm…exponent,' Shilpa said. 'How'd you hear of him?'

'Jai Uncle was talking about him yesterday,' Suraj said. 'Can I watch TV from today? It's more than a week since I locked myself in. Daadiji said it would be OK.'

'I suppose you can,' Shilpa said reluctantly. Anuj was travelling yet again. His mother had been in Shirdi when Suraj had locked himself into the TV room; she was back now, and was almost as upset by the TV ban as Suraj himself. Suraj ran to her room, whooping with excitement to tell her that the TV was within bounds again. Saira rolled her eyes in disgust, a very grown-up expression on her face. 'I think I'll leave now,' she said, gathering up her crayons and colouring books. 'Suraj and I have very different tastes in TV programmes.'

'I'll walk you home,' Shilpa said, hoping Saira wouldn't tell her off for the suggestion. Saira didn't object however, standing up and following Shilpa obediently to the lift.

Rakhi was clearing Saira's toys and books from the living room; she had a rather strained expression on her face. 'There's someone coming over to view the flat,' she said. 'Sandeep told the landlord last week that we're going to be moving out, and he's already put it on the market. Bloody money-minded Marwari.'

Shilpa couldn't help thinking that the landlord would have probably done the same even if he was a Buddhist monk, but she didn't say so.

'Is he renting it out, or selling it?'

'Renting it out for now.' Rakhi passed a hand over her face, and Shilpa saw with horror that she was very near tears. 'I'd spoken to him... before all this happened...and told him we'd be interested in buying the flat if he ever wants to sell it, and he said he'd think about it.'

'I'm sure things will work out,' Shilpa said awkwardly. 'Look I'll go now, I just came over because I didn't want to send Saira home alone.'

The doorbell rang, and Rakhi clutched at Shilpa's arm. 'That'll be them,' she said. 'The broker said they'd be here at ten. Don't go, I'd like you to be around, it won't feel so awful then.'

Shilpa stayed, but a few seconds later when the broker entered the room, she wished she hadn't. Because a step behind him, was Vikrant. It was difficult to say which one of them looked more taken aback. Shilpa recovered first.

'I thought you were buying a place,' she said.

'I haven't found anything I like yet,' he replied. 'So I'm looking for a flat to rent until I make a decision. And your husband was all praises for this building, I thought it would be a good place to begin.'

Rakhi was giving Shilpa an et-tu-Brute look, and Shilpa hastily introduced the two of them.

'Madam, if we could see the rest of the flat,' the broker prompted, and Rakhi glared at him as if he'd made an improper suggestion.

'Only if it's convenient,' Vikrant added, giving Rakhi a quick smile. 'I'd hate to disrupt your schedule on a Saturday morning.'

The smile hadn't changed, Shilpa noticed with a pang. Vikrant was dressed in jeans and a grey T-shirt today, and he looked a lot more like he did when he was in college. Rakhi wasn't particularly susceptible to charm, but the smile helped thaw her expression a little.

'You can see the flat,' she said, not very graciously. It didn't take them long—the flat had only two bedrooms, and even the broker ran out of things to say after a few minutes.

'Thanks for putting up with us,' Vikrant said to Rakhi. 'Shilpa, I've been meaning to call you—would you be free to talk sometime today?'

Shilpa was the kind of person who preferred to get unpleasant things over with as soon as possible, and she said, 'If you're done with viewing flats, we can talk now.'

'I have one more place to look at, but that's in this apartment complex as well,' he said. 'In the next building. I should be done in twenty minutes.'

'Right, I'll meet you in the garden then. It's on the first floor.'

Engrossed in her own problems, Rakhi wasn't disposed to be curious. 'We haven't even found a place for ourselves,' she moaned after the door closed behind Vikrant. 'Sandeep has a small flat in Bangalore that he bought years ago, we can always go there, but then we'll need to change schools for Saira, and there's the cost of shifting... I really don't know what to do.'

'Look for a cheaper flat in this area,' Shilpa advised as she left. 'Then Saira doesn't need to change schools. Maybe a building like where Nikita stays.'

Vikrant was already waiting in the garden when Shilpa reached. It was nearing the end of summer, and there were a few rain clouds overhead. Vikrant was sitting on a park bench looking up at them, his hands loosely folded across his chest. He turned around as Shilpa stepped into the garden, but he waited silently for her to cross the short stretch of grass that separated them before he spoke.

'This is a little awkward,' he remarked, his voice perfectly pleasant.

Shilpa sat down next to him. Little' is an understatement,' she said. 'Vikrant, I'm terribly sorry about what happened, and that I never called you and explained...'

'I think I've figured it out now,' Vikrant said. 'You met Anuj, didn't you?'

Shilpa nodded unhappily. 'I wasn't dating him or anything. But we were friends, and well, I knew I really liked him, and...'

Vikrant stayed silent for a while. 'You didn't feel the same way about me ever,' he said, and it was a statement, not a question.

'I was very fond of you,' she said. 'And of course...'

'And there was the sex.'

There was. It was horribly, horribly embarrassing to admit it, but the only reason she'd stuck with Vikrant for the three months they'd been together was because he was absolutely phenomenal in bed. Otherwise she'd always found him a little over-intense. Compared to the other interns she'd recruited at the same time, he took his work terribly seriously, not even taking time off for lunch. She'd been intrigued by him because of his looks and his undeniable talent, and one day during their lunch break, she'd insisted he come with her to the office canteen. Things had progressed very quickly from there, and before she knew it, they were in the throes of a passionate affair.

Four weeks later, she'd met Anuj. He was the exact opposite of Vikrant—he'd made her laugh, and she didn't know quite where she stood with him. Even his insecurities were endearing. The day she met him, she'd known he was the kind of man she'd like to spend her life with. Poor Vikrant, he hadn't stood a chance after that.

'I wish you'd told me about Anuj.'

'I wasn't sure how you'd react. I thought you might try to confront him or something…..' Anuj hadn't known about Vikrant, and Shilpa hadn't wanted to tell him. It was too early in their relationship—if he'd found out that she'd thrown over an existing boyfriend to date him, he'd have probably run a mile from her.

'Maybe I would have,' Vikrant said. 'I wasn't in a very rational state of mind.'

He'd taken to following her around, waiting for her as she left office each day and begging her to give him another chance. In hindsight, she could have handled it much better. Back then, she'd been torn between guilt and fear. Guilt because she knew she'd treated him badly, and fear that he'd tell people she'd slept with him.

Vikrant was in the last week of his internship when her boss had come across the two of them having an altercation in the office canteen. Her boss was an elderly man, and very protective, he assumed that Vikrant was harassing her, and she hadn't contradicted him. The security guards who'd dragged Vikrant off the premises had told her later that he'd stood outside on the road for hours afterwards.

'I'm sorry about your internship getting cut short,' she said. 'And the way my boss treated you. I shoudn't have let it happen.'

'It knocked some sense into me,' Vikrant said. He glanced at the small scar on his wrist. No one knew except his roommate and his parents, but he'd tried to slit his wrists a few weeks later. Well, no point talking about it now—there was something vaguely ridiculous about a failed suicide attempt. For a few seconds when he'd met Shilpa with her husband at the club he'd been tempted to make a scene, tell her exactly what he thought of her. While good sense had stopped him, he still needed closure.

'Are you going to take one of these flats?' Shilpa was asking.

'I liked the one your friend stays in. Would it bother you if I took it?'

Yes it would. Why couldn't he take a flat somewhere else, there were dozens of buildings with swimming pools in the area. Why did he need to be in Carlton Towers? She'd have paid over a year's salary not to have to see him ever again, except that a year's salary was probably what he made in a month.

'It doesn't matter,' she said finally. There was no point letting him know he was getting under her skin.

'Hey Mom!' Shilpa looked across the garden. Oh God, here was Suraj, down for his weekly dance class. She plastered an artificial smile on her face and waved. 'Hi Aunty,' the dance teacher called out. He was a muscle-bound youth in his early twenties, and Vikrant raised an eyebrow. 'Aunty?'

Shilpa shrugged, trying not to look annoyed. 'If you have a kid, it gives the world an unlimited licence to call you 'aunty'. I did think of telling him not to, but that would have been like Bindu in that awful movie where she keeps saying "*Bete, mujhe aunty mat kaho naa.*" To think I used to actually find that funny! Poor Bindu.'

Vikrant laughed in spite of himself. 'I can't quite take it in,' he said. 'You with a husband and a kid—you look just the same as you always did. Who's the girl with your son?'

'The maid,' Shilpa said. '*She* doesn't call me aunty thankfully.'

Vikrant got to his feet. 'I'll let you know if I decide to take the flat,' he said.

Shilpa looked up at him. 'Yes, all right,' she said, and hesitated. 'Come over for dinner some day if you're free.'

'I'm not sure,' Vikrant replied. 'I'm sorry, I'm still trying to come to terms with seeing you again.' He gave her a brief smile. 'I don't think I ever forgave you for dumping me like that without an explanation. But I'll see you around.'

Don't shift into the bloody building then, Shilpa felt like yelling after him. The last bit of her guilt was fading away. It was ten goddamn years, Vikrant needed to grow up and get a life. She hated the way he was making her feel, like she wasn't a good person. Or even worse, like she wasn't a good person, but had conned everyone around her into thinking that she was.

'I think I'll stay over with Nikita tonight,' Mrs Malhotra announced. 'She must be missing Radha, they had a terrible fight before she left.'

Having had a terrible fight sounded like a good reason for Nikita *not* to miss her mom. Shilpa didn't argue though. This particular visit had gone off pretty well so far, but she felt like having her home to herself for a bit.

~

'Have you completed that sweater for Jai?' Nikita demanded when she saw her aunt.

Mrs Malhotra had not only completed the sweater, she'd even bought Jai a pale blue button-down shirt to go with it. She was a good knitter, and Jai gave her a grateful smile as he accepted the little package. He hadn't brough any warm clothes with him when he left Jaipur, and he'd been wondering whether to invest in a jacket. He tried the sweater on, and Mrs Malhotra gave him a fond look. '*Kitna sona lag raha hai*,' she said. 'You can wear it at home at least, in the evenings.'

'It's very nicely made,' Nikita said. 'He can wear it outside as well. How come you never make me anything? I saw a really nice wrap in Zara, but it cost a bomb. Can you knit it for me if I show you the pattern?'

'I can do that,' Mrs Malhotra perked up immediately. 'Can I see it on your computer, or will I need to go to the store?'

'The store would be better,' Nikita said. 'But don't let them figure it out that you're only there to look at the design.'

Jai went with them. He liked Mrs Malhotra, and when she told him in confidence that Anuj would never wear any of the things she'd knitted for him, he felt a little sorry for her. More than once, he'd got the impression that Anuj was embarrassed by his loud, exuberant mother, but he hadn't realized that Mrs Malhotra was aware of it.

They met Naveen as they were stepping out of the store. 'Didn't find anything you liked?' he asked Nikita, gesturing towards her empty hands. 'No shopping bags?'

'Shhh', Nikita countered, looking around her in a very Bond-girlish way. 'We came here to steal a design.' Naveen looked puzzled, and she drew him aside and explained. He laughed. 'That's a brilliant idea,' he said. 'And I'm very impressed that your aunt's willing to put in all the effort for you.'

'What can I say, I'm worth it,' Nikita said. 'What've you been buying—diamonds for a new girlfriend?'

Naveen gave the jewellery bag in his hand a rueful look. 'Diamonds for my mom, actually. It's her birthday next week, and she's pickier than any girlfriend I've ever had. I'll probably be back next week, exchanging this for something bigger and better.'

'Such a sweet thought,' Mrs Malhotra said, beaming at him. 'I'm sure she'll love whatever you've got her.'

'Would you like to take a look? I don't want to open the bag here, but let me treat you all to some ice cream, and I'd love to have your opinion on what I've bought.'

Mrs Malhotra was dying to see what was in the bag, and didn't need a second invitation. Nikita linked her arm in Naveen's, and Jai didn't have a choice but to follow them. He felt an unfamiliar frisson of jealousy. Saloni was very close to Naveen, but that had never bothered him. Nikita making such an obvious play for him was a different thing altogether. Jai had a very primitive urge to yank her away and drag her home by the hair.

Naveen was opening the box and showing it to Anuj's mother. 'It's a mangalsutra pendant,' he said. 'She's always wanted one. What do you think, Jai?'

Mrs Malhotra passed the box to Jai, and he gave it a cursory look before handing it back to Naveen. 'Must have cost you a packet,' he said. 'The diamonds are excellent quality.'

'It's really pretty,' Nikita said. 'Though I honestly can't tell real diamonds from fake, they've always seemed a bit of a waste of money to me.'

Naveen smiled and put the pendant back into its box. 'I was planning to catch a movie after this,' he said. 'Anyone interested?'

Mrs Malhotra looked very tempted, but she knew where her duty lay. Naveen was exactly the kind of man her sister would choose for Nikita, and playing *kabab mein haddi* was out of the question.

'I'll get late for my puja,' she said, putting on a suitably regretful expression. 'But Nikita's free—Jai beta, you'll drop me home, won't you?'

'Interesting chap, this Jai of yours,' Naveen said, as he watched the two of them walk away. 'He seems to earn barely enough to make ends meet, has to be a tough life. And all he needs to do is patch up with his father to have a perfectly comfortable existence.'

'His dad doesn't want him writing the book about his granddad,' Nikita said. 'I assume some family skeletons are going to tumble out of the closet whenever the book's released.'

'I don't think so,' Naveen said. 'I've read most of the book, remember. There's nothing scandalous in it.'

'Doesn't need to be scandalous,' Nikita said. 'People get upset about the silliest things when it's to do with family. My mom stopped speaking to Sushma Maasi for a year because Maasi told a neighbour she dyes her hair. Anyway, it's not like Jai's losing out on much, not joining his dad's piddly business.'

Naveen stared at her. 'You really don't know, do you?'

'Know what? His dad's a jeweller in Jaipur or something, nothing great. And anyway, his sister's running the business now, there isn't anything for Jai to do.'

'You utter dimwit!' Naveen exploded. 'The man's heir to one of the largest jewellery businesses in the country—his father's a multimillionaire.' A multimiillionaire. Nikita's jaw literally dropped, and she was struck speechless for a few seconds.

'Well, how would I know,' she said weakly after a while. Then her sense of injury got the better of her. 'He never said! I just assumed his dad had some small-time jewellery store. And anyway, it's not particularly glamorous, it's just one step above being a shopkeeper or something.' The last bit didn't even make sense, but she was so muddled she didn't know what she was saying.

'It could be worse,' Naveen said drily. 'My father made his money supplying underwear elastic to every innerwear manufacturer in the country.'

Underwear elastic. OK, that definitely sounded worse.

'And when you have a surname like mine…' he continued.

'*Underwear ka elastic, Naveen ka bra*,' Nikita realized, and gave a little snort of laughter.

'Exactly,' he said. 'You can imagine what I went through in high school. Actually you can't. The only people who really understand are girls called Rupa.'

'*Rupa ka underwear aur banian*,' Nikita nodded in agreement. 'Yes, they must have had a bad time as well.'

'So about Jai, I thought you knew, and that's why you're so friendly with him.'

Nikita stared at him. 'What's that supposed to mean?'

'You don't treat him like your driver,' Naveen said. 'I met his sister when she was looking for a PR agency for a new line of jewellery, and I made the connection. I just assumed you'd always known that he came from a rich family.'

'Because I'm polite only to rich guys?' Nikita asked slowly.

'You're pretty clear that you want to marry one at least,' Naveen said. 'From what Saloni says you're…'

Nikita stood up. 'So Saloni thinks I'm a gold-digger does she? And what does that make her? I've always wondered why she got so interested in Jai all of a sudden. I bet she knew about his being rich all along.'

'Whoa, relax,' Naveen said, laughing. 'Saloni doesn't know about this. I found out by accident. Jai's sister is launching a new line of jewellery, and she's been speaking to me about handling the launch event. Something about her reminded me of Jai, and I asked if they were related.'

Nikita didn't want to get off the subject of Saloni, but Naveen's expression warned her not to go there. 'Have you spoken to Jai about it?'

'I asked him what his father does,' Naveen said. 'He didn't seem keen on talking about it, so I dropped the subject. Come on, let's get inside the cinema hall, the movie's about to begin.'

The film was good—it had a politically sensitive theme, but the director had done an amazing job of balancing the politics with the love story. Most importantly, he'd succeeded in not pissing anyone off. Nikita liked good movies, but not enough to brave angry mobs bent on burning the theatre down.

'I've sent Jai's book to the director,' Naveen said after the movie was over. 'I have a good feeling about it. It's not a theme Wayne Brothers would want to do a movie on, but it's exactly up Shirish's alley.'

'You're turning into Jai's fairy godfather, aren't you?' Nikita said cattily. She was feeling unreasonably upset. So far, she'd studiously avoided thinking of Jai as anything other than a good friend because he was so clearly ineligible. And now that she knew he was just as eligible as Naveen himself, there wasn't a thing she could do about it.

'Less of the fairy, more of the god,' Naveen said, sounding amused. 'He's a talented kid, could do with a boost.'

Heroically, Nikita refrained from doing a Kapil Dev impersonation, saying 'Boost is the secret of my energy.'

'It's amazing, the amount of trouble you're taking over him,' she said instead, flushing when Naveen raised his eyebrows. 'I mean it; you could have been furious with both of us when you found out he'd submitted his plot outline under my name.'

'Ah, but I couldn't imagine getting furious with you,' Naveen murmured, bending his head to drop a light kiss at the nape of Nikita's neck. Nikita had to grit her teeth to stop herself from jerking away, especially when his hand came up to caress her bare arm. There was something wrong, she thought confusedly as he pulled her closer, her body pressed against his side as he walked her into the restaurant where they were to have dinner. This was what she'd wanted, Naveen showing an interest in her. And he was attractive—his touch wasn't repulsive, it just felt all wrong, and she was incredibly relieved when he let her go. Luckily he hadn't noticed anything amiss.

12

Sunday mornings were Shilpa's days to laze around in bed until she absolutely had to get up. This Sunday promised to be better than usual. With Anuj out of town, and his mother paying a visit to Nikita, she didn't have to bother about breakfast. Suraj would get himself a bowl of cereal whenever he woke up, and she herself preferred fruit to a cooked meal.

When her phone rang, she almost didn't pick it up. It kept on ringing, and Suraj who'd crept into her bed in the middle of the night, was beginning to stir.

'Aunty, there's a fire in the building, you need to come downstairs!'

'What?' For a few seconds, Shilpa wondered if Suraj's dance teacher was playing a trick on her. Then the urgency in his voice penetrated her drowsy mind, and she sat up. 'Are you sure, Krish?' she asked.

'Of course I'm sure! Don't waste time, Aunty, just grab Suraj and get downstairs. The fire engines are on their way, but it's safer to be out of the building.'

Shilpa got out of bed as the boy rang off, and looked out of the window. There was a crowd downstairs—everyone was waving their arms and pointing at the building, but from the window, Shilpa couldn't see anything.

'What's happening?' Suraj asked. He was awake now, sitting up in bed with a bewildered look on his face.

'Krish's saying the building's on fire,' she said. 'Wait here, I'll go out and check.'

She crossed the living room and opened the front door, there was smoke billowing in the corridor, and she hurriedly slammed it shut. 'Suraj, come on!' she said, trying to keep the panic out of her voice. 'We need to leave now.'

'I am not going out in my pyjamas,' Suraj said firmly.

'Didi how bad is it?' Madhuri sounded worried, but not panicky, thankfully.

'Bad,' Shilpa mouthed to her. Aloud, she said, 'Suraj come on! Madhuri, you leave now, carry a bottle of water with you, and if the smoke's too bad, wet your dupatta and cover your face. I'll get Suraj.'

Suraj had run to his bedroom, and was pulling out a pair of jeans and a T-shirt from his cupboard. He pulled away as Shilpa tried to drag him to the door.

'I need to change!' he said, and hoping that the few extra minutes wouldn't cost them their lives, Shilpa helped him drag on his jeans and change his T-shirt. Then she grabbed her purse, car keys and a bottle of water and ran out of the flat holding on to Suraj's hand tightly. The stairwell was empty, and the smoke was thicker now. Realizing that she'd brought only one towel, she poured some water over it and gave it to Suraj to cover his face, using the bottom edge of her kurta for herself. Suraj was beginning to cough now, and Shilpa was seriously scared, wondering whether it would have been safer to have stayed in the flat. The source of the smoke wasn't visible, but it seemed to be growing thicker as they went down the stairs.

A burly fireman was coming up, seeing Shilpa struggling to keep Suraj upright, he reached out for the boy. Slinging him over his shoulder, he headed downstairs, while Shilpa was left to make her way down alone. The going was easier without Suraj, and she managed to get out of the building and on to the first floor podium without inhaling too much smoke. Suraj was standing next to Krish, staring wide-eyed at the building. Smoke was billowing out of the 3rd and 4th floor windows. Saira and Sandeep were staring at the building—Sandeep looked very tense, and Saira was near to tears.

'Where's your mom?' Suraj asked, getting the question in before Shilpa had a chance to open her mouth.

'She's still in there,' Saira said. 'She told papa to take me downstairs, and she went to ring the doorbells of everyone on the floor, to make sure that they got out safely. But she's not come down yet, and neither have our neighbours…'

'Their daughter is paraplegic,' Sandeep said. 'Saira thought they might need help getting her out. I should have gone in her place.'

'Then why didn't you?' Shilpa almost asked, and then she started feeling dreadfully ashamed of herself. It hadn't occurred to her to even ring her neighbours' doorbells before she ran down the stairs. Getting Suraj out safely had been the only thought in her mind.

'There they are!' Suraj yelled. Three firemen were helping carry out the paraplegic girl, while Rakhi was supporting the girl's mother. The girl seemed all right, but both women had inhaled a fair amount of smoke. Rakhi semi-collapsed into Sandeep's arms, making a weird choking sound that was scarier than anything Shilpa had ever heard before.

'The ambulance will be here in a minute,' one of the firemen said. 'She'll be all right; she was stuck on the 3rd floor for a while, that's where she must have breathed in some smoke. The girl's quite heavy, and these two had already carried her down five floors.'

'Can I leave Saira with you?' Sandeep asked. The ambulance was turning into the building. Rakhi had stopped choking, but she was coughing terribly, and there was blood on Sandeep's shirt.

'Yes, of course I'll take her,' Shilpa said. 'Call me if you need help, Sandeep.'

'I'll follow the ambulance in my car,' Krish volunteered. 'You take care of the kids, Aunty.'

Too shaken to even register the dreaded 'aunty' word, Shilpa nodded. 'Kids, come with me, we'll go to Nikita's flat,' she said to Suraj and Saira as they watched the ambulance whisk Rakhi away. 'Saira, your mom will be OK, don't look so upset.'

Saira nodded, biting her lip. 'I wish she wasn't so brave,' she said in a small voice. 'If she'd come down with us instead of trying to help Vidya she'd have been fine.'

Shilpa dropped down on her knees and gave Saira a hug. 'You should be proud of her,' she said. 'Look at the rest of us, we just ran out without thinking of anyone else.'

A second fire truck pulled up behind the one already there, and more firemen rushed out to enter the building. The smoke had grown a lot thicker, and was now pouring out of the lobby as well.

'It's a short circuit in the electrical duct,' one of the firemen was heard saying. 'And people had stored old wooden furniture and things in the duct—that's what caught fire first, and now the entire duct is up in flames.'

'Will our things be all right?' Suraj asked fearfully as he saw the firemen train their hoses on the building. 'The windows are open, everything will get *wet*.'

'That's the general idea,' Shilpa said. 'Things don't burn if they're wet.' Suraj was right though. In their zeal, the firemen were hosing more water into the flats than into the duct. In any case, weren't electrical fires supposed to be put out with sand?

∽

Nikita and Mrs Malhotra had just sat down to breakfast when Shilpa turned up at the doorstep with Madhuri and the two children in tow.

'*Hai Ram*!' Mrs Malhotra gasped out when she heard what had happened. 'Thank heavens you're all right.' She clasped Suraj to her generous bosom, and for good measure, pulled Saira in for a hug as well while Suraj squirmed in embarrassment.

'Your mom's better,' Shilpa told Saira. 'I just got a message from Krish. She'll have to stay in the hospital overnight though.'

'Does she need an operation?'

'No, they're just keeping her there to make sure she's completely OK.' She wasn't sure if that was correct—even if it wasn't, she could hardly tell Saira. Luckily, Saira seemed satisfied with the answer and didn't ask any more questions. Free to turn her mind to the pressing question of where they would sleep that night, Shilpa felt a rising wave of panic. The building electrician had told her that it would take at least a day to assess the damage to the central wiring, and probably longer before people could move back to Carlton Towers. If it had been just Suraj and her, there were dozens of friends whose homes she could go to. But with Madhuri, Saira and Mrs Malhotra thrown into the mix, she had no idea what to do. Nikita's flat was already bulging alarmingly at the seams.

'We can all adjust here,' Mrs Malhotra was saying comfortably. 'We just need a few extra mattresses, and the children could use Nikita's bed.' Shilpa caught the look of horror on Nikita's face and said quickly, 'Ma, I think we should take a couple of rooms in a hotel. Hopefully we'll be able to move back into our flat soon.'

Mrs Malhotra's expression suggested that they might as well withdraw all the money in their respective bank accounts and make a nice bonfire. Shilpa ignored it and started making a few calls. By the time she was done, she was inclined to agree with her mother-in-law. With no inkling on how long it would take till they could go back home, booking a hotel room could turn out pretty expensive.

Relief came in the form of a call from the mom of one of Suraj and Saira's classmates. 'Just read about the fire on the Net,' she said cheerfully. 'Send the kids over, Behram would love to see them. I'll drop all three of them off at school tomorrow.'

'We want to go!' Suraj and Saira chorused. 'Can we leave now?'

'I'll ask Jai to drop you if he's around.' Shilpa said. 'Ma, I'll take Madhuri and go back to the building to pack their things and ours. Should I get some of your bags?'

Mrs Malhotra shook her head. 'I have all I need,' she said. 'I'd packed some extra saris.'

Jai was nowhere to be found. He wasn't answering his cell phone, and his flat door was locked. Nikita finally volunteered to drive Shilpa and the kids to Behram's house.

'I thought Jai spent his weekends writing,' Shilpa said idly. They were waiting outside Carlton Towers—Madhuri had gone back upstairs to fetch an all important Nerf gun that Suraj had left behind.

'He's probably out somewhere with that slut of a Saloni,' Nikita replied, and Shilpa stared at her in astonishment. She'd sounded positively vicious, and very unlike her usual sunny self. Nikita flushed under her scrutiny.

'I don't like her much,' she said in explanation. 'From what I can see she's stringing both Naveen and Jai along. She's sleeping with Jai, and Naveen isn't exactly on brotherly terms with her.' She didn't add that Naveen wasn't on brotherly terms with her either. Shilpa was frowning, evidently on the brink of asking an uncomfortable question. Nikita hurried into speech. 'Isn't Madhuri taking awfully long?' she asked. 'It shouldn't take more than five minutes to climb the stairs, and Suraj said he left the gun lying on the shoe rack.'

'That's an intriguing statement,' a voice said behind them, and Nikita turned to look into the eyes of a perfectly gorgeous man. He was good-looking enough to make her lose track of what she had been saying. As she stared though, she began to notice slight flaws that hadn't caught her attention at first. The lack of humour in his dark-brown eyes, the tightness around the mouth, the slightly over-intense way in which he was looking at Shilpa. In turn, Shilpa looked rather uncomfortable. 'Hi Vikrant,' she said, her usual smile missing from her face. 'You, uh know about the fire?'

'Just heard,' Vikrant said. 'I had made an appointment to speak to the building secretary about moving in, and when I got here I found out what had happened.'

'Oh, so you've decided to take a flat here, then,' Shilpa said. She'd tried to keep her tone neutral, but it still came out sounding all wrong, as if she was saying, 'Oh, you've decided to take up serial-killing as a serious hobby, have you?'

'Yes, but in the other tower. It's a little bigger than the one your friend has. Though now I'm wondering if it was such a good decision, the fire could have happened as easily there.'

'Or in any other building in Mumbai,' Nikita said. 'You're in the wrong country if you're looking for world-class safety norms.' She turned to Shilpa and asked 'Should I go check if Madhuri's OK?' and Shilpa could have kissed her in gratitude for the interruption.

'I'll go,' she said. 'Maybe she forgot some of her own stuff and went back.' Dusk was gathering and soon it would be impossible to see anything inside the stairwell, and even though she wanted to get away from Vikrant, Shilpa didn't fancy the thought of having to climb all those stairs a second time. Drat Madhuri, if she'd come back when she was supposed to, they wouldn't have run into Vikrant in the first place.

'One of the kids still in the building?' Vikrant asked, sounding surprised. Nikita answered him. 'No, Shilpa's maid went in to fetch something around fifteen minutes ago, and she isn't back yet.'

'I'll come with you,' Vikrant said as Shilpa started towards the stairs. 'The building's deserted, its not safe going in alone.'

Shilpa was very tempted to say that if the building really was deserted it would be perfectly safe but she bit the words back. Madhuri's disappearance was worrying, and, however, uncomfortable Vikrant made her, it made sense taking him along.

The stairs were still very wet, and Shilpa held on to the banister as she carefully climbed up. Vikrant stayed one step behind her; he could have probably run up the stairs in half the time, and Shilpa wondered if he thought she was a wuss. If he did, it couldn't be helped. Better being a wuss than a middle-aged woman with a broken leg.

They were on the eighth floor when they heard it, a muffled cry that broke off halfway. Shilpa stopped immediately and listened, but there was no sound other than that of water dripping steadily from the various places where the firemen's hosepipes had wreaked havoc. The walls were streaked with soot and a strong smell of smoke and wet ashes hung around the stairs—the fading light made it look very much like a Ramsay Bros horror movie set and Shilpa wondered if she had imagined the sound.

'Did you hear something?' she asked Vikrant uncertainly. He nodded. The door leading from the stairs to the landing on the eighth floor was slightly ajar, and he pushed it open, stepping into the area opposite the lifts.

'There doesn't seem to be anyone here,' he said. 'Which floor is your flat on?'

'Sixteenth,' Shilpa said. 'Maybe we should go up and check there first.'

'Try calling out to the girl,' Vikrant suggested, and Shilpa obediently said 'Madhuri!'

No voice called out in response, but there was a scuffling sort of sound that could have been rats or mice running across the floor.

'Madhuri!' Vikrant called out, his louder and deeper voice echoing through the empty building.

'There's a fire refuge area on this floor, should we check that?' Shilpa asked.

Vikrant strode towards the partially shut door to the refuge area. It was the empty shell of a flat that had been kept vacant in accordance with fire department regulations. Ironically, in the excitement today, everyone had forgotten about it, and had rushed past the eighth floor to brave the choking smoke at the lower levels.

Vikrant pushed the door open, and Shilpa followed him rather unwillingly into the refuge area. It had just occurred to her that Madhuri might have gotten delayed because she had wanted to use the loo. Perhaps she might have already gone down the stairs past the eighth floor while they messed around. Just as she was about to mention this to Vikrant, her breath caught in her throat as she saw past him into the flat. There were two figures struggling silently at one end, the larger one a man with one hand clamped around Madhuri's mouth while the other hand grasped her cruelly by the waist.

Startled by the sound of the opening door, the man relaxed his hold on her mouth, seizing the opportunity, Madhuri bit into his hand with all her might at the same instant as Vikrant launched himself across the room at him. The man swore loudly, hitting Madhuri so hard that she went flying into the corner. As he turned to face Vikrant, Shilpa recognized Shinde, the building supervisor, his visage so contorted with fury that he hardly looked human any more. Blood was dripping from the hand Madhuri had bitten, but he was still twice as bulky as Vikrant. Vikrant was taller though, and in excellent physical condition, he evaded the man's first lumbering rush, and grabbed him around the throat from the back, one muscled arm almost choking him.

'*Saala, haraamzaada, chhupaa tha yahaan par...*' Madhuri had a deep cut where her forehead had hit the wall, but her spirit was completely unbroken. Trembling with rage, she stood and confronted the man.

'Madhuri, *chalo neeche*,' Shilpa said, tugging at her arm, but the girl refused to move. '*Maar daaloongi haraamzade ko*,' she said, her eyes darting around the room—clearly she was looking for a suitable murder weapon. The man was glaring at her, but slowly, sanity was returning to his expression as the enormity of the situation began to sink in.

'*Bhai...*' he choked out after a few seconds, and Vikrant gave Shilpa an enquiring look. 'I think you're cutting off his breathing,' Shilpa explained, staring at Shinde's goggling eyes and purple face in fascination.

'Well, I'm not letting him go until I have reinforcements,' Vikrant said. 'Perhaps if you could yell out to my driver from the window, he's standing near the car.'

Madhuri had in the meantime given up the search for a weapon, and she latched on to this suggestion with enthusiasm. Leaning out of the window, she shrieked out to Nikita 'Didi, can you please ask sir's driver to come upstairs, he's caught a monster, we need help. Quick, quick!' 'Don't leave the children,' Shilpa yelled out as Nikita made as if to move towards the building. 'Madhuri, go down and be with the kids.'

The driver came up in record time, and Vikrant released Shinde as soon as he burst into the room. Hot on his heels were an electrician and two inspectors from the fire department—they gawped at Shinde as he coughed, holding his hands to his throat.

'Take this guy downstairs,' Vikrant said, shoving him towards the driver. 'Madhuri, are you all right?'

'Yes,' Madhuri said, brushing away Shilpa's hand as she tried to examine the cut on her forehead. She was still spitting with fury. 'I can't believe that man had the nerve to touch me! If my father was still alive, he'd have castrated him! All this while I thought he was just an old lecher, and he wouldn't have the *himmat* to do anything to me. I'll fix him—I have friends in the area—my Rakhi brother is a policeman, he'll make sure this guy doesn't dare to even look at a woman ever again, I...'

'Thank sir for helping you,' Shilpa prompted gently, stopping the girl in mid-tirade. Madhuri turned towards Vikrant, her eyes still ablaze. 'Thank you,' she said. The interruption seemed to have made her realize what had almost happened, and she fumbled to adjust her dupatta. 'Don't let my mother find out,' she said abruptly to Shilpa. 'She'll get upset again.'

'She would need to know,' Vikrant said gently. 'Specially if this becomes a police matter.'

∾

But it turned out that it wouldn't be a police matter, because once Madhuri had a chance to think things out calmly, she said she wouldn't be filing a police report. 'No one will marry me if they know this happened,' she said. 'They'll think he did a lot more than he actually did. And I don't think he'd have really done anything, he lost his head and grabbed me when I screamed.'

'What if he molests someone else?' Vikrant asked.

Madhuri shook her head. 'As if my making a police complaint would make any difference.'

'I don't think making a big deal about this will help anyone,' Shilpa said, drawing Vikrant away. 'I'll speak to the society managing committee—Shinde will lose his job right away, I can guarantee that.'

Vikrant raised his eyebrows. 'That should have happened a long time ago,' he said. 'As soon as you found out that he was harassing the girl. It would have saved her from this experience if you'd done something right away.'

'Her own mother didn't want me making a fuss about it,' Shilpa burst out hotly. Not that she cared about Vikrant's opinion, but the condemnation in his tone stung. 'Vikrant you've been away from India for too long, you've forgotten how things work here.'

'Evidently,' he said, holding her gaze steadily. 'I remember a big fuss being made when all I had done was…'

'This is not about you!' she exclaimed, but he'd swung away without completing the sentence. Madhuri was finishing the Coke Vikrant had got her as Nikita cleaned up the cut on her forehead and covered it with a Band-Aid.

'Done?' Vikrant asked, leaning across to take the empty plastic bottle from her. She smiled up at him, and Shilpa thought that she looked far more grateful for the Coke than she had for Vikrant saving her from possible rape.

'Can we go now?' Suraj demanded. He was standing next to Nikita—Saira had fallen asleep in the car.

'Your Nerf gun!' Madhuri wailed in sudden dismay. 'Oh, and it's dark now. Give me five minutes, Suraj, I'll run up and get it.'

Shilpa was about to stop her when Vikrant said firmly, 'Oh no, you won't. I'm going to drop you back at your mother's, so you can recover from this whole mess.'

But Madhuri wasn't having any of that. 'I'm going with Suraj and Saira,' she said resolutely. 'They need someone to look after them, or they'll drive Behram's mother crazy. And I don't want to go anywhere near my mother for another week or so, she'll be very angry with me.'

'Poor girl,' Vikrant said as Madhuri got into the car. 'If the same thing had happened to someone in our class of society, the whole family would have rallied around to take care of her.'

There was a lot of truth in what he said, but by now Shilpa was completely sick of Vikrant. 'I'm sure,' she said shortly. 'But as she isn't, I'll do my best.'

Vikrant nodded, and stepped back as Shilpa got into the car. Nikita shot her a quick look as she put the car into gear and drove out of the gates. 'How do you know this guy?' she asked.

'He was a trainee in one of the firms I worked in a long while ago,' Shilpa said. 'And we met him again recently at one of Anuj's office dos.'

'Banker?'

'Private equity,' Shilpa said, expecting Nikita to immediately ask for his number. 'He's loaded. Unattached too, as far as I know.'

Surprisingly, though Nikita was shaking her head. 'Not my type. Too… I don't know, highly strung I guess.' She gave a self-deprecating grin. 'Not that I made much of an impact anyway—he barely noticed my existence.'

Which was a surprising thing in itself. Nikita wasn't conventionally beautiful, but she was striking to look at, and men usually noticed her over other, prettier women. Vikrant had hardly looked at her; his attention had been completely taken up by Madhuri.

It was after they'd dropped Madhuri and the kids off at Behram's sprawling old-fashioned flat in Malabar Hill that Nikita came back to the subject of Vikrant.

'The flat this chap is renting, is it the one Rakhi lives in now?'

'He looked at it, but I think he's renting another one. Don't talk to her about it, though, she's feeling really bad about having to move.'

They were just turning onto Peddar Road, and Nikita had to concentrate on her driving as a couple of bikers almost skidded under the wheels of the car. 'Morons,' Nikita muttered, as one of them turned to give her a cheeky wave. 'Suicidal idiots. Look at them in their black jackets—like a pair of bloody buffaloes. Their parents must be mad, buying bikes for snotty brats like that.' Shilpa nodded in what she hoped was a sympathetic manner. The day's events were catching up with her, and all she wanted to do was crawl into bed and sleep.

'You had something going with this Vikrant dude, *kya*?' Nikita asked casually when she stopped at the next signal. Shilpa snapped out of her drowsy state to stare at her in horror. 'Why…of course not! I've known him for a long while, he's a lot younger than me, why would you even think…'

Nikita gave her a wry look. 'Save it,' she advised. 'It's pretty obvious, you're so wary around him, and he's clearly not forgiven you for whatever you did to him. But if you like, I won't talk about it.'

'I'd have liked it even more if you hadn't brought it up,' Shilpa said. 'Don't tell Anuj, OK? I've been meaning to speak to him about it, I just don't know how to bring it up.' As Nikita's brow creased in thought, she added hastily, 'I don't need suggestions either—I'll figure out what to do. The light's turned green by the way, don't you think we should be moving?'

The driver of the white Innova behind them evidently agreed, judging by the way he was leaning on his horn. Nikita hurriedly put the car into gear, it jerked forward and stalled immediately. It took her several minutes to get started again. The Innova finally managed to reverse a bit and get into the next lane; the driver glared at them as he whizzed past. 'Now he'll go home and tell everyone how terrible women drivers are,' Nikita said fretfully as she finally got the car to move. 'But it's all your fault really, distracting me with your scandalous past.'

'A male driver wouldn't have been scandalized by my

past,' Shilpa said. 'Drive carefully now, you don't want to end up on the pavement again.'

They didn't discuss Vikrant again, but Shilpa stayed awake half the night worrying that she'd unconsciously mention him in her sleep. Given the size of Nikita's flat, she was sharing the bed with her mother-in-law, and muttering Vikrant's name out loud would be disastrous. Even if the muttering was more homicidal than amorous.

Jai turned up in the morning, his eyes heavy-lidded, but otherwise looking annoyingly cheerful. 'Where the hell were you yesterday?' Nikita asked grumpily as she gave him the car keys. Jai raised his eyebrows.

'Sunday, I had the day off, remember?'

'Not that way you dimwit,' Nikita snapped. She'd had an uncomfortable night on the couch, and was feeling unreasonably annoyed with Jai. 'You weren't at home, and you didn't even answer your phone when we called.'

Shilpa had wandered out in her pyjamas by then, and was blinking sleepily. 'I'm taking the day off,' she announced. 'Jai, you don't need to take the kids to school today, they're at a friend's place.'

'There was a fire in Carlton Towers yesterday,' Nikita told Jai. 'And Madhuri almost got raped afterwards. Shilpa's staying here with my aunt, and Rakhi's in hospital.'

Jai looked aghast. 'Madhuri... Is she all right? Who was it, Shinde?'

'If you knew Shinde would do something like that, you could have told us!' Nikita said. 'Shilpa would have got him chucked out, and yesterday's thing wouldn't have...'

'He did tell me,' Shilpa broke in wearily. 'So did Rakhi. Vikrant was right, I should have done something about it earlier. Jai, after you've dropped Nikita to work, can you take me to the hospital to visit Rakhi. In all the confusion yesterday I forgot to check how she's doing.'

Rakhi was a lot better, the doctors would be discharging her by evening. Her voice was still hoarse, and she couldn't talk much.

'You were amazing,' Shilpa said awkwardly. 'I didn't even think of the other people on the floor, I just rushed out.'

Rakhi smiled and scribbled on the notepad she was using to communicate—*Anuj wasn't around, Suraj would naturally have been your first priority. I knew Sandeep would take Saira downstairs.*

There was something in what she said, but Shilpa still felt uncomfortable. She'd always looked down on Rakhi, and realizing that she was better at handling a crisis had been a humbling experience.

13

Nikita stood on the pavement outside Flora Fountain, and peered hopefully on to the road. Jai had told her he would be there in a few minutes, but there was no sign of him. Although the monsoon hadn't set in fully, there had been a few pre-monsoon showers. Nikita looked at the wet roads and the overcast sky and grimaced. She was wearing a brand new silk churidaar-kurta set that had cost the earth, and she wasn't carrying an umbrella. If it started raining, it would be a sure sign that the gods disapproved of her new Shilpa-inspired style of dressing.

When Jai finally drove up, wheels screeching on the wet tarmac as he pulled to a halt in front of her, it was evident that he'd got caught in the rain earlier in the afternoon. His hair was wet, and his T-shirt was clinging damply to his chest. Privately, Nikita thought he looked rather hot, but she pushed the thought to the back of her mind.

'You didn't tell me you were the heir to a jewellery empire,' she said when Jai came to pick her up after work.

'I'm not,' Jai said shortly. 'My father and I haven't spoken to each other for years. When I left home, it was very clear that he was going to disinherit me.'

'I don't think it's all that easy to disinherit someone,' Nikita said. 'I'm sure he hasn't done any actual legal paperwork to cut you out of the business. You might want to check with your sister.'

'Even if he hasn't, I'm never going back to work for him,' Jai was saying. 'I tried it for three years, and I almost lost my mind. The work sucks the soul out of you.'

'But…' Nikita said and trailed off. Jai raised his eyebrows. 'But what?'

'Writing doesn't pay all that well, and it'll take a long time for you to establish yourself—doesn't it make sense to swallow a bit of that pride and go back? I'm sure your father would be more reasonable now.' Hastily, just in case he thought she was making a play for him because of his newly discovered millionaire background, she added, 'Specially if things are serious between you and Saloni. I mean if you guys are planning to get married and stuff…'

'But we aren't,' Jai said, sounding a little surprised. 'I'm sorry if I'm offending your sense of propriety, but we're together because we like each other's company. It isn't remotely serious.'

'Does Saloni know that?' Nikita frowned, trying not to show how deeply shocked she was. That was the problem of being a good *gharelu* Punjabi girl at heart, some of these big city ways were incomprehensible to her. And because she looked all edgy and sophisticated, people always found it incredibly funny when her old-fashioned sensibilities emerged. Jai was looking highly amused as well, though he was trying to hide it.

'Yes, of course she knows.' Jai hesitated a little. 'If there's anyone she's seriously interested in, I suspect it's your friend Naveen, but you've got in there ahead of her.'

This time, Nikita didn't even try to conceal her consternation. 'But…but…she could have hooked up with him any time! She's known him for much longer. And there isn't anything between Naveen and me...'

All the amusement seemed to have left Jai's face. 'You're right, Saloni could have hooked up with Naveen any time. I doubt he'd have married her though. His kind don't.'

Nikita struggled to follow him. 'Because...?'

'Because she's an actress. And she's had quite a few relationships. Naveen might strut around acting like a man of the world, but when it comes to marriage, he wants a nice, virginal girl like you who's had nothing to do with the big bad world of movies.'

And who was on the lookout for a rich man, so wouldn't expect her husband to have stayed celibate till he met her. Jai didn't say it, but the implication was there, and it made her feel incredibly small.

'I don't care for Naveen,' she said, trying to keep her voice steady. 'And it's not like he's asked me to marry him or anything. I'll keep out of his way from now on.'

'I didn't realize caring was required,' Jai said, and Nikita's eyes filled with tears. , She blindly leaned forward and put the radio on, keeping her head averted. Jai had no right to judge her, she thought fiercely, but he had anyway, and gone right ahead and jumped to all kinds of conclusions. He wasn't even wrong, technically—she *had* been angling for a well-off husband, and she'd made no secret of it. It was just that she'd assumed that she'd be automatically attracted to the man she married, she hadn't bargained for the repulsion she felt every time Naveen touched her. Even more worryingly, her evident discomfort seemed to intrigue Naveen; he'd started to treat her with a tenderness bordering on respect that was completely uncharacteristic. She felt like the fraud of the century.

'See you around then,' she said to Jai as they pulled up into the Shiv-Shakti Coop Housing Society parking lot. She didn't want him to know how deeply he'd upset her, and she ran up the stairs without waiting for him to park the car and catch up with her.

Mrs Malhotra was puttering away industriously in the kitchen when Nikita entered the flat. Nikita stopped for a second, she had completely forgotten about her aunt being there.

'I've made chicken butter masala,' Mrs Malhotra announced. 'Not too much butter, so even you health-conscious girls can eat it. Shilpa isn't as fussy as Anuj, thank heavens—he refuses to eat anything I cook, says it's got too many calories. Didn't do him any harm when he was growing up, all those calories...' She broke off when she got a good look at Nikita's face.

'What's wrong?'

'Nothing, something at work; will you get that Maasi, must be Jai returning the car keys.' She escaped into her bedroom, listening as her aunt opened the door and tried to persuade Jai to join them for the chicken butter masala dinner.

'I'll pack some for you then, if you're going to be back late,' Mrs Malhotra was saying. 'Put it in the fridge, you can have it for lunch tomorrow.'

'I don't have a fridge, Aunty.' There was a second of horrified silence—Nikita smiled in spite of herself as she imagined the expression on Mrs Malhotra's face. Not having a fridge would be just one step away from wearing animal skins and living in a cave.

Jai's voice was brimming over with amusement, and Nikita noticed for the first time how attractive it sounded. You could tell he genuinely liked Mrs Malhotra, and there was something very sweet about his taking the time out to bond with an elderly woman who was ignored for most of the time by her own son.

'If I may, I'll come over for lunch,' he was saying. 'If there's any of the chicken left over, I'd love to have it.'

'*Arrey*, if you're coming here, I'll cook a nice fresh lunch, no *baasi khana*, beta. Are you free around one o'clock?'

'Yes of course.' Jai said. 'Thanks, Aunty, I'll see you tomorrow.' He cast a wry look at Nikita's closed bedroom door as he left. She was avoiding him, that much was evident—he'd said way too much, must have offended her. There was something about Nikita that got under his skin. He'd known her for several months now, but he still hadn't got used to the mass of contradictions that she was.

༄

'You're such a nut,' Saloni said, half-despairing and half angry when Jai told her about the conversation he'd had with Nikita. 'Ten to one she'll go and tell Naveen everything, and that'll make things much worse. I wish I hadn't told you.'

'I'm sorry,' Jai said, pulling her into his arms. 'And I'm sure they won't say anything, it's just that they make me so angry sometimes, people like Nikita and Naveen.'

'The rich and the wannabe-rich, who wants them when we have each other,' Saloni said, reaching upwards to kiss Jai on the mouth. Jai winced. His own net worth was probably thrice that of Naveen's. He hadn't been entirely honest with Nikita. There were the shares he owned in his father's company, and there was the money he had inherited from his grandparents—all of it was just a phone call away. He wouldn't even need to speak to his father to claim the money, it was all there, and his sister would hand it over the day he asked for it.

Saloni misinterpreted the reason for his silence. 'Getting a bit too heavy for you, all this 'being there for each other' stuff?' she asked. She wasn't in the least bit in love with Jai, but she still found him incredibly attractive. And she really liked him as well, it was difficult not to. The yearning she felt for Naveen, however, was completely absent. She had come very close to succumbing and getting into a meaningless, one-sided affair with Naveen—meeting Jai had given her a way out. A no-strings relationship with a man who treated her like an equal was the ideal antidote to Naveen. Jai had begun to seem a little distracted of late, and she suspected he was more interested in Nikita than he let on.

'No, it's not too heavy,' Jai said slowly after a while. 'I was just wondering. We like each other, we're great in bed together, but there's something missing, right?'

'True love, that's what's missing,' Saloni said, her lip curling in a surprisingly cynical smile. 'Are you still looking for it, Jai? I was, for many years, but I've given up now. I can't have the man I want, not in the way I want him. Till then, I'm happy with the man of the moment.'

Her expression was challenging as she looked at Jai, but it softened when she saw the understanding in his eyes. She snuggled closer, hiding her face against his chest. 'We never fall for the people we should, do we?' she said, her voice muffled. He didn't say anything, but he held her a little tighter.

༄

Nikita had been right in thinking that Naveen was intrigued by her withdrawing every time he touched her. He knew she wasn't playing hard to get; there wasn't a hint of coyness in her expression, and she looked genuinely uncomfortable.

The simple explanation that she didn't like his touch hadn't occurred to him, and he reintensified his efforts to woo her. Slowly, over the next couple of months, as the monsoon waned, Nikita began to melt under his attentions. It was difficult to resist all that polished charm when it was focused solely on her, and he made no move that could be considered remotely amorous—he barely touched her. And seen across the tables in expensive restaurants, his lean and rather cynical face began to look as attractive as it had seemed when she first met him.

'Got you a little something from Paris,' he said one evening, reaching across to take her hand. He'd been away for more than a week, and the first thing he'd done when he returned was to ask Nikita out for dinner. They were in one of the restaurants at the Shangri-la hotel, and Nikita was doing her best to pretend as if she ate out at places like this every other day.

'You shouldn't have,' Nikita said half-heartedly. She'd had two glasses of wine already, and Naveen's hand resting lightly on hers didn't feel as objectionable as before. And there was the gift, of course. Perfume or a scarf, most likely, it wouldn't be anything as personal as clothes. Nikita tried not to look too eager as he pushed a box across the table. It was white and oblong, and when she opened it, all it seemed to be full of was tissue paper.

'Am I missing something?' she asked, looking up at him with a slight smile. 'Not April yet, is it?'

'Look a little more carefully,' Naveen said. She pulled away a couple of layers of the delicate paper, and uncovered a little red box. With her heart thumping loudly, she fumbled at the catch with clumsy fingers. Earrings, it has to be earrings, she said feverishly to herself. Naveen was leaning back, a slight smile playing on his lips. The gasp of wonder when she finally opened the box was entirely genuine—her eyes were huge as she stared at the platinum ring inside. A perfect solitaire of god knows how many carats winked at her. It was flanked by two smaller, equally flawless baguette diamonds in a deceptively simple setting. All in all, the ring was practically a work of art.

'Like it?' Naveen asked.

What's not to like, she almost said, then bit her tongue. Everything would be spoilt if she made a flippant remark right now.

'Does this mean...' she hesitated a little, not wanting to sound presumptuous. It looked like an engagement ring, but what if it was a cocktail ring or something, with Swarovski crystals in it—she'd never been a good judge of jewellery.

'Yes, it does.' Naveen was openly smiling now. 'Nikita, would you do me the honour of becoming my wife?'

It didn't even sound cheesy when he said it, Nikita thought. Or maybe that was the effect of the diamonds, for if he was asking her to marry him, they definitely were diamonds and not glass.

There was a little pause, as Nikita looked up to study Naveen's face covertly. It was probably the confidence in his expression that clinched it for her, the slightly arrogant look that said 'What's not to like', meaning the man himself, not the diamonds.

'Yes,' she said, her voice sounding thready and very young even to her own ears.

'Yes what?' he prompted.

'Yes, I'll marry you.' He broke into a smile, and for a second, Nikita thought he would get up and come across to kiss her. He didn't, gesturing to a waiter instead and asking him to fetch them a bottle of champagne.

He kissed her in the car though, when he was dropping her back to her flat, and this time Nikita didn't cringe away. The feel of his dry lips against hers was slightly repelling at first, and she could feel him holding back, controlling the extent of his desire, and perversely, she wanted to break that control. She pressed closer to him, trusting more to blind luck than any kind of seduction skills—it seemed to have an effect, but just as things got a little more interesting, he broke away from her, leaning back in the seat.

'Maybe when we're alone together,' he said softly, but she saw his hands shaking a little as he rolled the car window down and lit a cigarette. He didn't ask her if the smoke bothered her, and she didn't resent the omission; he'd told her once that smoking helped him calm down, and she felt a little thrill at the power she seemed to have over him. But when she slept that night, she dreamt of fast cars and expensive holidays, not of the man who was going to give them to her.

'I have news,' she said the next morning as she bounced into Anuj's flat. Anuj and Shilpa looked up from their breakfast. It was a Saturday, and both of them were at home. Rakhi and Sandeep were there as well; they were due to move out of Carlton Towers that weekend, and all their things had been packed up in readiness for the move. Nikita checked when she saw Rakhi. Shilpa might have warmed up to the woman after the fire, but Nikita still disliked her deeply. As far as she was concerned, even winning a Param Vir Chakra for bravery didn't make up for being a nag.

'Oh, look at you, all matching-matching,' Rakhi said cattily, taking in Nikita's lime-green top, worn over white capris and teamed with flip-flops, bangles and earrings in the exact same shade of green. Nikita grinned at her. 'Yes, even my bra matches—wanna see?' She twanged the strap out of her sleeveless top, and Rakhi recoiled as if it was a cobra. Anuj looked a little scandalized as well, but both Shilpa and Sandeep laughed.

'So what's the big news, kiddo?' Sandeep asked.

'I'm engaged,' Nikita announced as she plonked herself down on a chair and grabbed a pancake from the stack on the table. 'To Naveen.'

'Naveen Kabra?' Rakhi asked. She'd heard about him from Anuj's mother.

'Yes, see, now my surname will match my bra as well,' Nikita said irrepressibly.

'Be serious, Nikita,' Anuj said, and Nikita promptly sobered up at the note of authority in his voice. Anuj took his duties as an older male cousin very seriously. 'Have you told Radha Mausi?'

'Yes, of course. She's terribly thrilled.' She would be, Shilpa thought. Ever since her husband had died, Mrs Dewan's ambitions had centred around her daughter marrying a rich and influential man.

'So when's the wedding?' Anuj asked.

'End of the year most likely. Look at my ring, isn't it nice? I wish Sushma Mausi was around, she'd have loved to see it.'

'Send her a picture,' Shilpa suggested. 'I'm surprised she hasn't called yet, Radha Mausi mustn't have told her. Have some breakfast, Nikita—Saira and Suraj made the pancake batter, there's enough for an army.'

'Chocolate sauce or maple syrup?' Nikita asked Suraj. 'Which do you think?'

'Both.' Suraj was very positive. 'Nutella as well. Don't mix them though, they taste better separate.'

Nikita was halfway through breakfast when Jai arrived. He was helping Sandeep and Rakhi move, and had come over to pick up the keys to their new flat. Automatically, she turned the ring around so that the diamonds were not visible. She could have saved herself the trouble, Sandeep beamed at Jai and said, 'Have a chocolate, Jai, Nikita's just got engaged, and we're celebrating.'

The chocolates were in an unopened box left over from Anuj's trip to the US. He'd got back to Mumbai just when Carlton Towers had been restored to a habitable condition after the fire. Mrs Malhotra had left soon after he returned—this had been one of her more pleasant visits, and Shilpa wondered later if it was because Anuj had been away for most of the time.

'Have you had breakfast, Jai?' she asked. His expression was rather stiff, and as usual, Shilpa wondered if it was because of something one of the others might have said to him. She still over-compensated madly for his relatively menial position in the Malhotra–Dewan household, not realizing that he found it easier to deal with Rakhi's unabashed snobbishness. At least he knew where he stood with her. 'I've had breakfast, thanks,' he said. 'Nice ring, Nikita.'

Nikita nodded and bit her lip. 'You'd know, I guess,' she said. 'Trained as a jeweller and all.' It came out sounding all wrong, and Jai's lips compressed in response.

'Well, anyway,' he said. 'Congratulations. Sandeep Sir, should I go on to your new flat and get it cleaned up a little?'

'Hang on, I'll send Madhuri with you.' Shilpa bustled out to call Madhuri, and Nikita followed Jai with her eyes as he went out to wait on the landing. He hadn't even asked who the man was—probably it was so self-evident that he didn't need to ask. And calling Sandeep and Anuj 'sir'; she wasn't sure if he did thus sarcastically, or if he was trying to emphasize the divide between them.

Rakhi got up with a sigh. 'I guess we should go back to the flat,' she said. 'The movers will be here soon. Thanks for looking after Saira, guys.'

'Has Sandeep got a job?' Nikita asked in an undertone after they left.

'Shilpa got him in touch with a BPO in Malad,' Anuj said. 'Something might work out soon. Not the best role in the world, but it's not terrible either. It'll keep them going for a while in any case.'

He didn't mean to sound condescending, Shilpa thought; it just came out that way. She jerked her head towards the children playing in the next room, and made a shushing gesture.

'Let's change the topic,' she said, and Anuj nodded immediately.

'Bring Naveen to our anniversary party next month,' he said to Nikita. 'It would be a good opportunity to meet him.'

Their tenth wedding anniversary was coming up, and Anuj had decided to throw a party for 'close' friends (including his boss and half his office) and family (represented by Nikita) to celebrate. Shilpa would have far preferred a quiet dinner for just the two of them, but she hadn't protested. In ten years of marriage, one of the things she'd learnt was when to pick her battles. At least Anuj wasn't expecting her to cook; he'd hired a catering firm, complete with white-gloved waiters to serve the food and clean up afterwards.

'Should I go and help Rakhi?' she asked doubtfully. Rakhi might see it as interference, or worse, as gloating over their situation.

'Naah, she's a cow,' Nikita said, getting to her feet. 'I'll see you later, guys.'

Rakhi was blinking back tears as she watched the movers pack up their belongings. Sandeep was downstairs, getting permission for them to use the luggage lift to move the cartons and furniture. She'd cribbed often enough about their flat being small, but it was home, and Carlton Towers was like an extended family. The building they were moving to was like a clone of Shiv-Shakti, where Nikita and Jai lived. While it was called Sagar Darshan Coop Housing Society, the only view from the windows was of other people's living rooms and bedrooms. There was no play area for children downstairs, and though Shilpa and several others had said that Saira could come over to play in the Carlton Towers garden every day, Rakhi didn't see herself taking them up on the offer. It would be an imposition, and other residents had every right to object if they wanted to. Also, it was probably better for Saira to make a clean break.

'It's not too bad, is it?' Sandeep asked once they'd finally got everything moved and unpacked. The flat was even smaller than their earlier one, and their carefully chosen furniture looked oversized and a little out-of-place.

'It's horrible,' Rakhi said viciously, and had the empty pleasure of seeing Sandeep's brave expression falter. Good, she thought as she went into the bathroom and slammed the door behind her. Let him realize what he's done.

14

Two days before their wedding anniversary, Shilpa found out that Anuj had bumped into Vikrant at the gym and invited him to the party.

'You hardly know him!' she said, for once, really angry with Anuj. 'I can understand you inviting Rishi, but this is the absolute limit! Call him up and tell him he can't come. Or I'll do it if you can't.'

Anuj stared at her. 'Don't you think you're overreacting a little, Shilpa?' he asked. 'Granted, I should have asked you before inviting him, but it was a spur of the moment thing.'

'I don't want him here, that's why I'm overreacting!' Shilpa said furiously. 'It's bad enough, him moving into the building, but now he's trying to muscle his way into our home. I've had enough of him.'

Finally, it dawned upon Anuj that there was something more behind Shilpa's anger than just annoyance at his having invited an extra person to dinner.

'When you say you've had enough of him...' he said slowly.

'I mean precisely that,' Shilpa said icily. 'In more ways than one. You remember I told you I was with someone before I met you?'

Anuj frowned. She'd said something to that effect when they'd just started dating, but it hadn't bothered him much;

there was something very virginal and untouched about Shilpa, and even when he'd realized that he wasn't the first man she'd been with, the initial impression had stayed. He'd always assumed that the man she'd fallen for had let her down in some way, she was always so disinclined to talk about him.

'It was Vikrant,' she said, looking straight at him. 'I didn't mean it to happen, but it did, and it went on for quite a while. I really don't want to see him more than I absolutely have to.'

'This was when he was an intern with your old firm?' Anuj asked, trying to understand what had happened.

Shilpa nodded. 'He was only nineteen,' she said. 'I was around twenty-four—I recruited him actually. He was very intelligent, semi-genius level. And he was so good-looking, I couldn't take my eyes off him even when I was interviewing him.'

Anuj stayed silent, and she continued, forcing herself to speak calmly, almost as if she was discussing the weather.

'We used to work on the same floor. He was lonely; he was working on an advanced project while the other trainees hung around in the canteen or surfed the Net. He used to come over and talk to me whenever he saw I was free.

'I guess you could say I seduced him. I took him home one day when my parents were out of town, and well... I knew what was going to happen, he'd made it very clear he had a crush on me. It became like an addiction, I couldn't do without him, we used to sneak out of office sometimes, and meet at the flat he was staying in. It was an office flat they'd allotted the trainees, five of them were sharing it, but it was empty during the day. I even took him to a hotel once, but that felt sleazy, so we didn't go there again.'

She fell silent, and Anuj swallowed a couple of times before he spoke. Shilpa's voice had been completely deadpan, without expression, but that emphasized the intensity of what she was saying. It was a completely new side to her—he knew that he hadn't ever inspired that kind of physical passion in her, not even during the first few months.

'What happened then?' he asked, his voice sounding remote and very unlike his own.

'And then...well, I met you.' It was the last thing he'd expected her to say. Her tone suggested that the statement was an explanation in itself, but Anuj felt far from enlightened. Some of his confusion must have shown on his face, because she went on.

'I wasn't in love with him. I knew almost on the day I met you that this was going to be the real thing, and I dumped him, pretty much without explanation. Told him never to contact me again.'

From her expression, Anuj gathered that Vikrant hadn't taken the dismissal well.

'He used to wait for me outside the office, then my boss saw him and threatened to lodge a formal complaint with his engineering institute. That's when he stopped trying to speak to me. His project was almost over anyway, so he went back to his institute.'

'Not that bad then.'

Shilpa hesitated. The last bit was something that even Vikrant probably didn't realize she knew. It could be left unsaid, but now that she'd started talking, she might as well tell Anuj everything.

'He tried to kill himself—slashed his wrists—his roommate found him just in time; he could have died...and I didn't even go and visit him in the hospital. He probably still thinks I don't know about it... That was the week your parents had come down from Chandigarh, and you introduced me to them for the first time.'

Anuj remembered that week very clearly. He'd been worried that Shilpa would be put off by his loud, over-exuberant mother. She had been a little remote and preoccupied, but she'd explained it by saying that work was stressful. Even in his wildest flight of fancy he would never have believed that she was upset because her ex-lover had just tried to kill himself.

It all still seemed rather unbelievable, more like the plot of a movie than something that had actually happened in real life.

'Why didn't you ever tell me?' he asked, and the question quickly brought Shilpa back to her usual self.

'I don't know—it was just so, so *weird*,' she said. 'Like it was a bad dream or something. You were pretty conservative, and I didn't want to scare you off by telling you about it, and later on, well, it just didn't seem relevant anymore. Not the details at least, I did tell you that I had a relationship.'

Except that the relationship had turned out to be very different from the bloodless, one-sided one he'd imagined. Anuj felt a wild desire to laugh. His nicely ordered world had just been turned topsy-turvy, and the funniest thing was that Shilpa didn't even realize she'd done it. He thought back to all the times he'd come close to being unfaithful to her. He knew now that he would never have actually cheated on her—Shilpa was too important to him. For the first time though, he wondered whether *she* had always been faithful. He'd always been so *sure* of her, so confident that with her, what he saw was what he got. Compared to his own rather temperamental family, Shilpa was like an oasis of calm. There was an aura of class around her, perhaps because of her Navy background and the tony schools she'd been to. Even now, he couldn't imagine her having a passionate affair with a boy five years younger.

Vikrant Sinha. Anuj had felt rather inadequate besides him when Rishi had introduced them. Several years younger, he was a hundred times more successful, perhaps Shilpa compared the two of them now and wished she'd chosen Vikrant all those years ago. A sudden thought struck Anuj.

'So is he…bothering you or something? Is that why he's rented a place here?'

'He's not bothering me,' Shilpa said. 'I think he rented a flat here because you praised the building when we met for dinner at Rishi's club. But he's not forgiven me either. He never did have much of a sense of humour, and he's very bitter, he doesn't miss an opportunity to take a dig at me.'

Right then, Anuj felt that his own sense of humour had been surgically extracted from his system. He could see absolutely nothing funny in the current situation, not even in his having invited his wife's ex to their wedding anniversary dinner. If Shilpa had chosen him over Vikrant for his sense of humour, she'd be within her rights in asking for her money back.

'Don't worry about it,' Shilpa said, getting to her feet. 'It's quite likely I'm overreacting—I'm feeling a lot better now that I've told you. Don't un-invite Vikrant, it'll look really peculiar.'

Anuj was less convinced about the cathartic effects of a confession. Maybe it did the person who was doing the confessing some good, but in this case at least, it had left the listener in a complete mess. His phone rang, and he frowned as he looked at the display. He was in no mood to speak to his mother, but he knew she'd call the landline next if he didn't answer.

'Did you hear Nikita's news?' Mrs Malhotra demanded.

'Nikita's... oh yes, of course.' For a few seconds, Anuj had completely forgotten about his cousin's engagement. 'She came over last week to tell us, we're both very happy for her.'

'I told Radha we'd help with the trousseau,' his mother was saying. 'There won't be any dowry of course, given that they've fallen in love, but she'll need some jewellery and a really good send-off.'

The whole thing sounded more like the launch of a ship than a wedding, Anuj thought, not being able to concentrate. He kept imagining Vikrant and Shilpa together; it was considerably worse than thinking of her with a nameless man, and he felt a strong urge to throw up. Mrs Malhotra twittered on, and Anuj tried to force himself to listen. Apparently, he'd already agreed to fund at least part of the wedding reception they were planning in Chandigarh—if he continued to let his mind wander, he'd be paying for the honeymoon as well.

~

Back in her flat, Nikita was going through a similar discussion with her mother. 'Mom, I haven't even thought about what kind of wedding I want,' she said finally in exasperation. 'I'll talk to Naveen and then I'll call you, OK?'

'Has he introduced you to his parents?'

'They live in Delhi, Mom. I'll meet them when they're in town next. I've spoken to his mother on the phone.'

'Did she talk to you properly?'

'What kind of a question is that, Mom, of course she talked properly!' Nikita sounded casual about it, but she'd been pretty nervous before she spoke to Mrs Kabra. Then she'd realized that Naveen's mother was even more nervous than she was. She didn't speak English too well, and she was clearly in awe of her son's chosen bride. Naveen's father, the underwear-elastic king, spoke English quite well, though he was not half as sophisticated as his son.

'When can you come down to Mumbai and meet them?'

'Oh, I can't come to Mumbai, travelling there is just too stressful,' was her mother's surprising reply. 'Why don't you bring Naveen to Chandigarh for a visit?'

'You'll need to meet his parents as well, and I can't get them down to Chandigarh,' Nikita said. 'There are all kinds of details to finalize about the wedding, and his mother sounded terribly confused. And then there's the shopping to be done.'

'It'll be easier for you to decide what you want, it's your wedding after all.' Nikita started to protest, but her mother cut her off ruthlessly. 'I'm very tired,' she said. 'I've been working hard for so many years, I need a rest. You can manage the arrangements for the wedding on your own quite well.'

'Right,' Nikita said, too stunned to react. She'd just assumed her mother would be as excited about the wedding as she was, but she sounded positively tepid. Being 'very tired' was hardly an excuse; she'd taken voluntary retirement a couple of years ago, and since then had spent most of her time relaxing at home.

Mrs Dewan rang off a few minutes later, and Nikita put the phone down, uncharacteristic tears pricking at her eyelids. Unconsciously, one of the things driving her to marry Naveen was the thought that her mother would approve. From ever since she could remember, her mother had been obsessed about finding a suitable man for her to marry. Even when she'd completed her CA course and landed a good job, her mother hadn't ceased to worry. If anything, she'd worried even more, because having a career knocked out various rich-but-poorly-educated businessmen from the list of eligible grooms.

Nikita was still brooding when the doorbell rang. Hoping it wasn't the *presswala* to whom she owed a staggering sum of money, she went to open the door. Jai was leaning against the door jamb, his eyes crinkling up in amusement at the look of relief on her face. 'Expecting a bank collections agent, were you?' he asked, strolling into the flat.

'Almost as bad. I've not paid the ironing guy for three months, and every time he lands up asking for money, it's on a day I have only ten rupees in my wallet.'

'You could try paying him in shoes,' Jai remarked, carefully stepping over the several pairs piled up in a brightly coloured heap in the middle of the hall. 'You have enough to fit an entire family of giant caterpillars.'

'Funny, funny,' Nikita said, kicking some of the shoes aside as she followed him into the room. 'To what do I owe the honour of this visit?'

'Well, it's the end of the month…'

'Do I need to pay you as well? But I thought I already…' Her voice trailed off in an undignified little squeak as she realized he was laughing at her.

'Anuj paid me,' he said. 'Remember the deal with Shilpa? They pay my salary and for the petrol, and you provide the car.'

'Oh yes.' Nikita breathed a sigh of relief. 'I completely forgot about that. So why're you here then?'

'So welcoming,' he said, his tone mocking her gently. 'I thought I'd generally drop by, check if you'd like to watch TV together for a bit or something. You said Naveen's out of town, and you'd be bored out of your wits hanging around alone.'

'Where's Saloni?' Nikita asked suspiciously, and Jai grinned. 'She's out of town as well,' he said. 'Gone off to do volunteer work at one of the villages her pet NGO supports.'

'She's too good to be true,' Nikita said, sighing as she plonked herself down in front of the TV. 'Be a sweetheart and go make two packets of Maggi *na*, please, Jai. Ranjana's taken the day off. I'll surf the TV for a bit and find a nice movie for us to watch.'

'There's a Bond movie starting at 8.00 pm,' Jai said as he sat down next to her and grabbed the remote. 'Which is two minutes from now. Go make the Maggi yourself—I want to watch the opening credits.'

They ended up ordering pizzas finally; Jai had to pay, and Nikita promised faithfully to pay him back once she finally got around to visiting an ATM. He shrugged. 'Don't bother about it. This can be my treat for your engagement.'

'I thought you didn't approve of my engagement,' Nikita said.

'I think you're making a mistake,' he replied, and the words were so matter-of-fact that they took a few seconds to sink in. 'But it's entirely your business. Pepperoni or barbeque chicken?'

'One slice of each,' Nikita said, and grabbed the plate from him crossly once he'd put the slices on it. '*Why* do you think I'm making a mistake? Or is this one of Saloni's recycled opinions?'

'He's not your type,' Jai said promptly. 'He's moved from a rich-but-crass background to being a Page-3 personality, and that part of his life is very important to him. You'll not fit into his social set, and you'll regret marrying him once the glamour wears off—you're a Maggi and pizza type of girl, he's a caviar and champagne kind of guy. Oh, and you don't care two hoots for him.'

'How would you know?' Nikita asked furiously. He was right, of course, but somehow that made it a lot worse.

Jai shrugged. 'Call me immodest, but I know a fair bit about women. I've seen you with him, you don't look in love. Neither does he for that matter, but he's figured that the only way he can get you to sleep with him is by marrying you.'

Having completed his little speech, Jai turned his eyes back to the TV, apparently completely immersed in the movie. Nikita glared at him in impotent anger. 'You can't just say things like that,' she said finally. 'Who died and made you a world authority on relationships?'

That made him smile slightly, though he kept his eyes on Sean Connery and his antics with one of the more voluptuous Bond girls.

'It's just my opinion,' he said mildly. 'You can ignore it—I could be wrong.' That took the wind out of her sails a little, and she sat back against the cushions to bite into a slice of pizza. Her phone was ringing in the next room, but she ignored it. It was probably her mom in any case, calling to remind her of some detail that she needed to take care of for the wedding.

'These old movies were pretty politically incorrect, weren't they?' she asked, as Bond gave the girl a playful spank on her bottom. Jai grinned. 'They're far more fun to watch,' he said. 'I like the girls better too, nice and curvy, not like the stick-insects you see on the screen nowadays.'

Nikita gave her own size-zero curves, or rather, absence of curves, a rueful look, just as Jai looked towards her. 'Sorry,' he said, though he didn't look apologetic in the least. 'But as I'm giving you my opinion on a lot of things today, I do think you could do with some more meat on your bones.'

It was the first time Jai had ever commented on her looks, and Nikita felt quite unnaturally flustered. And it wasn't even a compliment, if anything, he sounded more like a farmer checking out the livestock.

'That's why I'm eating pizza,' she came back at him. 'I can't help being skinny, my metabolism's wired to keep me that way. No wonder you like Saloni, she's got padding in all the right places.' Oops, that had come out sounding a little bitchier than she'd intended. Oh well, in for a penny, in for a pound.

'Don't you find me attractive at all, Jai?' she asked with genuine curiosity. 'I thought you did at the beginning, but now you treat me like I'm part of the furniture.' A coat-hanger, probably. Or a carom board, like one of her school friends had called her when she was in the awkward flat-chested teenager phase. Maybe carom boards weren't furniture though, and she did have a bosom on her now, not the impressive kind like Saloni's, but perfectly respectable. She took a peek at it to make sure it was still there. Yep, perfectly respectable. When she looked up, she realized that Jai was sitting very still, staring at the screen as if frozen in time.

'Well?' she asked, her voice a little more challenging this time. And a lot more confident.

Jai cleared his throat. 'Well, you're very good looking, of course,' he said finally, still not looking at her.

'So's John Abraham,' Nikita said. 'That's not what I asked you.'

'Well, ummm, he's a man...'

'And I'm not,' Nikita added helpfully. 'Just in case you hadn't noticed. So do you find me attractive or not?'

By now Jai's ears had turned an interesting shade of pink. 'I've always thought you're attractive,' he said.

Nikita scooted a little closer to him. She wasn't sure what was driving her, but after the things he'd said about her and Naveen, she wanted to make him a little uncomfortable.

'How attractive?' she asked, putting a hand on his arm. Now that she was near him, she could smell his cologne, the one he said his aunt had given him. It was a smell she associated with Jai now, and unconsciously, she leaned a little closer. He was wearing a short-sleeved shirt, and her hand was touching his bare skin. She moved her hand up his arm a little, enjoying the feel of the smooth skin covered with just the right amount of hair, and the strength of the muscle underneath. He tensed up immediately, and she stroked his arm again in a soothing movement.

'Relax, I'm not hitting on you,' she said teasingly, but there was something wonderfully thrilling about being so near him. Rather the way she'd felt as a kid when a neighbour had left a perfectly frosted cake in their refrigerator to be picked up in the evening. She'd held out the whole afternoon, and then, when her mother had gone for a bath, she'd opened the fridge and run a finger oh-so-slowly around the edge of the cake, and then licked the chocolate icing off her finger. Her mother had never found out, nor had the neighbour. Smiling a little at the memory, she rested her cheek on Jai's shoulder, nuzzling against the soft cotton of his shirt.

Jai recovered his wits at about the same moment, and taking her by the shoulders, he turned her around to face him.

'I find you terribly attractive,' he said firmly. 'But I'm in a relationship with someone else, and so are you. We shouldn't be talking about this.'

His hands were large and warm and strong, and Nikita found that she quite enjoyed the feeling of being pushed around masterfully. Realizing it, Jai let her go in a hurry and stood up, thrusting his hands into his pockets. 'I should go,' he said, but he made no move towards the door.

'Don't be silly,' Nikita said, patting the settee next to her 'Come and sit here, I want to watch the rest of the movie.' Reluctantly, Jai sat down again. They spent the next few minutes watching Bond extricate himself from various improbable situations, and then Jai said abruptly, 'Why did you ask?'

Nikita curled herself into a corner of the settee, and gave him a smile that was curiously catlike. 'Because I wanted to know.'

He made an impatient gesture with his hands. 'Yes, of course, but *why?* What possible difference could it make to you?'

Good question, Nikita felt like saying. Because it wasn't just curiosity that had made her ask. Pride, of course, was part of it, and knowing she had the power to make Jai's heart beat just a little faster. But most of all, she was intrigued by her own reactions to him. Even now, she could hardly stop herself from reaching out and touching him; knowing that he was attracted to her had resulted in an immediate shutdown of all her inhibitions. Praying she wasn't about to make an almighty fool of herself, she sat up and looked directly into Jai's eyes. He held her gaze, his eyes still stormy and troubled, and she hesitated a little before bringing her mouth close to his.

She'd expected him to jerk back in horror, but he stayed very still, closing his eyes when her lips touched his. Swallowing a little in nervousness, Nikita pressed herself closer to him, and then, the last shred of self-consciousness deserted her, and she kissed him hungrily, as if she couldn't have enough. For a few seconds, Jai responded as eagerly, but then he made a strangled sound in his throat and tore his mouth away.

'I should go,' he said hoarsely, and got to his feet. 'I'll see you tomorrow.'

Nikita should have felt offended by his reaction, but the after-effects of the kiss had made her euphoric, and going by the way Jai's hands were shaking, he wasn't exactly unaffected either.

'So that's what it's supposed to be like,' Nikita said aloud, once Jai had left. Her phone was ringing again, and she wandered in to answer it. It was her mother, and after hesitating a little, she let it ring. She was in no mood to talk about the wedding right now, she wasn't even sure if she wanted it to happen at all.

15

Suraj was in deep disgrace—allowed out of his room for a short while to greet the guests at the anniversary party, he'd been rude to Rishi. Privately, Shilpa didn't blame him, Rishi had ruffled Suraj's hair and said in a patronizing tone 'You've really shot up, young man! Amazing!' To which Suraj had retorted, 'Normal children don't shrink.' Anuj was livid, and Shilpa had had to swing rapidly into damage control mode.

'I don't see what was so rude about what I said,' Suraj said rebelliously after Shilpa marched him to his room. 'Adults are so annoying, they *always* say I've grown. As if I could do anything about it! And Rishi Uncle said it was fine, but Papa still forced me to apologize.'

'Rishi Uncle is Papa's boss,' Shilpa said wearily. 'You can't talk to him the way you do to my friends. Go to bed Suraj, the party will go on for hours. You can keep your reading light on if you like and read for a bit.'

'OK,' Suraj said, looking very sulky. 'Can I not brush my teeth or change into night clothes?' Thwarted in both these very reasonable requests, he grew even grumpier. 'You look weird with make-up on,' he informed Shilpa as she paused by the door to switch off the light. 'Like the picture of the lady on the box of the herbal cream that Daadi uses.'

'Thanks a bunch,' Shilpa said as she went out. 'The lady on the box is twice my age, she's the one who invented the cream forty years ago.' The anniversary party was already turning out to be a royal nightmare. The caterers had goofed up, bringing in double the order of non-vegetarian starters and nothing at all for the vegetarians. The Patels had landed up early, and Anuj was focusing on them and completely ignoring his other guests.

The doorbell rang, and Madhuri opened the door to let Vikrant and Nikita in. 'Hey Madhuri, looking good,' Nikita said, breezing in with a determinedly cheerful look on her face. Madhuri grinned at her—she liked Nikita, even to the extent of trying to copy some of her mannerisms. Vikrant smiled at Madhuri, and she blushed. He'd featured in her dreams pretty regularly ever since he'd rescued her from Shinde, but seeing him in real life only emphasized the gulf between them.

'Hey, Vikrant, great to see you,' Rishi said, striding across the room to shake Vikrant's hand. Shilpa's eyes flew to Anuj's face—his lips had tightened a little, but he greeted Vikrant perfectly cordially.

Nikita came across to Shilpa, her eyes scanning the room to find a familiar face. 'Congratulations,' she said, kissing Shilpa lightly on the cheek and handing her the gaily/brightly wrapped gift box in her hand. 'Ten years, huh? Amazing.'

'Amazing that we stuck together, you mean?' Shilpa asked in an undertone; there was no one else within earshot, but as soon as the words were out of her mouth, Shilpa realized that she sounded just like Suraj.

Nikita grinned. 'Well, that too,' she said. 'What I meant to say was more along the 'wow, time has really flown' lines.'

'Hmmm. Where's Naveen?'

'Bollywood launch party. He'll try to come by later.'

'I hope he can, it would be nice to meet him. And I've been meaning to ask, what's happening on the Wayne Brothers movie?'

'Oh they're doing a talent hunt for the lead pair now,' Nikita said. 'Jai's taken his money and gotten out, the script's being done by a professional scriptwriter.' She looked around the room again. 'I've never met any of these people. Aren't Rakhi and Sandeep here?'

'Sandeep had to work—he's not home yet,' Shilpa said, though her lips twitched a little. Nikita must be really desperate if she wanted to know where Rakhi was. 'I told Rakhi to come over on her own, but she's insisting she needs to wait for him. I don't think things are going too well there,' she added in answer to Nikita's raised eyebrows.

'That woman's a nightmare. *Chalo*, I'll go and introduce myself to a few people then. I think Anuj needs your help entertaining his boss's wife.'

Anuj needed to be surgically detached from his boss, Shilpa thought savagely. There were other people from his office clustered around Rishi, but Rishi himself was concentrating on Vikrant. Who in turn, was looking completely disinterested.

Shilpa went across to Payal, who seemed to be fascinated by Vikrant, and was evidently getting in the way of whatever important discussion Rishi wanted to have with him. Unfortunately, as soon as Shilpa came up, Vikrant detached himself from Rishi and joined her. It was difficult to say who was more disappointed, Payal or Rishi. Shilpa could see Anuj's bonus shrinking just a little as Rishi gave her a beady-eyed look.

'I don't see your son around,' Vikrant said.

'He's been sent to bed,' Shilpa said. 'He was here for a bit, but then he started mouthing off to the guests, and he had to be removed.'

'Oh come on, he wasn't trying to be rude. All children are like that—mine are positively embarrassing at times. My daughter met one of my oldest friends the other day and told her 'Aunty, you look like my neighbour's maid',' Payal said. 'I've been trying to explain to her that it's really not done, saying something like that, but she just doesn't get it!'

'I don't get it either,' Vikrant said abruptly. Shilpa felt like clutching at her hair in despair. Rishi was already looking annoyed that Vikrant had been hijacked; all she needed now was an impassioned argument between Payal and Vikrant on the subject of the rights of the lower classes.

'Sorry?' Payal asked, raising her eyebrows.

'Why is it rude? If she'd said that your friend looked like your neighbour, you wouldn't have been upset, would you?'

'It's not the same thing,' Payal said, clearly not getting the point.

'I think what Vikrant's trying to say is that the maid is a human being too—there's no harm in saying that someone looks like her,' Shilpa interjected.

'I'm not saying she isn't a human being, but really!' Words seem to fail Payal. 'She's dark, and, well she's not particularly good-looking.'

'And your friend is? Good-looking I mean?'

Payal gave a tinkling little laugh, the kind that made Shilpa long to strangle her.

'Oh no, not really, actually she does look a bit like the maid, it's just that Sanjana can't be saying things like that.'

Vikrant seemed dispose to argue the point further, but Shilpa gave him a pleading look, and he took the hint and changed the topic.

Nikita was wandering along the balcony disconsolately. She'd surveyed the room for a third time, and on sober reflection decided that she didn't want to introduce herself to any of the rather stuffy-looking bankers or their wives. The last few days had been rather upsetting. Jai had gone all stiff and formal on her; he still landed up punctually to ferry her to work and back, but he refused to make even the slightest conversation. As for touching, she might have been a leper going by the way he was treating her. And Naveen had been terribly busy. She took a sip out of her drink and gazed moodily out at the Worli skyline.

'Nice view isn't it?' a voice said, and Nikita turned to smile at Sandeep. 'Thank heavens you're here!' she said. 'I was getting bored out of my wits—soon I'd have started biting people and barking at the furniture.'

'I'm glad I saved you from that,' Sandeep said solemnly. It was a relief to see Nikita; it had been a long day, and Rakhi's nagging followed by the prospect of an evening spent with a bunch of ex-colleagues hadn't helped matters. The new job was taxing without being stimulating, and sometimes he wondered what would happen if he just chucked everything up. There might be a vacancy for a sanyasi in an ashram somewhere. Wearing orange robes and smearing ash on his face seemed preferable to a life spent listening to Rakhi catalogue his inadequacies.

Nikita laughed. 'Where's Rakhi?' she asked.

Sandeep sighed. 'I got home a couple of hours later than I'd said I would,' he said. 'She's not pleased. And our tenth wedding anniversary is coming up as well—there's no way we can throw a party like this.'

'Wouldn't a romantic dinner be a better idea anyway?'

'I tried that last year,' Sandeep said gloomily. 'But I made a booking for the wrong night by mistake. When we went to the restaurant, they were full, and we had to wait for more than an hour to get a table.'

Nikita laughed. 'So how many carats did that add to the rock?' she asked. Sandeep looked genuinely confused. 'Carrots to the rock?' he asked, visions of hares and tortoises crowding into his mind.

'Carats, not carrots,' Nikita explained patiently, though she couldn't suppress a derisory snort of laughter. 'Did you have to buy Rakhi a bigger diamond to make up?'

'No, but she wasn't pleased,' Sandeep said sadly. 'Didn't talk to me for a whole day.' Nikita didn't ask why they hadn't done the sensible thing and gone to another restaurant. Presumably Rakhi had insisted on dining at that particular restaurant and no other, and poor, meek Sandeep hadn't had the guts to protest.

'*Mard ban, yaar,*' she said impulsively. 'Tell your shrew of a wife to back off and let you have a life.'

Sandeep gave her a comical grin. '*Mard hota toh Rakhi se shaadi nahin karta,*' he said. Neither of them noticed Rakhi who'd just opened the balcony door to step out; Nikita gave Sandeep a consoling hug.

'Poor you,' she said. 'Liking the new job?' Rakhi didn't stay to hear the answer. She turned back and pushed through the guests in the living room blindly.

In the kitchen, Vikrant was talking to Madhuri as he helped her load a tray with the cheese and mushroom canapés she'd made for the starving vegetarians. 'Don't you want to do something else with your life?' he asked. 'You seem a bright girl, you can't cook and clean for the rest of your life.'

'I'm doing my BCom,' Madhuri said warily. Still dazzled by Vikrant, she was finding it difficult to figure him out. He was Anuj and Shilpa's friend, so he had to be at least as well-off as they were—by Madhuri's standards, that qualified as stinking rich. But he treated her like an equal, and she found it disconcerting. She hadn't been able to help noticing how good-looking he was, almost like a film actor. And his clothes were lovely; covertly, her eyes slid over the perfectly cut shirt and the faded jeans.

Rakhi walked in at that moment, her eyes glittering with anger and hurt. By her standards, she'd done her best by Sandeep, she'd stood by him even when he was sacked and she'd agreed to leave her lovely little flat for the poky hovel he was making her live in. He should be grateful to her, instead of which, he was laughing at her behind her back, that too with Nikita. Rakhi felt positively wild with fury every time she thought of it.

'Get me some water,' she said curtly to Madhuri.

'Whatever happened to saying 'please'?' Vikrant murmured, and Rakhi glared at him. Rationally she knew that no part of what had happened to her was his fault, but he had come to view her old flat and that was bad enough.

'I don't need lessons on manners from you,' she snapped. 'Thanks, Madhuri.'

'Ah, but you do admit you need them from someone.'

Shilpa stuck her head into the kitchen in time to hear the exchange.

'Vicky, stop being rude to my guests,' she said. 'Why're you hiding in the kitchen anyway? Rishi's been hunting for you, I think he's probably knocking on the loo doors now.'

Unconsciously, she spoke to him the way she used to many

years ago, even before they'd started dating, and Vikrant's rather brittle expression softened.

'I think I'll stay right here then,' he said, as Rakhi stomped past him. 'I've been working like a dog all week, I don't want to talk deals right now.'

In spite of herself Shilpa felt sympathetic. People badgered her at all times because she worked in HR, and with the onset of the recession it had only worsened. It wasn't the same thing as being chased after for multimillion dollar deals, but the feeling of never being allowed a break was similar.

'Let me introduce you to some of the other guests,' she said. 'Believe it or not, there are some nice people around.'

Vikrant hesitated, biting his lip. 'Can I talk to you for a minute,' he asked. They were alone in the kitchen—Madhuri had carried the tray of canapés out for the vegetarians the caterer had overlooked.

'I guess so,' Shilpa said unwillingly. Anuj wouldn't be thrilled to find them together. He'd been withdrawn and rather strange ever since her big revelation, and Shilpa had begun to wish she hadn't told him.

'Look, I didn't mean to cause trouble between you and Anuj,' he said, his voice low. Shilpa raised her eyebrows. 'What makes you think you have?'

'He keeps looking at you, and then at me, and back again,' Vikrant said drily. 'It's not difficult to figure out what he's thinking. And given that it's your anniversary, neither of you look very happy.' Hmmm. That was one of the things about Anuj that Shilpa found endearing and terribly irritating at the same time. Anyone who looked at him could figure out what was going on in his head, it was as if he had thought bubbles coming out of his brain/head like Mickey Mouse.

'It's the thought of me having slept with someone he actually knows,' Shilpa said. 'Even if it was in the distant past. Vikrant, can I be honest?'

He nodded.

'If you were really concerned about causing trouble, you wouldn't have taken a flat in this building, would you? Why act concerned now?'

Vikrant didn't get a chance to answer as Nikita breezed into the kitchen right then. She shot them both a look, and went to the fridge. 'I need some ice,' she said, and then in an aside to Shilpa, 'What's eating Rakhi? She's acting like a prize bitch.'

'Leave her alone, can't you,' Shilpa said. 'First Vikrant, then you, why do you guys talk to her if you don't like her?'

Nikita gave Vikrant a cheeky grin. Anyone who'd managed to get on Rakhi's wrong side within five minutes of meeting her immediately climbed several notches in her estimation.

'Poor thing, if everyone who disliked her stopped talking to her, she'd have no friends left,' she said. Vikrant smiled briefly. Nikita's edgy looks and bordering-on-rude conversation had been a little off-putting at the beginning, but he was beginning to quite like her. The short dresses helped—she had fabulous legs.

Shilpa noticed the smile as well as the quick glance of appreciation, and a germ of an idea sprang into her head. 'Where's Sandeep?' she asked Nikita. 'I wanted to introduce Vikrant to him, but I've been so run off my feet, I haven't had a chance to breathe.'

'No probs, I'm fab at introducing people,' Nikita said. 'Come on, Vikrant. Sandeep's a doll—he's the only reason people tolerate Rakhi, though Shilpa won't admit it.'

Heaving a sigh of relief as they left the kitchen together, Shilpa turned her attention to the canapés. There were still dozens of unfilled ones sitting on the counter and smirking up at her. She grabbed a spoon and started filling them up, feeling positively murderous. The caterers deserved to be shot, or better still lynched by the vegetarians and hung up on a tree by their heels. Her own wedding anniversary, and here she was, slaving away in the kitchen.

'I'll do them,' Madhuri said, coming back with the empty tray. 'You go and have a good time, didi,' Shilpa did the last one in the row and handed her the spoon. 'I'll go and check on Suraj then,' she said. It was only partly an excuse; it was highly probable that left alone in his room, he was up to some unspeakable mischief.

As it turned out, though, he was fast asleep, his head pillowed on an assortment of extremely uncomfortable looking books. Shilpa tugged them out one by one, replacing the last with a pillow. Suraj grunted ungratefully and rolled over to his other side, presenting Shilpa with an unobstructed view of his little behind. She was rearranging the blankets around him when Anuj came in to find her.

'Everything OK?' he asked, looking at Suraj. 'Poor guy, he hasn't had much fun today.'

Shilpa turned to him, eyebrows raised, and he shrugged his shoulders. 'I'm sorry,' he said. 'You were right, we should have just celebrated with family. Having a big party was a bad idea.'

He looked so remorseful that Shilpa melted. 'It's OK,' she said in a whisper. 'Our actual anniversary is next week, we can celebrate it properly then. And I loved the gift.' It had been a surprise, a truly beautiful antique bracelet in rose gold—for all her worrying about their mortgage, she was still a sucker for jewellery.

Anuj put an arm around her and laid his cheek on the top of her head. There were a few seconds of peaceful, companionable silence. This was what a marriage was about, Shilpa thought hazily, while Anuj thought—Thank heavens I didn't do anything stupid with Diya.'

Shilpa was about to say that they should be heading back to their guests, when the sound of raised voices made her jerk away abruptly. 'Who's that?' she said.

'Sounds like Rakhi,' Anuj said grimly, striding out of the door.

It was. Seeing Sandeep standing with an arm around Nikita as he happily chatted with Vikrant had finally driven her over the edge. Not having the guts to confront Sandeep with what she'd overheard, she had picked a quarrel with Nikita on the flimsiest of excuses.

'You're a cheap woman with low morals,' she was shrieking at Nikita. 'Look at the way you dress, you look like a hooker in that skimpy dress.'

'Hopefully a highclass hooker,' Nikita drawled. Her nostrils flared with anger, but she had enough control to realize that a cat fight at her cousin's wedding anniversary bash was distinctly avoidable. 'Though I'd love to know where you get your information on brothel fashion from. Not first-hand I presume?'

'You complete bi...'

'Rakhi!' Sandeep said, and the word was like a gunshot, startling even some of the people who were standing around, pretending not to listen, but lapping up every word. Rakhi broke off mid-sentence to stare at him in shock. She'd never heard that particular tone in his voice before. But Sandeep had finally had enough.

'You've either had too much to drink, or you've lost your mind,' he said, his voice taut with anger. 'At the very least, you could have some consideration for Shilpa and Anuj. Come on, put that glass down, and let's go home.'

Later, Shilpa wasn't sure if she'd jogged Rakhi's elbow as she tried to soothe her. Rakhi was holding herself very stiff, and when she felt Shilpa touch her, she jerked away, and the wine glass went flying out of her hand. It didn't hit anyone, though the sound that it made as it shattered was very loud in the suddenly silent room. Some of the wine splashed on to the wall, but a lot of it ended up on Rakhi's own dress. She stood frozen in place, as Sandeep gave her a long look and swung around on his heel, marching out of the flat.

It was a pity Rakhi hadn't waited till after dinner to throw a tantrum, Shilpa thought as she took her inside to change. The woman was positively shaking in shock, and could give no coherent reason for behaving the way she had. Finally, Shilpa had to tuck her into bed with a glass of water, and an extra-large handkerchief before she rejoined her guests.

'It's the strain,' Payal was saying knowledgeably when Shilpa came out of the room. 'Her husband's just lost his job, and they've apparently moved to some hideous place, and it's all pretty grim.' Some people nodded sympathetically, others recoiled as if unemployment was catching even when mentioned by an unconnected third party.

'Let's have dinner,' Shilpa said abruptly. Her head was pounding now, and she wanted everyone out as fast as possible. Luckily the caterers had managed to lay out a fairly creditable buffet at one end of the large living room—this time, thankfully, the vegetarians hadn't been neglected. Payal looked a little disappointed at being cut short, but when Rishi headed for the food she trailed after him rather like a rag doll being dragged along by a surly urchin. Anuj shepherded the rest of his colleagues towards the buffet as well, while Shilpa was left to deal with the remaining guests.

'Is she OK?' Vikrant asked in an undertone. 'Your friend, Rakhi.'

Shilpa shrugged. 'I don't think so, but honestly, I don't care as long as she doesn't break out of the bedroom and start throwing my best glassware around.' She gave Nikita a brief look. 'I'll find out later what really happened.'

16

'I didn't know you were going to be here,' Naveen said as he spotted Saloni on his way into the preview screening. She gave him a quick smile. 'I've done a bit part in the movie,' she said. 'It's a blink-and-you'll-miss-it role, but they were still nice enough to invite me for the premiere.'

'Sit with me, you can tell me which part not to blink at,' Naveen said, and laughing, Saloni allowed herself to be led to the row of plush seats at the back of the theatre. She was acutely aware of his arm casually slung across her shoulder. In the light coming from the screen, Naveen's rather harsh features were accentuated so that he looked hawk-like, almost predatory. Saloni gave a wry little grin. He could look like a vulture for all the difference it made. If anything, she was more attracted to him now, after the self-enforced separation. Naveen had probably not even noticed that she'd been avoiding him. In fact, she'd have been surprised to know that he *had* noticed, and very uncharacteristically had missed her.

The role wasn't as short as Saloni had made it out to be, and she was surprisingly good. After the credits rolled, several people came up to congratulate her. Naveen smiled. 'After this and the Wayne Brothers movie, you'll be set,' he said. 'I wish Jai had agreed to put his name to the story, we could have done a neat PR piece on the two of you dating.'

'If Jai hears that, he'll change his name and flee the city,' Saloni said, laughing. 'On the other hand, I've nothing against a bit of free PR—tell me whom I should date and I'll make it happen.'

She was joking, but Naveen gave her an odd look. He had once, oh-very-obliquely, suggested a quick roll in the hay together, and he'd held out the lure of a part in a movie he had a stake in. She hadn't slapped his face and stormed off, but she hadn't looked like she was bowled over by the idea either. Since then, she'd laughingly kept him at a distance. Something told him that she wasn't completely indifferent to him—if he hadn't been engaged to Nikita, he would have tried his luck with her again. Even while he was engaged to Nikita... no, better not. He sighed. Turning respectable was a bore at times.

'How's your little NGO doing?' he asked. The contrast between Saloni's over-the-top item-girl looks and her catalogue of good deeds was a never-failing source of wonder to him. 'Donations pouring in?'

Saloni grinned. 'Like you care,' she said. 'You're one of those money-grabbing plutocrats who hates the thought of people getting something for nothing.'

'I'm not that terrible,' Naveen protested. 'I give money to all kind of charities, as long as I get a tax break. I just can't bear the thought of mingling with the great unwashed masses myself. And I don't know why that NGO needs you anyway—you're a dentist, not a doctor.'

'This might come as a shock to you, but underprivileged people do have teeth,' she said. 'And it's tough getting them proper dental care. All the funding goes towards treating AIDS and cancer and tuberculosis, and no one wants to donate money for root canals and braces.'

'That's an interesting way of looking at it,' he said. Actually it wasn't; the thought of the aforesaid unwashed masses in conjunction with rotting teeth made his stomach turn. But Saloni obviously felt very deeply about the whole thing. She was looking at him expectantly now, rather like a nun would look at a sinner returning to the fold, and he felt compelled to continue. 'There would be a lot of other things like that, right? That underprivileged people don't have access to, and that no one sponsors because the things aren't seen to be important or sexy enough.'

'Heaps,' Saloni said cheerfully, not fooled one bit by Naveen's sudden interest in social causes. 'On that note, would you like to do something for my 'pet NGO'? They don't get to watch movies—will you sponsor a free show?'

'Depends on what I'd get for it,' Naveen said, looking straight into her eyes. To hell with being respectable. What Nikita didn't know wouldn't hurt her, and a girl like Saloni was completely wasted on that idealist author chap.

This would be a good time to slap his face and ask him if he had a *maa–behen* at home, Saloni thought, matching his gaze squarely. On the other hand, she was tired of pretending.

'Are you propositioning me?' she asked finally.

Naveen grinned, looking almost wolf-like. 'Propositioning,' he said musingly. 'That's a word I've never heard a girl say in real life. Maybe you should start English classes for Bollywood starlets.'

'Whom you proposition on a daily basis,' Saloni said, recovering her poise. 'Maybe I should teach them simpler words first. Like 'no' for example.'

'You're the only one who's ever said no,' Naveen remarked, as he linked his arm through hers and walked her to the exit. 'It's surprising what a little bit of power can do for you.'

He sounded unusually cynical, and Saloni stopped in her tracks.

'It's not just that,' she said.

Naveen laughed. 'Money then?'

She shook her head vigorously. 'You're an attractive man,' she said. 'Granted, the starlet-types might be sleeping with you because they think you'll help their careers. But Nikita's...'

'Nikita wouldn't have looked at me twice if I hadn't had money,' Naveen interrupted. 'She'd have been off like a shot with someone like your Jai.'

Saloni stared at him. 'Why are you with her then?' she asked. 'I thought you guys were in love?'

'Really?' Naveen said mockingly. 'You're a bad liar, Saloni.' Unlike him, he thought. The line about women wanting him only for his money had worked. Pity he hadn't used it on her earlier—it was the item-girl-vs-Mother Theresa thing. Making her feel sorry for him was clearly the way to go.

'Well, not head-over-heels in love, maybe,' she amended, wondering how she'd got herself into the conversation in the first place. 'Why didn't Nikita come, though?'

'Her cousin's wedding anniversary,' Naveen said and grimaced. 'I'm supposed to be on my way there, actually. Are you off to Jai's place? I can drop you off on the way.'

Saloni declined the offer. Jai was on standby for the party, presumably to fetch ice and booze if Anuj ran out of either, or to drop inebriated guests home. He definitely wasn't on the guest list.

'See you soon then,' Naveen said as he hailed an auto for her. 'Dinner sometime soon?'

Saloni shook her head. 'I don't think it's a good idea,' she said as she got into the auto. 'I like you a bit more than I should.' Her voice was airy, but her vision was blurred with tears, and her voice shook a little as she sank back on to the seat and gave the driver directions to her home.

~

It was past eleven, and the traffic had thinned, it took Naveen just around half an hour to get from the western suburbs to Prabhadevi. Expecting the party to be still in full swing, he was a little taken aback to see that people were almost through with dinner. 'Boring party?' he whispered to Nikita in an undertone.

She rolled her eyes. 'Anything but. I've just had a terrible scene with Shilpa's best friend.' Naveen looked around instinctively, and she shook her head. 'She's sulking in one of the bedrooms. Probably waiting for all of us to go before she emerges.'

'Ah, then we should probably stay on for a while,' Naveen said, giving Nikita a wicked look. 'Wouldn't do to make it easier for her.'

Shilpa heard the tail end of the exchange and felt like tearing her hair out. As if Nikita wasn't bad enough on her own, her fiancé had to positively egg her on to behave in an even worse manner. Nikita herself was now studying Payal carefully across the table, as if she was a being from an alien planet.

'I'm planning a grand party for Rish's fortieth,' Payal was saying to a bunch of banker's wives. 'He's been working so hard, he deserves a treat, and you know what they say—nowadays life begins at forty …'

'Funny how you never hear a twenty-year-old say that,' Nikita remarked idly, earning herself several glares. Rishi, however, laughed. 'I can see that Suraj gets his outspokenness from his aunt,' he said.

'You should meet my mother—Nikita is a *chooi-mooi ka phool* compared to her,' Anuj replied with a wry grin. Somehow the exchange eased the awkwardness lingering in the room after Rakhi's tantrum, and Shilpa felt herself relax for the first time in the evening.

Vikrant was the first person who got up to leave; a lot of the female guests seemed to wilt once he was out of the door, nudging their husbands to remind them how late it was. By one o'clock, all the guests were gone, even Nikita and Naveen, and Shilpa went to tell Rakhi that it was safe to come out. Sandeep had left without waiting for dinner, and Jai had to drop her home.

'I want a divorce,' Rakhi said when she finally got home after apologizing yet again to Shilpa and Anuj. She'd meant to sound decisive and in control, but her voice sounded petulant even to her own ears.

Sandeep gave her a long look.

'A divorce,' he repeated finally. 'Sure. When?'

Rakhi looked as if he'd slapped her.

'As soon as possible,' she said. When he still didn't seem perturbed, she pressed on, 'And I'd like us to start living apart right away, so if you could find another place to stay...'

Contemplating complete freedom for a few seconds had gone to Sandeep's head with a rush. Quite suddenly he knew he didn't want to see Rakhi ever again—the door of the cage was open and he was damned if he'd let her continue to bully him.

'You'd be the one who'd need to find another place to stay,' he said quietly. 'It's a rented flat, and I'm the one paying the rent—I'm not planning to move out. You're welcome to stay on for as long as you like. Or, if you're very keen on this particular flat, you're welcome to take on the lease. I'll rent another place for myself.'

Rakhi went very white. 'I don't have any income, Sandeep,' she said. 'You know that. It's only fair that you pay the rent.'

Only fair to whom? The landlord? Sandeep's lip curled up in distaste.

'I don't see it that way. I haven't deserted you or been unfaithful to you, and I haven't been cruel either. You're the one who wants to live apart. I've no objections, but I'll be damned if I pay for your whims.'

'But...' Sandeep cut Rakhi short. 'I've done the best I can for as many years as I could stand it, and now I've had enough. You can take me to court if you want, but I won't give you a paisa.'

'What about Saira?' Rakhi asked in a voice she could hardly recognize as her own.

'You're welcome to ask her to live with you once you find a place of your own. Till then, I'll ask my mother to come over and help out.'

It was like a nightmare, Rakhi thought, and one that she'd dreamed up all on her own. She'd meant to teach Sandeep a lesson—the thought that it might backfire hadn't even occurred to her. She tried to back-pedal.

'I think we need to discuss this sensibly,' she said. 'Maybe tomorrow, when we're less tired. We've both said a lot of things we don't mean.'

'Speak for yourself,' Sandeep said. 'I haven't said a thing I don't mean.' And with that, he went into their bedroom, and went to sleep.

~

'Madhuri, there's a set of someone's car keys lying on the microwave,' Shilpa said the next morning. The caterers had done most of the clearing up after the party, but the flat was still a mess. The keys were a mystery—how had the owner got home? Unless he'd been too drunk to drive and had hitched a ride with someone else. Or he normally carried a spare key around.

'They're Vikrant sir's,' Madhuri said.

Shilpa frowned. 'Are you sure?'

'He had them in his pocket, and he took them out when he was searching for something else.' She didn't add that she'd purposely not reminded him to pick them up again. 'I can go drop them off if you like.'

Ranjana was chopping an onion, her eyes screwed up firmly to stop the tears. She put the knife down and glared at her daughter. 'I'll give them to him,' she said. 'I've got to go to his place next to cook lunch.' Not content with moving into the building, Vikrant had also hired the same cook. And there was a high chance he'd come looking for the keys himself, better to get them out of the house before he landed up, Shilpa thought.

'No, he might need to go out before you're done, Ranjana,' she said. 'Go now, Madhuri, he lives on the 13th floor in the B-Block, where Saira used to live earlier.'

Madhuri nodded. She knew perfectly well where he lived, just as she knew that he was doing laps in the swimming pool right now. The pool was clearly visible from the kitchen window, and she could see his perfectly toned body cutting through the water like a knife.

She dawdled a little, fetching her dupatta and combing her hair. Ranjana was fuming in the kitchen—her daughter's crush on Vikrant was painfully evident. Pointing it out in front of Shilpa was impossible though, and she had to content herself with grumbling under her breath in Marathi. '*Beshrampori… ghari chal changla dhada shikavate,*' she said, but Madhuri was already out of the door.

Singing to herself, Madhuri went down to the podium level and crossed to B-Block. She'd timed it just right; she had left Shilpa's flat just as Vikrant had hoisted himself out of the pool. By now, he'd have showered and been on his way home, she just needed to make sure she was waiting outside when he returned to his flat.

Vikrant was deep in thought when he got into the lift. Somehow, all his pent up angst against Shilpa had vanished the previous evening. Maybe it was seeing her with her family and friends, but he'd finally accepted that there wasn't much he could do about the way she'd treated him ten years ago. Sure, he could make Anuj jealous, but that was a rather paltry revenge, especially since he didn't even find Shilpa attractive any more. That was the thing with women of the wholesome girl-next-door type—everyone wanted to marry them and take them home to mother, but once a guy actually did it, the rest of the male species lost interest. Shilpa was good-looking still; she hadn't aged much, but on the whole she had as much sex-appeal as the women in the Johnson's Baby ads.

Having settled this to his own satisfaction, Vikrant grinned to himself. So here he was, stuck living in a building that wasn't really convenient either for work or for anything else, and he'd lost interest in the long-term plan of revenge that had made him take the flat in the first place. Oh well, at least the building had a good pool, and leases could always be terminated.

He came out of the lift, running his hand through his rumpled, still-wet hair. Madhuri was ringing the bell to his flat, though she knew perfectly well that no one was at home. She turned as the lift door opened, her face breaking into a happy smile.

Vikrant smiled back at her. He'd seen the girl around the building often, usually with Shilpa's son in tow, and he liked her cheerfully intrepid attitude to life.

'Keys,' Madhuri said, holding them up in case he didn't understand what she was saying. The years he had spent living in the US had added a twang to Vikrant's Hindi that Madhuri privately found rather funny.

'Thank you,' Vikrant said, taking them from her. He was careful not to touch her hand, and Madhuri felt vaguely disappointed. Shilpa and Anuj hugged and touched their friends all the time, and Madhuri had been left with the impression that the *bhabhis and bhaiyyas* were very free with each other. She wouldn't have minded Vikrant's hand brushing hers—she was at an age when her hormones had more-or-less taken over her head, and Vikrant looked a lot like her favourite film star.

'Would you like a Coke?' Vikrant asked as she hesitated on the doorstep, clearly unwilling to leave. He remembered how grateful she'd been for the Coke he'd bought her the evening Shinde had assaulted her—she probably didn't get to drink it often.

'Yes,' Madhuri said, and remembering her manners added, 'Thank you.'

Vikrant unlocked his front door, and went into the kitchen. 'There's only Diet Coke, is that OK?' he called out.

'Yes,' she said, and then in a burst of confidence. 'I've never had it—what's the difference?'

'No sugar,' Vikrant said, handing her the can. 'But it tastes sweet, they use an artificial sweetener.' Madhuri popped the tab on the can; she'd done it often enough for Suraj, though he wasn't allowed cola, only canned juices once in a while. She took a sip of the fizzy drink, and gave Vikrant a shy smile. 'It's nice,' she said. 'I can't tell that it doesn't have sugar in it.'

'I can,' Vikrant said. 'But I drink the stuff, even though it's supposed to give you multiple sclerosis. How're your studies going?'

'I don't get much time to study,' she said, wondering what multiple sclerosis was. Vikrant for all his film-star looks sounded distinctly kooky to her at times. 'I'll take a few days off before my exams—my mom will help out with my work then.'

'And after you've done your BCom, what next? Will you do a CA course or something?'

Madhuri shook her head vigorously. 'I'll open a beauty parlour,' she said. 'I'm going to do a beautician's course, and for a while I'll work in a beauty parlour. And when I've saved up enough, I'll open a parlour of my own. Maybe I'll even...'

The doorbell rang, and Vikrant went to open the door. Ranjana stood outside, breathing a little heavily as if she'd run all the way.

Vikrant held the door open, and Ranjana came into the kitchen, glaring at Madhuri.

'Shilpa bhabhi's waiting for you,' she said, and added in Marathi, 'How long does it take to drop off a set of keys? And how dare you drink saheb's cold drinks?'

'He offered it to me,' Madhuri said sulkily. 'I'm going now.' Seeing her mother in her cheap synthetic sari standing next to Vikrant had brought home the vast difference between them. Suddenly she felt cheap and a little stupid with all her planning and strategizing to meet Vikrant alone. He might be a little different from the rest of the rich folk she'd known, but he was as out of reach as the Bollywood stars he resembled.

'And don't come here again,' Ranjana said. Vikrant had gone into the living room, and she could talk a little more freely. '*Je hote sarva mala kalta aahe haa.*'

'Of course you do, you're like Ma Kali, you know everything,' Madhuri said and slipped neatly out of the door before her mother could react.

'Bye Vikrant sir,' she called out, and Vikrant said goodbye in return. He'd figured out that Ranjana wasn't too pleased with her daughter, but he wasn't perceptive enough to figure out what it was all about. The idea of Madhuri wanting to set up a beauty parlour of her own had caught his fancy—it seemed like such a sensible, down-to-earth kind of ambition compared to the wild business plans put up by the supposedly highly qualified entrepreneurs he interacted with at work.

'She's a smart girl,' he told Ranjana. 'Do you really need her to work? She should be concentrating on her studies, at this age.'

'I have a son to look after as well,' Ranjana said shortly. 'Madhuri will need to get married soon anyway—it's all right as long as she passes her BCom.' In that she was lying; she was as fiercely ambitious for her daughter as she was for her son, but she thought mentioning marriage would be a warning to Vikrant not to encourage the girl in her fancies. She stopped chopping vegetables for a few seconds to gauge his reaction.

'Seems a pity,' Vikrant said, frowning slightly as he opened the fridge to take out a second can of Diet Coke. 'She'd do well with just a little more attention to her studies. By the way,

Ranjana, I've been meaning to tell you, don't cook rice for me, I prefer rotis for dinner.'

Ranjana put the rice tin back in the cupboard, and shut the door with a louder-than-usual slam. Either the sahib hadn't got what she was trying to say, or he was deliberately ignoring it. She'd have to take Madhuri in hand, make sure she didn't get ideas above her station. Time for a mother–daughter chat, and if talking didn't do the trick, a few whacks with a belan would, Ranjana thought, punching the atta viciously. Daughters were a pain.

17

Meeting up with Jai and Saloni had to be the worst idea Naveen had ever had, Nikita thought. Officially, the reason was to celebrate the finding of a publisher for Jai's book. Naveen had got him an introduction to a couple of people he knew in the industry, and the rest had been easy. Once editors actually read the book, they fell over themselves to offer him a contract.

Jai was looking awkward and ill at ease, and she herself felt absurdly guilty every time she looked at him. Perhaps she should have told Naveen about the kiss. But then she'd have to tell Jai she'd told Naveen, and he in turn would have to tell Saloni—it would have all become even messier. Thankfully, Naveen's Man Friday had gone home to his village, and Naveen had decided that a dinner at Yauatcha would be simpler than organizing something at home as he'd originally planned. Nikita had been there before, and obviously so had Saloni. Jai was the only one who'd wrinkled his nose up and said 'I didn't know there were any restaurants in BKC other than Pizza Hut.'

'So how's that friend of Shilpa's doing?' Naveen asked. 'The one who threw her glass of wine at you?'

OK, he was officially messing with her head now. 'She didn't throw it *at* me,' Nikita said through gritted teeth. 'She was upset, and the glass slipped from her hand.'

'It's quite amusing, the whole situation,' Naveen said. 'Maybe you could work it into a book, Jai. An Indian version of the US teen movies. All the pretty girls ganging up against the ugly duckling.'

'That is such a load of bullcrap,' Saloni said lazily. 'I don't know what it's like in the US, but in India it's the ugly unpopular girls who're the bitchiest.'

'Not very politically correct, are you?' Naveen said, sounding amused.

She shrugged. 'It's the truth. What d'you think, Nikita?'

'Doesn't apply to this case. Rakhi isn't ugly, she's normal looking, just a little out of shape. And there's no one ganging up against her—apparently she and Sandeep are getting divorced, that's what triggered the tantrum. She's very proper normally, not at all the glass-throwing type.'

'Ah, so she did throw the glass.' Saloni sounded amused.

'Let it go,' Jai said in an undertone, but Nikita wasn't fazed. 'If she had thrown it, she'd have got her face slapped. You're welcome to think what you like, of course.'

Naveen stepped in hastily before Saloni could retort. 'Jai, you never did tell us. Why's your father so against you writing this book about your granddad? From the parts I've read, it seems quite unobjectionable.'

'I haven't read it yet,' Nikita said. 'You told me it was about your grandad's days as a freedom fighter.'

'Yes, it's fictionalized, but that's broadly it. My grandad was with the Congress for a while, but he didn't think they were doing enough to get independence for India. Then he heard about Subhas Chandra Bose and the INA, and he decided that that was a cooler way to fight for his country. Most of the book is about his days in the INA and how he met my grandmom and married her.'

'Which part did your dad object to?'

Jai thought it over. 'Umm, well, pretty much all of it, actually,' he said. 'He's a staunch Gandhian, and while he tells people that my granddad took part in the independence movement, he's very careful to avoid the details.'

Nikita laughed. 'Oh God, and now you've decided to spill the beans in public. No wonder he's upset!'

Her phone rang as she spoke, and she pulled it out of her little sequinned evening bag. 'It's my aunt,' she said, cutting the call and putting the phone on the table. It rang again, almost immediately, and kept ringing while Nikita stared at in irritation. Mrs Malhotra was normally very good with the phone, messaging to ask if it was convenient before she called.

'She seems really desperate to speak to you,' Naveen said lazily. 'Maybe you should go out and call her back before the restaurant throws you out.' Yauatcha was unashamedly upscale, and heads were already turning at Nikita's 'lungi dance' ringtone.

Nikita obeyed. There was something about the way Naveen said these things that made her feel terribly conscious of being a small-town girl with no background to be proud of.

'Hi Maasi,' she said, trying not to sound resentful.

'Nikita beta, thank God you called back, I was about to try Shilpa in case she knew where you were!'

'Is everything all right?' Nikita asked, wondering what the fuss was about. 'I was out for dinner with friends…'

'Your mother's very ill,' Mrs Malhotra interrupted, her voice shaking. 'She's in hospital, the doctor said it's something in brain, like a blood clot, an anorexic or something like that…'

'An aneurysm,' Nikita said automatically. The last few weeks, she'd had a vague sense of foreboding. Life had been going particularly well—she'd got a promotion, and there was her engagement to Naveen—she'd wondered when things would begin to go wrong. Now that they had, her mind seemed to be working with unusual clarity. She could even remember a Reader's Digest article she'd read on aneurysm, right down to the diagrams. 'Can I speak to her?'

'No, she...she can't talk, she's... Nikita, beta, you need to get here as quickly as possible, it's really bad. I'll call Shilpa and ask her to help you with the flights and things—if you could reach Chandigarh by tomorrow?'

'I'm with Naveen, he'll help,' Nikita said. 'I'll be there as quick as I can, Sushma Mausi. Take care, and thanks for letting me know.' She cut the call while her distraught aunt was still mid-sentence. The hubbub in the restaurant seemed very far away as she walked slowly back up the plexiglass stairs, past the large aquarium and the impressive wine rack, back to where Naveen and the others were sitting.

'My mother's very ill,' she said calmly. 'I need to leave for Chandigarh right away.'

Jai and Saloni both looked up, but Naveen stood up and came to her side. Probably she looked more upset than she felt, she thought as she felt his arm come around her and guide her to a chair.

'How ill?' he asked, his hand on her arm. She shook his hand off gently. 'I think she's dying,' she said baldly. There was nothing that Mrs Malhotra had said that implied this was true, but Nikita knew it was. 'I need to leave tonight.'

'Eat your dinner first,' Naveen said, pushing a plate towards her. 'I'll get someone from my office to book the tickets.'

He got up and went out of the restaurant to make a call to the nameless someone, and Nikita pushed the plate away again. 'She can't talk,' she said to no one in particular. The compassion in Jai and Saloni's eyes was bothering her, and she felt the need to make it clear that everything was under control. 'I think they're trying to schedule a surgery for tomorrow morning.'

Naveen managed to get her a ticket on the earliest flight the next morning. Unconsciously, she'd assumed he'd come with her, and she was a little shaken to realize that he wasn't planning to.

'I'll send a car to take you to the airport in the morning,' he said. 'And we'll keep in touch over the phone—cheer up, it's probably not as bad as your aunt made it sound.'

'I can drop her,' Jai said quietly. 'Actually, if you could take Saloni home, Naveen, I'll drive Nikita back.' Naveen assented readily. His conscience was pricking him a little; he could have cancelled his meetings for the next day and gone with Nikita, but there was a lot of money at stake, and there wasn't anything practical he could do to help in any case.

Shilpa was waiting for Nikita when they got back and Jai drew her aside when Nikita went in to change.

'How serious is it?' he asked her, keeping his voice as low as possible.

'It's bad. The aneurysm's ruptured, I don't think she'll last the night,' Shilpa said.

'Can you go to Chandigarh with Nikita? She's not in a very good state.'

'There's no one I can leave Suraj with,' Shilpa said. 'Anuj is out of town. Isn't Naveen going with her?'

'Apparently not.' Jai exchanged a quick look with Shilpa—it was evident that she shared his low opinion of Naveen's priorities.

Mrs Dewan lingered on for two days after Nikita reached Chandigarh. She didn't open her eyes though, and when her heart finally stopped beating, Nikita wasn't even in the hospital—she'd gone home to bathe and change while her aunt sat by her mother's bedside.

'At least she didn't suffer much,' Mrs Malhotra said, her eyes awash with tears as she took in Nikita's stony expression. 'Think of it as God's will, beta, there was nothing you could have done.'

It would have helped thinking of it as God's will if she'd believed in God in the first place, Nikita thought drearily as Anuj and the pundit performed the last rites for her mother. She could have fought to do the rites instead of him, but the rule book said they had to be done by a man, and she didn't have the energy to protest. She hadn't even changed into white clothes, wearing a blue cotton kameez over jeans, and tying her hair back with an ancient scrunchie. Someone gave her a dupatta to cover her head with during the ceremony, and she obeyed silently. She felt curiously detached from her surroundings. There were mutterings among friends and relatives that she wasn't looking as afflicted as she should be. 'Unfeeling girl', was the phrase she overheard someone use, and she almost told the man that he was right—she genuinely could feel nothing.

Naveen was waiting for her at the airport when she came back. 'You poor thing,' he said, pulling her into a warm hug. He'd sent flowers, expensive ones, and called often though the calls had been mainly one-sided with her giving monosyllabic answers to his questions.

There was something different about her, Naveen thought, as he took in her appearance. Partly because she had omitted to put on the kohl she usually wore like armour—without it, her face looked naked somehow, and very young. Her expression had a brittleness that hadn't been there before, and she had dark circles under her eyes.

'Are you all right?' he asked. He found it difficult to deal with other people's emotions, and he hoped she wouldn't start crying. He'd rescheduled his day to be able to meet her flight, and in his book that was the maximum that he could be expected to do.

'I'm OK—nothing wrong with me,' she said in a tone that suggested that she was surprised by the question.

'Great,' he said, realizing it was the wrong thing to say the second the word left his mouth. 'I thought we'd go to my place for a while, so that you could rest a little. We can figure out tomorrow what we need to do next.'

'I need to go to work tomorrow,' she said. 'And I can't come to your place now, Naveen; I'd prefer to go home. Is Jai here?'

'No, he isn't,' Naveen said slowly. 'I'll take you home if that's what you really want, but I don't think you should be alone today.'

She didn't reply, and Naveen's sense of unease deepened. He was relieved that she wasn't weeping all over him, but the degree of detachment she was showing had to be abnormal.

When they reached her flat, she wheeled her bag in, and placed it carefully in a corner of the living room. When she turned around, she looked almost surprised to see Naveen still there.

'I'll be OK on my own,' she said. 'I need to unpack, and I

have to get organized for office tomorrow. You can go back to work if you'd like.'

Naveen wanted nothing more than to be a hundred miles away from the automaton his fiancée seemed to have turned into, but in the current circumstances he could hardly say so.

'Are you sure?' he asked.

Nikita nodded, and as he turned to go, she said, 'And Naveen?'

He turned back, and she looked at him silently for a while.

'I think you should have this back,' she said, slipping his ring off her finger. 'I don't think I can marry you after all.'

Naveen looked at the ring she put in his palm—the diamonds winked up at him cheekily. Nikita's announcement had come as a shock, but not as a surprise. She'd been distancing herself ever since her mother fell ill, even insisting that he not come for the funeral.

'May I ask why?' He wasn't feeling angry, or even unhappy, just curious.

'You were the kind of man my mom wanted me to marry,' she said after a pause. 'She's not here anymore, so what's the point?'

What indeed. Naveen left the flat silently, wondering why he hadn't lost his temper. He wasn't particularly vain, but he had a fairly good sense of self-worth—being jilted by someone like Nikita was a severe dent to his ego. Only he knew that she wasn't doing it out of malice, and in a way, he was happy to be out of a relationship that was going nowhere.

Jai was coming up the stairs as he went down them. 'Hi Naveen,' he said. 'Good to see you. Nikita back?'

Naveen nodded. 'She is. Any chance you and Saloni might hitch up soon?'

Jai laughed. 'Very unlikely. We've decided to take a break from each other, actually, figure out what we really want out of life.'

'Pity,' Naveen said, passing him and heading down the stairs. 'I have a perfectly good engagement ring here that I don't need any longer—you could have used it.'

It was unlikely Jai would have wanted to ask any questions—if he did, Naveen didn't give him the opportunity, heading out of the building while Jai was still staring after him.

Feeling rather troubled, Jai climbed the remaining steps to his flat. He paused outside Nikita's door for a minute. There was no sound from within, though the living room light shone from under the door. Jai raised a hand to ring the door bell, but at the last minute he changed his mind and turned towards his own flat. Nikita probably needed time to herself—she wouldn't thank him for turning up suddenly if she was in a state.

'People are splitting up all around us,' Shilpa said. 'First Rakhi and Sandeep, and now Nikita. Even Jai's no longer with that pretty actress–dentist girl.'

'Maybe we're a malignant influence,' Anuj suggested. 'One look at us, and people realize that matrimony isn't all that it's cracked up to be. I feel sorry for Nikita, but in the long run, I think she's better off not marrying Naveen.'

'She's had a bad time after Radha Mausi died,' Shilpa said. 'And she's bottling it up—I tried talking to her a few times, but she doesn't want to discuss it. Or the Naveen thing either.'

'She probably wants to be left alone for a while. I guess it's better than wanting to move in here, like…'

Shilpa gave him a warning look. Rakhi had been staying with them for the past week, her break with Sandeep apparently irreconcilable. They could hardly have said no, not when she'd landed up on their doorstep the day after the party, looking as white as a sheet and carrying her belongings in two huge suitcases. Sandeep's mother had come down to look after Saira, who was far less upset by the split than anyone had anticipated. 'It's fun being with dad, and I can come and see mom whenever I want at your place,' she'd told Shilpa in a burst of unsolicited candour. Luckily Rakhi hadn't been around, or she'd have spontaneously combusted.

'But seriously,' Anuj said in a lower voice, 'how long is Rakhi planning to stay here? And why is she with us? Doesn't she have parents she can go to, or other friends?'

'Apparently not,' Shilpa said with a sigh. 'Sandeep and she eloped when they were in college, and her parents never forgave her. So they're ruled out. And most of her friends are wives of Sandeep's colleagues or parents of Saira's friends. I think it's a little awkward for her to go to any of them.'

'So we're stuck with her for good then,' Anuj said gloomily. 'Oh well, at least there's someone responsible around the house when Suraj gets back. That Madhuri of yours gets flightier by the day.'

If even Anuj had noticed how distracted Madhuri was, it was definitely bad. Shilpa frowned. She'd seen Madhuri wandering around downstairs when she was supposed to be on her way to the grocery store. She also seemed unusually keen to take Suraj to the swimming pool in the evenings. Shilpa hadn't yet made the connection with Vikrant, and she'd assumed that the girl had a secret boyfriend, one of the swimming instructors perhaps, or maybe even the muscle-bound physical trainer who managed the building gym.

'Aren't you back from the school yet?'

'Just got back—do you need to go somewhere?' Jai had planned to call Nikita and check if she was okay with him visiting her later in the day. Her call had come as a surprise.

'Office,' Nikita said. 'This is the time I normally leave—did you forget?'

'You're going to work today?' Jai asked stupidly. 'Yes. I'm already waiting downstairs, it'd help if you got the car around quick.'

She was so obviously struggling to sound normal that he didn't snap at her, even though her tone bordered on the offensive.

'Be there in a minute,' he said. It took him more than that to get the keys and head downstairs, but Nikita didn't crib further. They didn't talk during the drive to Nikita's office—Nikita was fiddling with her BlackBerry all the way. Jai gazed after her as she got down from the car and walked towards her office. She'd lost some weight, but the kohl was back, and she was dressed in efficient black. Looking at her, no one could tell that anything was wrong. Jai still felt deeply uneasy. The silence wasn't like her.

Rolling down the window on impulse, he called out her name; she turned, her face politely blank.

'Take care,' he said, feeling a bit stupid, but ploughing on. 'And call me if you want to be picked up early or if you need anything.'

Nikita bit her lip and nodded, her eyes suddenly wide and vulnerable. Jai wanted to get out of the car and put his arms around her, absorb some of the pain. Instead, he gave her a quick smile and waited till she walked into her office building before he drove off.

※

'You aren't with Jai anymore?' Naveen asked. Saloni gripped the phone hard. Naveen hadn't lost any time, she thought, her heart beating so loudly she wondered if he could hear it. It was only a couple of days since Jai had messaged to tell her about meeting Naveen outside Nikita's flat.

'It wasn't working out,' she said, trying to keep her voice as neutral as possible. She sounded a bit like the Doordarshan weather lady, but better that than letting him know how shaky she was feeling.

'Nikita and I broke up as well,' he said. 'But I suppose you already know that. I'll come to the point, Saloni. I've always found you very attractive, and we're both single now—should we try giving it a go?'

It sounded as if he was asking her to test-drive a scooter, Saloni thought a little hysterically. The new Naveen Kabra two-wheeler, especially designed for ladies, would you like to take a spin? No responsibility taken for broken bones or bruised hearts.

'We knew each other before we met Nikita and Jai,' she found herself saying. 'And we were both single then as well. What's changed?'

There was a slight pause. 'Me, I guess,' Naveen said finally. 'This engagement with Nikita—I realized I was looking for all the wrong things in a wife. I'm not asking you to marry me,' he added hastily, just in case she got the wrong idea. 'I just think we're suited to each other. And if things work out, well we could consider marriage then.'

'Even though I'm an immoral actress-type?' Saloni asked, unable to keep the wryness out of her tone.

'Even though you are,' Naveen agreed. He knew where that was coming from; he'd told her once that his father, the underwear-elastic king, thought that actresses were just a notch above bar-girls. At that time he'd been trying to get a message across. Saloni had been showing signs of getting a little over-serious, cooking him meals and offering to sew buttons on a shirt he'd been about to throw away. Very seventies movie type; he'd started to feel like he was turning into Amol Palekar.

Saloni stayed silent, and Naveen shrugged. 'Let me know when you want to meet up,' he said and cut the call. One thing he'd learnt over the years was never to be on the defensive with a woman. Girls like Nikita would walk all over you, while the Salonis of the world turned into smothering earth goddesses, and before you could say 'Kamasutra', you'd be stuck with a wife and four snivelling children.

'I need a drink,' he said to no one in particular and walked across to the 'Jain' bar his interior designer had made for him. Cunningly designed to look like a bookshelf, it concealed an array of bottles that would have made an alcoholic weep with joy. He was pouring out a whisky and soda when his phone rang. He ignored it, and it stopped after a few rings. The phone pinged once, and he grinned as he looked at the sender's name—Saloni was messaging him to ask if they could meet for dinner.

18

It was almost dark, and the last lone bulb in the Shiv-Shakti stairwell had fused a couple of nights ago. Jai climbed the stairs to his flat, cursing mildly under his breath. The person who'd designed the building—almost definitely not a qualified architect—must have done it without using a spirit level. The stairs all sloped ever so slightly to the right, and Jai found himself gravitating towards one side without meaning to. The first three floors were pitch-dark, but luckily there was some light on the fourth, the most treacherous flight of steps to his own flat. It was only when he reached his floor that he realized the source—Nikita's door was slightly ajar, and light was streaming on to the landing and the stairs. Nikita herself was nowhere in sight.

Hesitating a little, Jai pushed the door open. It was dangerous, Nikita leaving the flat unlocked like this. As Anuj had pointed out on several occasions, the security arrangements in the building were pathetic. The solitary watchman looked as if he belonged in a home for geriatrics, and the wall around the building was low enough for a ten-year-old to jump over.

Nikita was sitting at the dining table staring at the wall opposite her. She turned when Jai entered the room, but she didn't look surprised to see him.

'You OK?' he asked. 'I'm sorry I came in without knocking, but the door was open—I wasn't sure if you were at home.'

'It's OK,' she said drearily. 'I must have forgotten to shut it when I came in. You can close it when you leave.'

Her tone was hardly welcoming, but Jai pulled out a chair from across her and sat down.

'Are you all right?' he asked.

If she hadn't looked so expressionless, he would have thought she was affronted.

'I'm fine,' she said stiffly.

But she was clearly anything but. 'Have you had dinner?'

Nikita shook her head. 'Not hungry.'

'Do you want to come out with me? No where fancy, maybe Subway or that little Chinese place around the corner.'

'I said I'm not hungry.'

Hesitating even more than he had when he'd first pushed her door open, Jai put a hand on hers.

'I'm really sorry about your mom,' he said softly. 'I can't begin to imagine how you must be feeling.' There was a pause, and he wondered if he'd have done better to keep his mouth shut.

'I didn't realize she was ill,' Nikita said finally. 'All this while she kept saying she was tired and she felt dizzy and had headaches—and I thought she was making a fuss about nothing. She used to do that sometimes, pretend to be ill when she wasn't.'

'You couldn't have known,' he said, his heart going out to her. It was all very well talking about survivor's guilt, but from what Shilpa had said, there was very little she could have done even if she had known.

'But I should have,' she said, shaking his hand off. 'I should have! But I was so obsessed with Naveen and my job, and about stupid things like Rakhi abusing me at that party... Even Anuj tried to tell me that things weren't OK with her, and I refused to listen.'

She fell silent for a few seconds, twisting the dupatta in her hands over and over before she spoke again.

'You remember the story about the boy who cried Wolf?' she asked. Jai nodded. 'No one ever thinks about how the villagers felt—the ones who heard him calling for help and ignored him—and then they later found he was dead. I bet they didn't say 'Oh look, serves him right...'.'

'Try and get some sleep,' Jai said gently.

'I can't sleep,' Nikita said wildly. 'I can't, I can't.'

'Come here,' he said, drawing her into his arms. 'Shut your eyes and try to relax a little.'

She came to him, putting her head against his chest, though her body was still stiff and unyielding in his arms. Jai held her close, stroking her hair as she took a few deep shuddering breaths. Her frame was slight, almost like a child's, and Jai felt absurdly protective.

It was past eleven when he left her flat. She'd calmed down after a while, talking a little about her mother in happier days, when her father was still alive. Jai went into the kitchen and made them a couple of sandwiches for dinner—neither of them was very hungry. Just before he left, she looked up at him and said, 'Jai, I know I shouldn't be saying this, it's such a personal thing, but you should contact your parents. Life is so short, it's silly letting old *jhagdas* keep you apart.'

If she hadn't been in such a fragile emotional state, Jai would have told her to get a job writing soppy cards for Hallmark. As it was, he just nodded, but his cynicism must have showed—Nikita gave a watery laugh, and took his hand. 'Sorry,' she said. 'My mom and I spent the last ten years sniping at each other—I'm the last person who should be doling out advice.' Her smile wavered a little. 'It's just that I can't believe she's gone; I did love her deep down, I just never got around to telling her.' Jai hugged her again, but it was growing late and he didn't trust himself to be around her any longer and not tell her how he felt about her.

He'd realized it the day Naveen told him that their engagement was off. He'd had to exercise supreme self-control not to start grinning like an idiot at the thought of Nikita being single and un-entangled again. However annoying and materialistic she was, the initial attraction had never faded, and her present vulnerable state increased her appeal if anything. The trouble was that she wasn't reacting to him as a man any longer, more like a convenient shoulder to cry on. Jai grimaced. Being Nikita's best friend had never seemed as unappealing as it did today.

◆

'So do you want me to sponsor this for her?' Shilpa asked. Vikrant had just finished outlining a complicated plan under which Madhuri could continue working for Shilpa, but at the same time training to be a beautician.

'No, why would I? I'll pay for her training, it's just that she's keen to continue working for you, and I wouldn't want to put you in a spot—I know you depend upon her to look after Suraj.'

'Why?' Shilpa asked, and as Vikrant opened his mouth to answer. 'Not why you don't want to put me in a spot. Why would you want to sponsor Madhuri's beautician's course?'

She looked like she genuinely wanted to know—saying that it had just seemed a good idea wasn't going to convince her.

'I like the kind of drive and energy she has,' he said slowly. 'And that she wants to be self-reliant, not just get married and have babies. I don't believe in anonymous charity; I prefer my money going to support someone who's going to make good use of it.'

'Have you spoken to Ranjana?'

He looked puzzled. 'Do I need to?'

Shilpa heroically suppressed the urge to say 'Well, duh?'

'I think you do,' she said instead. 'Ranjana may not be OK with Madhuri accepting the money.'

Vikrant still looked puzzled; and sighing, Shilpa explained. 'In case you hadn't noticed, Madhuri's nursing a huge crush on you. Ranjana's pretty upset. And if you start handing the girl money now…'

It was no use. Vikrant seemed constitutionally incapable of understanding Ranjana's point of view, and after a bit, Shilpa gave up trying. 'It's like he lives in an alternate universe,' she told Anuj when she repeated the conversation to him a week later.

'He's spent his adult life in the US,' Anuj replied. 'And from what you say about him, he was always a bit idealistic about class differences.'

'I guess,' Shilpa said, giving a little sigh. 'Are you meeting Sandeep today?' Rakhi had finally moved out of their flat and gone to live in the Bangalore flat she owned jointly with Sandeep. Though she'd always liked Sandeep more than Rakhi, Shilpa found herself firmly on Rakhi's side. Sandeep was being completely unreasonable. His latest take on the situation was that as the Bangalore flat had been paid for out of his earnings, he didn't owe Rakhi even a paisa more. Saira was staying with him and his mother while Rakhi tried to find a job in Bangalore.

'Yes, at around six.'

'I know it's not easy, but try and talk some sense into him if you can,' Shilpa said.

'I will.' He hesitated a little, and said, 'Shilpa, you know I love you, right?'

She gave him a surprised look, and he flushed. 'It's just that I don't think I say it often enough. I'd hate anything like what's happening with Rakhi and Sandeep to happen to us.' His voice had an unmistakeable ring of truth to it. He didn't say it, but finding out about Vikrant had shaken him up more than a little. It was the first time that he'd actively thought about the possibility of Shilpa leaving him. And Shilpa was no Rakhi—if she left, she would take Suraj with her. The mere thought had been enough to drive other women, including Diya, clear out of his head.

Some of what he was feeling came through, and Shilpa came across to give him a quick hug. 'I love you too,' she said softly. 'Go on now, you'll be late.'

Sandeep was already at the bar when Anuj entered the little old-fashioned restaurant on the Mahalakshmi race course.

'We used to sponsor the races every year,' he said nostalgically as Anuj joined him. 'That's the kind of stuff I miss about the bank.' It was also the kind of thing that had got him sacked; spending lakhs on a bunch of largely unprofitable customers hadn't done the P&L a lot of good.

'How's the new job going?'

Sandeep shrugged. 'As well as could be expected. I need to thank Shilpa properly—I'd have been lost without her. It's been almost a decade since I last had to look for a job. I had no contacts at all.'

Anuj, who socialized with headhunters at least once several times a year, and felt naked if he didn't have at least one alternate job offer on hand, tried not to look shocked.

'Always good to build a network,' he said. 'It's helped me a lot.'

'I can see that,' Sandeep said, making a generous gesture that seemed to encompass Anuj and all the symbols of his material success. There was a brief pause as the bartender refilled Sandeep's glass.

'How're things with Rakhi?' Anuj blurted out. 'I mean, I haven't spoken to her properly since she moved out of our place—any chance of you guys getting back together?'

'Zilch,' Sandeep said tersely.

Anuj put his glass down. 'I don't need to know,' he said awkwardly. 'I wouldn't even have brought the topic up if it hadn't been bothering Shilpa so much.'

Sandeep didn't seem to have even heard him. 'Rakhi's parents created a god-awful fuss when we got engaged,' he said. 'My family wasn't good enough for them, I didn't have enough money, even my education was all wrong as far as they were concerned.

'She had money; her grandmother managed to send it to her in some roundabout way. I had started working in the bank then, but I didn't really like it. It was the peak of the dot-com days, remember? 2000 and 2001, it was crazy. A friend and I decided to work on this online movie ticketing portal. We had big ideas, and we thought we'd be millionaires overnight.'

'Didn't we all,' Anuj said. This was the kind of conversation he understood. 'I didn't have the balls to quit banking though.'

'I wish I hadn't had the balls either,' Sandeep said, taking a swig from his glass. 'They got cut off anyway, once Rakhi figured out I'd pissed away all her money.' He caught Anuj's eye. 'Oh, she knew I was putting it into the business,' he said. 'I didn't swindle her out if that's what you're thinking. She had more confidence in my business plan than I had myself. It was only later once the money was gone that she started saying that I'd hoodwinked her. Anyway, I had to drag my sorry ass back to the bank, and move from one mind-numbing role after another, and whatever I did wasn't good enough for her. Not enough money, no flat of our own...'

He went silent for a bit, and Anuj transferred his gaze to the TV that was playing an IPL re-run

'If nagging was an Olympic sport, Rakhi would have brought home the gold,' Sandeep said, surprising a snort of laughter out of Anuj. 'My life's been hell for the last ten years. For a long time I thought I actually deserved it, and I kept my mouth shut, then it became a habit. The official Mr No-Balls, that's who I am, now.'

'I think she realizes that,' Anuj said quietly. God knows he hadn't wanted to have this conversation, but now that they were being all soul-baring with each other, he might as well try and get his one-point agenda across. 'She won't be such a nightmare to live with if you go back to her.'

'No fucking way,' Sandeep said. 'She's not getting me into her net again. I've made out a cheque and sent it to her—it's exactly the amount that she put into the business, plus the interest she'd have got if she'd left it in a fixed deposit. Bloody spent the weekend calculating it, had to dig out the fixed deposit rates for the last ten years. That's all she's getting from me. And she can keep the Bangalore flat as well.'

'What about Saira?'

'She'll be fine.' Sandeep was finally beginning to look a little ashamed of himself. 'It's not the best thing for her, but having a father in a lunatic asylum would be worse, and that's what Rakhi would drive me to if I went back. She can have custody if she wants as long as I get decent visitation rights—my mother's a bit too old to manage a kid.'

Sensing Anuj's shock, he smiled briefly. 'You're a pretty conventional dude under the surface, aren't you?' he said. 'You think that we should patch up for Saira's sake.'

Not wanting to admit it, Anuj stayed silent. 'You see, the kid has a lot of her mother in her,' Sandeep said. 'And she's been trained to think of me as a loser. I'm fond of her, but I can live with seeing her once a week, and maybe having her with me for a couple of weeks during the holidays.' He hesitated a little. 'I might as well tell you,' he said finally. 'There's someone else.'

'Another kid?' Anuj asked involuntarily, reddening as Sandeep gave a shout of laughter. 'Not another kid, man, that would be pretty fast work. Another woman. She's OK with me as I am, and she's pretty damn successful herself, doesn't need me to play the provider. I'm on the right side of forty—I'm planning to settle down with her, maybe have another couple of kids. Rakhi couldn't have any more children, I don't know if Shilpa told you. I've always been in favour of large families.'

He slid off the bar stool. 'See you around, Anuj. Good talking to you.' He was gone with a wave of his hand, and Anuj was left trying to make sense of what he'd just heard.

'I felt an utter fool,' he told Shilpa gloomily later. 'I always thought Sandeep was the ultimate family man, and all the while he's been living it up with a girlfriend on the side.'

Shilpa couldn't help laughing, in spite of her indignation on Rakhi's behalf. 'What are you upset about?' she asked. 'Sandeep having a more *rangeen* life than you, or that you didn't figure it out earlier?'

Anuj thought it through. 'I think because I took him at face-value,' he said finally. 'Evidently I suck big-time at judging people.'

Shilpa got up and gave him a hug. 'That's because *you're* the nice, uncomplicated family man at heart,' she said. 'In spite of the cool man-of-the-world image you work so hard on.'

'I need to speak to you, didi,' Ranjana said, popping her head around the door, just as Anuj put his arms around her and things began to get interesting. Shilpa gave a sigh. 'The lives we lead,' she said. 'I'll be back in a minute.'

It took longer than a minute though, and when she came back, she was in no mood to carry on from where they'd broken off.

'Damn Vikrant,' she said feelingly. 'Ranjana wants to send Madhuri to live with her aunt in the village.'

'But what about us?' Anuj asked, sounding appalled. 'What about us', pretty accurately summed up Shilpa's feelings as well. But Ranjana had been immoveable.

'She's getting all kinds of fancy ideas living in Mumbai,' she had said grimly. 'The quicker she gets them out of her head and settles down the better. Don't worry, I'll find you someone reliable to help with Suraj.'

'But I like Madhuri!' Shilpa's voice had sounded whiny even to her own ears. 'I'm sure she'll be fine if you just speak to her…'

'I have,' Ranjana had replied. 'It didn't help.' And that was that—she didn't budge an inch, not even when Shilpa offered to give Madhuri a fifty per cent pay hike.

∽

Vikrant looked dumbfounded when Shilpa told him.

'Why's she sending the girl away?'

'Presumably because of the raging crush she has on you,' Shilpa said drily. 'I tried to tell you, Vikrant—it was a pretty impractical plan helping Madhuri live a middle-class life.'

'It's totally unfair,' Vikrant said angrily. 'So what if she has a crush on me; she'll get over it, she's just a kid. She won't get this kind of an opportunity again.'

Shilpa gazed at him with narrowed eyes. In spite of his twenty-nine years, Vikrant looked rather like a kid himself, all het up and indignant. For the first time, the suspicion crossed her mind that he wasn't completely indifferent to the girl. Madhuri was attractive, and her unconditional devotion to Vikrant had to have an appeal.

'With that class there's only one respectable way out,' she said. 'And I'm sure you're not ready for that kind of commitment.'

'Are you suggesting I marry her?'

Shilpa met his gaze squarely. 'Well, why not?' she asked. 'If you claim that class differences don't matter to you, that's the best way to prove it.'

She felt positively Frankenstein-ish as she watched him think. The idea of marriage had evidently never crossed his mind before.

'I'm not sure I feel that way about her,' he said in a low voice, flushing as Shilpa shrugged and retorted, 'Then don't interfere in her life anymore—let Ranjana take her back to their village.'

'But I wanted to help her, and I've only made things worse!' Well, he'd chosen a particularly dim-witted way of helping her, Shilpa felt like saying, but she stopped herself. Anuj was right; all those years of living in the US had evidently helped Vikrant forget how things worked in the real world in India.

'I'd suggest you leave them to sort it out,' she said. 'In the meantime I'll look for a replacement maid.' It wasn't as easy as it sounded; with the number of new buildings that had cropped up between Parel and Prabhadevi, the demand for maids had far outstripped the supply. Even Ranjana was not able to get her a substitute.

'Mumbai's turning into an absolute nightmare to live in,' Shilpa said crossly, a week after her talk with Ranjana. Madhuri was under self-imposed house arrest, moping around the flat, and annoying everyone, especially Suraj.

'We could always move,' Anuj said.

'Where to? Delhi's not safe, Bangalore's bursting at the seams, and anyway I thought that Mumbai's the only place to be in your industry.'

'Within India, yes,' Anuj said, and Shilpa looked up sharply. Anuj very rarely threw out a remark without a purpose.

'Are you saying we should emigrate?'

'It's an option.' He looked so innocently ingenuous that Shilpa sighed and put down her book.

'Have you got an offer overseas, is that it?'

He nodded, looking a little shamefaced. It wasn't the first time that Shilpa had seen through one of his conversational gambits, but it was one of those *kya karein control nahin hota* things. After so many years in the corporate world, he found it difficult to come out with what he wanted in a straightforward manner.

'I've been exploring options—there's not much scope for me in the India office—the next step is Rishi's job, and he's going to be around for a while. There's a role in London…'

'Which you've already applied for?' Shilpa's brows contracted. She wouldn't put it past Anuj to have accepted the offer—she had a mad impulse to go and check his passport to see if he'd already got a work permit.

'I haven't applied for it, the regional office sent out a feeler, and Rishi asked if I'd be interested. I haven't said anything yet.' Most wives would be happy at the thought of their husbands getting promoted, he thought resentfully. Shilpa's expression resembled a cat that had been left outdoors on a rainy day.

'What would I do in London?'

'You could get a transfer too, Anuj said. 'Your firm has a pretty big presence there, right?'

'Anuj, my firm has a pretty big presence in Nairobi and Papua New Guinea as well,' Shilpa said exasperatedly. 'It doesn't mean there are roles for me there. And there's Suraj's schooling to think of—and we'd need to get household help or put him in daycare.'

'They do have schools in London,' Anuj murmured, and when Shilpa glared at him, he said, 'Look, all I'm saying is that we should consider it. If I do take up the role, I'd be going there on ex-pat terms—if you wanted to take a break and have a second baby, we could afford to do that.'

The thing with wishes was that if they suddenly came true on a Sunday morning they tended to knock you off balance. It was all very well to *say* that she wanted to take time off from work and have a second baby. The thought of actually doing it immediately was scary—images of Suraj's colicky, two-hours-of-sleep-a-night babyhood flashed through her head. 'Don't freak out, we can take some time to think it over,' Anuj said, correctly reading Shilpa's frozen expression.

'No, let's do it,' Shilpa said suddenly. Anuj stared at her. 'Do you mean it?' he asked.

'Yes,' she said firmly. 'We can come back to India after a couple of years, and I can always find a job then even if I don't get one in London. But I want to have another baby right away.'

∽

'If you're going to London can I come with you?' Madhuri asked a few days later. 'You'll need someone to look after Suraj. And I can now manage to speak English.'

'What about your mother?' Madhuri looked down and fiddled with the end of her dupatta. 'She'll be OK, as long as I'm not in Mumbai. She's got some idea about me and Vikrant sir, she's so stupid, it's not like he'd ever look at me… Anyway, I'm eighteen now, she can't stop me.' Her voice trailed off, and her eyes looked suspiciously damp.

'Damn Vikrant,' Shilpa said again, this time to herself. He really had no idea of the mess he'd created.

'I'm happy for you to come along,' she said to the girl. 'We'll have to get your passport done and everything, and I'll need to check the rules they have, I think they're pretty strict. What about your plans to become a beautician? And college?'

'My exams will be over next month,' Madhuri said. 'And the other thing, I don't want to do it anymore. I'm happy working for you.'

So that was what life did to young girls, Shilpa thought. Convinced them that a life of drudgery was better than having a dream. Vikrant and Ranjana had a lot to answer for.

Nikita shrugged when Shilpa told her. 'She'll probably make more money working for you in London than she would have here,' she said. 'Stop trying to solve the world's problems, Shilpa. If there's anyone who should be bothered about this whole thing, it's Vikrant.'

'He's bothered all right,' Shilpa said drily. 'There's very little he can do, that's all. How are things with you, Niki? Any chance of getting back with Naveen?'

Nikita shook her head. 'I think he'll end up marrying Saloni,' she said. 'They're suited for each other, and she's been in love with him for a while.'

'Is Jai upset?'

'I'm not sure,' Nikita said. 'I don't think he was serious about Saloni, but he's been a little different ever since they split up.'

It was difficult to put a finger on what exactly had changed in her relationship with Jai, Nikita thought as she walked back to her flat from Carlton Towers. He had been a complete tower of strength when she'd been going through a phase of intense depression after her mother's death. Somehow, he'd always known exactly what she needed to keep her from breaking down completely, and she'd begun to rely on him in a way she'd never relied on anyone before.

For the last week though, she'd been feeling a lot better. She was past the initial crippling wave of grief, and had begun to come to terms with what had happened. Work had helped, and so had Jai's support. What was bothering her was that as she recovered, Jai was slowly withdrawing from her. It was almost as if he didn't want to be around because he felt she didn't need him any more.

She ran into the subject of her thoughts as she climbed the stairs to her flat. Jai was coming down looking quite unfairly handsome in a dark blue T-shirt and khaki shorts. He gave her a quick nod, his eyes meeting hers, and then looking away quickly.

'Good evening,' she said, giving him a sunny smile. 'Off somewhere?' It was a pretty stupid question, she realized as soon as she asked, but he answered it literally. 'Need some groceries,' he said. 'I was about to start cooking dinner, and I found there was exactly one potato in the flat.'

'You can have dinner with me,' Nikita suggested, feeling unreasonably hurt when he hesitated. 'Come on, Jai. It's Friday, and I hate the thought of eating alone anyway. You can bring your potato along if you want.'

He laughed at that, but he turned to climb the rest of the stairs with her. 'I needed shaving cream as well,' he said. 'And bread for tomorrow's breakfast.'

'I'll lend you the bread,' Nikita promised as she tried to unlock the door to her flat. 'And you can always try growing a beard. It would look pretty sexy actually.'

The thought of Nikita finding him sexy sent a sudden flash of heat curling through Jai's body. He'd tried very hard to suppress his growing attraction towards Nikita, telling himself that she was still grieving, and that it was too soon after her break-up with Naveen. Also, he had no idea what Nikita's feelings towards him were. Most of the time she treated him like a good friend. Sometimes though, she said or did something that made him think she perhaps wasn't quite as indifferent to him as she pretended to be.

'Do you want dinner right away, or do you have time for a drink first?' Nikita asked.

Jai glanced at his watch. It was only eight o'clock, and in any case, he didn't have any place to go or anything better to do.

'I have all the time in the world,' he said, leaning back against the wall as he watched Nikita struggle to unlock her front door.

She gave a sigh of relief as she finally got it open. 'I swear that door hates me,' she said as she went in and clicked on the light. 'Will you be an angel and try and find the bottle-opener for the wine? It should be in one of the kitchen drawers. Suraj was using it to make a cork sculpture the last time he was here, and I'm not sure where he put it. I'll hunt for the booze.'

The bottle-opener finally turned up inside the pressure cooker. Feeling mildly triumphant, Jai went back into the living room. Nikita had unearthed a half-full bottle of vodka, and an extremely expensive red wine, and was thoughtfully examining the label on the wine.

'This costs as much as a dinner in a five-star restaurant,' she said without looking up. 'What a waste.'

'Why'd you buy it then?'

'I didn't. Naveen gave it to me—he hates drinking Indian wine.'

'Maybe we should stick to the vodka then,' Jai said, feeling suddenly uncomfortable. 'Keep the wine for a special occasion.'

'This *is* a special occasion,' Nikita said firmly, taking the bottle-opener from him. It was a complicated gadget, and it took her a little while to remove the cork. 'Ahh, finally,' she said, as she got it out. 'Naveen gave me the bottle-opener too—the first time he tried to open a bottle of wine here, he had to use a screwdriver, and half the cork went into the bottle.' She looked up and gave Jai and impish grin. 'Till I met him all I drank was Breezers and beer.'

It was the first time she'd mentioned Naveen since she broke up with him, and Jai wasn't sure if it was a good sign. She didn't sound as if she was missing him, but she could be just putting on a brave front.

'Are you in touch with him?' Jai asked tentatively, and she shrugged.

'We text each other once in a while,' she said. 'But we're not planning to get back together if that's what you're asking. He and Saloni seem pretty happy together.'

Jai grinned. 'I know,' he said. 'I met Naveen last week about my book.'

'Wasn't it awkward?' Nikita asked curiously. 'Given that you and Saloni were…ummm…'

'Not really,' Jai said. 'It's difficult to explain… Saloni and I weren't a proper couple like you and Naveen anyway.'

Nikita made a face. 'I guess I'm not as sophisticated as you guys,' she said. 'Too much of a small-town girl at heart.'

Jai gave her a surprised look. It was the first time Nikita had admitted to a lack of sophistication. Also, it sounded completely incongruous coming from her. His lips twitched a little as he took in her skin-tight neon-green trousers and off-the-shoulder top. With her spiky hairstyle, kohl-rimmed eyes and swinging mini peacock-feather earrings she looked like she'd stepped out of an MTV Roadies video.

'Yes, you're a complete *gaon ki gori*,' he said. 'So what's the special occasion?'

Nikita carefully poured the wine into two glasses and handed him one before answering.

'I'm celebrating my return to the land of the living,' she said, and grimaced as she clinked her glass against his. 'God, I sound horribly self-obsessed don't I? What I mean is that I've decided to stop moping around and get back to living my life. And the way I want to live it, not the way other people want me to.'

'That's not being self-obsessed,' Jai said softly. He'd known enough about Nikita's relationship with her mother to understand that her expectations from her daughter had been high. Nikita herself was ambitious as far as her career went, but it was her mother who'd wanted her to marry a rich man. Left to herself, Nikita would probably never have got engaged to Naveen. And Naveen in turn had all sorts of expectations from his future wife.

'You're very sorted, aren't you, Jai?' Nikita asked, looking up at him. 'You know exactly what you want, and you're not bothered about stupid things like money and status and all that.'

'It's easy not to worry about money when you know its there if you really need it,' Jai said, shrugging. 'From what you've told me about your childhood, it's perfectly natural for you to want a stable income.'

Nikita nodded, taking a big swig of wine. 'Jai...' she said. 'I've been meaning to say this for a while... Thanks for being around. I think I'd have gone stark raving mad these last few weeks if it wasn't for you.'

Her brown eyes were looking straight into his, and Jai found himself suddenly at a loss for words. 'It's fine,' he said awkwardly. 'That's what friends are for.'

She gave him a little smile. 'We're going to stay friends, aren't we?' she asked. 'I know I'm not always easy to deal with, but I'll make more of an effort to behave.'

Jai swallowed. Even at her prickly best, Nikita was madly attractive—in her current mood, she was pretty much irresistible. The impulse to bend down and kiss her was immense, and he had to tell himself sternly that it wouldn't be fair to her. She might be over the worst, but she was still in an emotionally vulnerable state that he couldn't take advantage of.

'Don't make too much of an effort,' he said, trying to keep his voice as normal as possible. 'I've got so used to you being rude and tactless that I won't be able to handle it if you turn angelic overnight.'

Nikita's expression lightened immediately, and she punched him in the shoulder. 'I'm never rude,' she said. 'Come on now, drink up that wine, we've got an entire bottle to finish.'

Jai obediently swigged back the rest of the wine in his glass and held it out for a refill. Common sense was telling him to get the hell out of Nikita's flat before he ended up doing something stupid, but his body was refusing to budge.

Nikita was thinking exactly the opposite. Jai was finally behaving normally with her and she herself was feeling alive and happy after a long, long while. She hadn't missed the times Jai's gaze had lingered on her lips and body, and she was incredibly aware of his nearness. She was gathering courage to reach out and touch him, perhaps stand on tiptoe and press her lips to his, when he spoke.

'I'll be going out of town for a few days.'

She looked up in surprise—this was the first time he'd mentioned it. 'Where to?'

'Delhi. I have a meeting with my publishers to finalize some of the details for the book launch.'

'How long will you be away?'

'A week. The meeting's tomorrow evening, but I have a few friends there, and I'll stay back and spend a few days with them.'

Nikita digested that slowly. Somehow, it had never occurred to her that he'd have friends from his previous life, since before he came to Mumbai.

'I'll miss you,' she said slowly.

'I'll be back before you know it,' he said, ruffling her hair lightly. 'Come on, let's have dinner. I need to go pack.'

'I thought you had all the time in the world,' Nikita said snidely before giving up with good grace. She knew she hadn't imagined the expression in his eyes earlier, but for some reason he'd evidently decided that she was off bounds for now. Perhaps it was some sort of misplaced loyalty towards Naveen because of the help he'd taken to get his book published. Whatever it was, it was damned inconvenient—Nikita felt like screaming at him as she laid the table for dinner. She wasn't ready to sleep with Jai just yet, but she really, really wanted to kiss him. The memory of their last kiss was seared into her brain, and now that she was unattached again, she couldn't wait to repeat the experience. Somewhere, deep inside, she knew that she was very close to falling in love with Jai, but she didn't want to think about it right now. There was a good chance that Jai didn't return the feeling. Being attracted to her didn't automatically mean that he was in love with her, and she didn't want to deal with the heartbreak that would result if she found out that he didn't want to have anything to do with her in the romantic way.

'When's the book launch?' she asked.

'Two weeks from now on Thusday. Will you be able to come?'

'Yes of course,' Nikita said, then clicked her tongue in exasperation. 'Oh no,' she said. 'That's the day our global CEO is in town—there are some meetings I can't duck.' He looked disappointed, and she immediately felt better.

'I'll be praying for you though,' she said, giving him an impish smile. 'And I'll get everyone I know to buy your book.'

He laughed, and the conversation moved to more general topics. The awareness between them was as strong as ever, but so was the unspoken agreement that they weren't going to do anything about it right now.

'Dessert?' Nikita asked once they were done with dinner. Jai shook his head. 'Not for me,' he said. 'Come on, I'll help you clear up.'

He picked up their plates and carried them to the kitchen sink while Nikita put the leftovers into the fridge.

'There's a box of Lindor dark chocolates here,' she announced as she poked about in the bottom shelf of the fridge. 'Sure you don't want some?'

Jai crossed the kitchen to come to her side. 'Just one perhaps.'

'Coming up.' Nikita took the box out, and straightened up, almost colliding with Jai as she did so. One of her peacock feather earrings brushed against his chest, and the clasp snagged on his T-shirt.

'Oops,' she said, laughing, though she was intensely conscious of his proximity. She could hear the steady thump of his heart, and the woody smell of his cologne was tantalizing.

'Here, give me the chocolates,' Jai said, taking the box from her and abstracting two before he set it on the top of the fridge. He popped one into his own mouth, and the other into hers before taking the earring in one hand and trying to disentangle it from his T-shirt. It took a while; the clasp had gone through the cloth, and some careful manoeuvring was required to get it out without ruining the shirt.

'All done,' he said finally, and Nikita stared up at him, still recovering from the feel of his fingers against her mouth as he'd slid the chocolate in. He gave her a quick smile, bending down to press a brief kiss next to her mouth.

'Good night,' he said quietly as he raised his head. His breath smelt of red wine and cocoa, and Nikita put her hands up and clutched his T-shirt.

'Don't go,' she said softly, as he ran his thumb slowly over her bottom lip, making her quiver with desire.

'I'll see you when I'm back from Delhi,' he said, and before Nikita knew what was happening, he stepped away and was out of the door without turning back.

She could have felt upset at his rapid exit, but Nikita knew that he was quite as affected as she was. He'd left in a misguided attempt to protect her from things getting too serious too fast, and she found herself grudgingly admiring him for his self-control.

'The next time, I'll lock the door behind him and throw away the key,' she informed the refrigerator as she put the chocolates back. 'Let's see how long his chivalry lasts then.' But she was smiling as she latched the door and went to bed, and when she finally fell asleep she dreamt about Jai all night long.

19

'Why are you doing so much for Jai?' Saloni asked. 'I mean, not to sound self-centred or anything, but he was my ex-boyfriend—it seems a bit weird, you being his self-appointed fairy godfather.'

Naveen gave her an amused look. 'Do you feel awkward about it?' Saloni and he had been together for a couple of months, and their relationship had progressed beyond the lets-take-off-our-clothes-and-jump-in-bed level to something a tad deeper. Marriage wasn't completely ruled out. Naveen had even progressed to checking out engagement rings at his favourite jeweller. Of course, he'd chickened out at the last minute and bought her a bracelet instead, but there was still hope.

'Awkward?' She shook her head. 'Not really. I still like Jai, and I think it's great you're helping him, I'm just not sure why.'

'It's something I've wanted to do for a while,' Naveen said. 'I usually work to get press coverage on new movies or product launches or polishing up a celeb's image. Time I branched out a little, created a celebrity myself.'

Saloni arched her eyebrows. 'Are we still talking about Jai?'

Naveen laughed. 'We are. Oh, the raw material is all there—he's written a good book, some would even say an outstanding book. But without me, it's unlikely he'd have even found a publisher. And he has subzero knowledge on how to market himself.'

'I thought it was the book he needed to market,' Saloni murmured.

'People will buy the book only if they're intrigued by him,' Naveen said. 'Wait and watch. There's the personal angle as well, of him having left home to write this book. Then it's a historical novel, so he has an open field—all the bestsellers today are written by hotshot MBA types who spend more time on marketing than on their grammar. And he's perfect for the camera, every female journalist in town who claps eyes on him will immediately be drooling over him.'

For a second, Saloni felt vaguely upset at the thought of drooling female journalists. Then, as Naveen put a casual arm around her shoulders and drew her close, she forgot about Jai. After all, he'd been just a pleasant interlude—Naveen was the real thing.

Naveen grinned to himself. For all her movie career and NGO work, Saloni was still remarkably naïve. And, as he'd discovered very early on, part of the truth was always more believable than complete fabrication.

On the actual day of the book launch, Jai paced the back area of the bookstore nervously, feeling a bit like an expectant father. Naveen's team had done an excellent job building up the hype around the book, and the media turnout for the launch was impressive. Jai's stomach churned as he thought of the ordeal ahead of him. Naturally self-effacing, standing up in front of a dozen journalists and telling them his book was the greatest piece of writing to come out of India after the Mahabharata was a daunting prospect.

'Jai, come on, you need to get up on the dais,' the PR girl hissed, and he bit his lip. Given a choice, he'd like to walk rapidly away from the bookstore and never come back. He'd badly wanted Nikita to be there, but her meeting with her company's global CEO had clashed with the launch time. His trip to Delhi had got extended, and he'd not been able to meet her after he got back. Since the dinner at her flat he'd had a lot of time to think, and he'd finally come to terms with the fact that he cared very deeply for Nikita and was perhaps even in love with her. Maybe she didn't feel the same away about him right now, but she was definitely attracted to him, and he knew he'd be able to bring her around in time.

Right now though, he needed to stop thinking about his love life and go out there and talk about his book. There were almost a hundred people in the audience. He didn't know more than three or four of them—the rest were journalists, book critics and prospective readers, and to Jai they looked as intimidating as a pack of ravenous wolves.

'You'll do great,' Naveen said, giving him an encouraging thump on the back. 'The build-up's there, all you need to do is look brooding and intense. Stick to the script, and don't lose your temper with the journalists.'

It took Jai less than ten minutes to realize that the last bit wasn't a facetious add-on. Some of the journalists were the eager and starry-eyed kind, others were cynical sharks in human clothing. The graceful Bollywood movie star, who was the celebrity guest at the launch, cut the ribbon and made the kind of speech that sounded good and meant nothing. The publisher then spoke fulsomely about having been bowled over by Jai's talent when he saw his manuscript. To the best of Jai's knowledge, he hadn't yet read the book. After that, Jai was left to the mercies of the journalists.

'So is this just one large publicity stunt, Jai?' one of the scruffier specimens asked. 'Is the book even based on your grandfather's life? I Googled him and couldn't find any mention of a freedom fighter by that name.'

'That would be because they didn't have Google in 1947,' Jai said gravely. The women journalists giggled, and even some of the men laughed. Naveen smiled as well, but the look in his eyes said 'Be careful.'

'Jokes apart, the book's based on my grandfather's diaries which are available for anyone to see,' Jai said.

'Is it true that you worked as a driver to support yourself while you wrote the book?'

'Yes, I did.'

'Will you be writing another book about your experiences?'

'I'm not sure, but it's possible.' He'd prefer to have a few teeth extracted without anaesthetic, but that was neither here nor there.

'Did your employer know that you write?'

'She did.' Jai's eyes automatically sought Shilpa's in the audience. Shilpa gave him a thumbs-up and several of the photographers turned to take a quick shot of her. Shilpa was wearing a particularly flattering dress, and for once had put some make-up on—she looked elegant and very cool and collected.

'So, ma'am, what do you think of Jai's book?' one of the journalists asked.

'I think it's wonderfully well-written,' she said. 'But he's the person best qualified to talk about it.'

Naveen gave her a quick smile of appreciation. It was rare to find someone who didn't try and grab the maximum possible airtime when given a mike. Shilpa had shifted the attention back to Jai in a way that was graceful and charming at the same time. 'She's got class,' he muttered to Saloni, and she nodded in agreement. She'd met Shilpa only once, but had liked her.

'You did well,' Shilpa said to Jai as they left together half an hour later. 'And there were journalists from some pretty well-known publications out there—if you're lucky, your book will be a bestseller.'

'I doubt it,' Jai said gloomily. 'The publisher told me that they put out more than two hundred books this year. And that's just this publisher, there are dozens more out there. The bookstores are full of new books. I'll be lucky if I sell five hundred copies.'

'You could explore that movie deal Naveen was talking about,' Shilpa suggested, but Jai refused to be cheered up. The euphoria of finally having the book out in bookstores had ebbed away, and he was wondering what to do with the rest of his life.

'I don't want to have anything to do with movies,' he said. 'I'll start looking for a job, that's the only thing left.'

He sounded so glum that Shilpa laughed. 'You sound as if a job is only a notch above eternal slavery,' she said. 'Actually I have an idea about that. Want to come over to my office and discuss it?'

It was past eight, but Jai agreed, as Shilpa's office was on the way to Carlton Towers. Besides, he didn't want to go home and brood, and Nikita wouldn't be home from work yet.

In that he was wrong; more keyed up about the launch than she cared to admit, Nikita was already home and pacing her living room. She didn't want to call Jai or Shilpa in case the launch was still on, and every once in a while, she'd stick her head out of the door to see if the lights were on in his flat. Of course if they were, she'd have to kill him for not coming over first to tell her how the launch went off.

The lights were still off, and Nikita turned back disappointed, when she heard a kind of gasping noise from the stairwell. She put her head over the banisters and saw a rather plump woman leaning against the wall, trying to catch her breath.

'Are you OK?' Nikita called out. Jai had bought some bulbs and replaced the lights in the stairwell, but she couldn't see much of the woman's face, just that she was fair and quite young.

'Just about. Could do with a hand, though.'

'Yes, of course,' Nikita said, hurrying down the stairs. She took the woman's arm, and realized that she wasn't fat, just very pregnant.

'Umm, are you sure you should be climbing stairs?' she asked worriedly as she half-dragged, half-lifted her up the remaining stairs.

'Probably not, but the lift seems to have been abducted by aliens,' the woman said, sounding remarkably cheerful. 'Thanks a million. You must be Nikita?'

Nikita nodded, but the woman seemed to have lost interest in her, sitting down with a thump on the last step. 'Oh hell, he's not back yet,' she wailed, looking at the locked door of Flat 405. 'What a bummer. Any idea where he is?'

'You mean Jai?' A pregnant woman so eager to meet Jai that she'd climbed four flights of stairs to find him... Nikita tried to do the math in her head. How long had it been since Jai had suddenly appeared in Shiv-Shakti Housing Society?

He'd never told her what the fight with his father had been about. Oh Lord, could he be married to this woman? She was wearing something that looked like a very fancy mangalsutra around her neck. What about Saloni then? And of late, he'd seemed interested in Nikita again...

'I'm his sister,' the woman said drily, as Nikita gaped at her. 'Any idea where he is?'

'He's gone for the book launch,' Nikita stammered, trying to gather her wits. *Not* his girlfriend/wife then, what a relief.

'The launch got over an hour ago,' Jai's sister said impatiently. 'I spoke to Naveen. That's why I came here, I thought he'd be back. And you're here, it's unlikely he would have gone off to celebrate with anyone else.'

Nikita flushed hotly. 'Any chance I could wait in your flat?' Jai's sister continued. 'I'm Pooja by the way, and I'm rather tired of sitting on the floor.'

'Yes, of course,' Nikita stammered. All her natural confidence seemed to have deserted her—in any case, even though she looked about fifteen months pregnant, Pooja seemed more than a match for her.

'Ah that's more like it,' she said, sinking into the sofa. 'Now I hope that boy doesn't take too long.'

'Would you like some water?' Nikita asked. 'Or tea or something?'

'I'll take the something,' Pooja said, raising her hand. 'Or no, on second thoughts, maybe just the water.'

Nikita had pulled herself together by then. 'So you know Naveen?' she asked, handing Pooja a glass of water. 'Would that explain his interest in Jai's career?'

'Sharp,' Pooja commented. 'I guess I was stupid, telling you I'd spoken to Naveen. But those stairs were torture, I wasn't thinking straight.'

She took a swig of water and continued, 'Yes, you're right of course. I did ask Naveen to keep an eye out for my baby brother. Jai's talented, but he isn't street-smart—that book of his would have sunk without a trace if Naveen hadn't given it a push. Now, at least, it stands a decent chance.'

'You're paying Naveen to do the PR?'

Pooja gave Nikita an amused look. 'It doesn't work that way, pet,' she said. 'Naveen won the pitch to do the launch and the PR for my new jewellery line. He already knew Jai— he'd even read part of his book, I just had to drop a few hints. Maybe I didn't negotiate quite as hard as I normally would have over the launch costs, but who's to know if he'd have dropped his rates even if I had?'

Nikita looked mildly shocked, but the shock turned to horror as Pooja put the glass down abruptly and clutched at her stomach.

'Honey, I hate to alarm you, but would you have something as handy as a gynaecologist tucked away somewhere?' Pooja asked, beaming at Nikita. 'Because I have a feeling that this baby of mine is in as great a hurry to meet her uncle as I am.'

'So we're setting up an internal communications team,' Shilpa was saying. 'And we've discussed it a lot—the one thing we don't want is a typical corporate type running things. We have all kinds of people in the company, right from workers to hotshot MBAs, but we need someone who's genuinely empathetic and has excellent communication skills... I thought of you immediately'

Her phone trilled to life, and she gave him a quick smile 'Excuse me a second,' she said and turned to take the call.

Nikita was shrieking into the phone. 'Is Jai with you? His sister's here and she's gone into labour; Naveen said Jai's left the bookstore, and I can't get through to him. I'm taking her to the hospital right away, come quiiiiicckkk, I know nothing about babies!'

'We need to go,' Shilpa said, jumping up and dragging a surprised Jai out of the door. 'I'll explain on the way.'

∽

'What do you mean, you can't admit her, you moron?' Nikita demanded, almost dancing with anger. 'It's an emergency, you geddit? She's about to have the baby, right here!'

'Ma'am, you'll have to move your car, it's blocking the way,' a security guard interjected, and Nikita almost slapped him. She'd had to rouse half the building to help her carry Pooja down the stairs again, but no one had agreed to come with her to the hospital. She'd assumed Shilpa and Jai would have reached before her, but they hadn't, and Pooja's pains were just ten minutes apart now.

'I'll move the car, just give me a minute,' Nikita said distractedly.

'And I'll go ahead and have the baby, shall I?' Pooja asked. 'Right here, I think, since no one's willing to let me into the actual maternity ward.' She sounded remarkably composed for someone who had to be in terrible pain. The security guard and the receptionist fell back and a nurse went off to fetch a doctor.

Luckily, she didn't have the baby in the reception hall— Shilpa and Jai pelted into the hospital, with Naveen at their heels. 'Saloni will get the car sorted out, give me the keys,'

Shilpa said. 'I've called my gynaecologist, he'll be here in a few minutes. It's Dr Merchant,' she said to the nurse. 'He's already called someone—he asked me to speak to Simone—they should have a room ready by now.'

Dr Merchant's name got things moving. A wheelchair appeared, and Jai helped his sister into it, his eyes wide with worry. 'Does it have to be a male gynaecologist?' Pooja asked, her pretty brown eyes looking troubled for the first time that evening.

'You almost had the baby on the street,' Jai retorted. 'Right now you should be grateful even if an orangutan comes along and delivers it for you.' He'd got over his initial panic and was working himself into a temper. 'What were you *thinking* coming all this way alone? Who allowed you on a flight? And where's that numskull husband of yours?'

'I took the train,' Pooja said, looking as dignified as it was possible to look scrunched up in a wheelchair. 'And Jignesh had a relative to visit in Kandivali, he went there.'

'And left you to wander around on your own? I knew he was stupid, but this is criminally careless, he should be...'

'Jai, I don't think you're helping,' Nikita murmured, laying a soothing hand on his arm. 'You can sort all this out later.'

'Sir, if you could all wait outside,' the nurse said. 'Dr Merchant will be along in a minute, and he'll need to examine the patient. Also, hospital rules allow only one visitor at a time.'

'Yes, take him away Nikita,' Pooja said. 'Serves me right for coming all this way to meet my bratty little brother. Where's that nice lady who came with him? She could sit with me till the doctor comes. I liked her.'

'If you mean me, I'm right here,' Shilpa said, walking in. 'Out you go, both of you.' Jai looked disposed to argue, but a particularly strong contraction gripped Pooja. 'Owwwwwwwwww...' she moaned, directing the sound right at Jai. 'I think we should get her ready for the labour room,' one of the nurses said.

Contraction over, Pooja beamed at them. 'I don't think you need to see this, Jai,' she said, but he was already out of the door, almost colliding with Dr Merchant as he rushed into the room.

'So this is the young lady who's caused so much trouble, hey?' they heard him say as the door closed behind him.

Not having Pooja around to yell at, Jai reverted to panic mode. 'What if something happens to her?' he asked. 'I could kill Jignesh, he knows how headstrong she is, I can't believe he let her out of his sight!'

Prudently, Nikita decided not to tell him that Pooja's labour had probably been brought on by climbing four flights of stairs. 'Let's see if all the admin stuff is sorted out,' she suggested. 'I hadn't managed to do anything more than give them her name.'

Naveen was at the counter though, flashing his teeth and his credit card at the lady in charge of patient registration. From the complete dragon she'd been when Nikita had come in, she seemed to have turned into something approaching a human.

'He seems to have it under control,' Saloni muttered, as Naveen shamelessly name-dropped and charmed his way into having the lady fill the forms for him. 'I think you'll need to sign, Jai, you're the only immediate relative here.'

Left alone with Saloni, Nikita said awkwardly, 'Thanks so much for coming here, and helping out with the car and stuff.'

'No worries,' Saloni said, smiling briefly. 'Here are the keys, by the way. Naveen's driver parked the car in the BMC parking lot a little further down the road. We'll need to leave now, got a dinner to go to.'

Speaking of which, she hadn't had dinner either. Nikita gave Jai a hopeful look once he had finished speaking to his brother-in-law. 'Can we eat?' she asked. 'It's almost ten. They have a little canteen in the hospital.'

Jai hadn't had dinner either, but he was too nervous to swallow a bite. Nikita finally gave up on him and concentrated on her own meal, giving his hand reassuring pats between mouthfuls.

Shilpa found them when Nikita was halfway through her gulab jamun. Jai sprang to his feet, almost sending the table flying.

'Is she OK?' he asked. 'The baby?'

'Both fine,' Shilpa smiled at him. 'Dr Merchant said you can go and see them in fifteen minutes... In fifteen *minutes* Jai, relax, and don't go charging off, you don't even know where to find them.'

Pooja was looking quite unfairly radiant, cuddling a bald and squirmy little infant. 'Say hello to your niece,' she said holding her up for Jai to see. 'There, baby, that's your grumpy Uncle Jai. He's run away from home, but if you ask him nicely he'll come back.'

'No I won't,' Jai said, but he was smiling. Nikita felt an unfamiliar pang of jealousy as she watched him gaze at the baby. This is what Jai would be like when he fell in love, she thought, as his eyes melted and he dipped his head to place a reverent kiss on the baby's tiny fist. Supremely unappreciative of the honour being done to her, the baby wrinkled up her face, turned bright red and began to bawl.

'Oooh, don't cry, it's OK, I know he's ugly, but he's really quite nice, wait till you get to know him better,' Pooja said, rocking the baby till she calmed down.

'You're a natural,' Shilpa said, looking amused. 'It took me days before I was comfortable holding my own son.'

'Got lots of practice with thingie here,' Pooja said, nudging Jai with an elbow. 'Horrible little monster he was too, though he's turned out OK.'

'Pooja, you were only six when I was born,' Jai protested.

'So what, I used to look after you all the time.' She evidently had a lot more to say, but then she took a good look at his face. 'You OK, baba? What's wrong?' Jai shook his head blindly, shying away from Pooja's hand as she tried to stroke his face.

'I was so scared,' he choked out, placing his head against the cold railing of the hospital bed. 'You came all this way to see me—what if something had happened to you or the baby? If Nikita hadn't been there…'

Pooja promptly handed the baby to a waiting nurse. 'Here, put the creature back in her cot,' she said abruptly. 'Come here, Jai, don't be a nut. Nikita *was* there, and if she hadn't been, I'd have yelled till someone came. And see, I got that lovely Dr Merchant to deliver the baby, did you look at him, wasn't he cute? All that thick white hair, and he has the sexiest eyes, Jignesh will die of jealousy when he sees him.'

Jai didn't say anything, but he turned to Pooja and let her hug him tenderly.

'Come on, time for us to go,' Shilpa said, tapping Nikita on the shoulder and winking at the nurse. The three of them left the room together, and the nurse asked, 'Husband? But he looks so young?'

'Brother,' Shilpa said. 'They're meeting after years. It's a long story, but if you're on duty tomorrow, I'm sure Pooja will tell you the details.'

20

'Oh bloody hell,' Shilpa said as they got into the car and she took her phone out of her bag. There were eleven missed calls and multiple messages from Anuj. She called him back as Nikita pulled on to the main road. 'Anuj, relax, I'm OK. No, something did happen, I'll explain when I get back. The car's parked in office, Nikita's dropping me home.'

There was an outburst from the phone, and Nikita grinned, imagining Anuj in a flap. Poor guy, he must have been frantic, but yelling at Shilpa now wasn't going to get him too many brownie points.

'Jai's in hospital. No, nothing's wrong with him... Anuj I *told* you the car's parked at my office. His sister just had a baby... Yes, a BABY, one of those little things that grow up into human beings... Anuj, can we just leave it, I'll explain when I get back.'

'If Anuj is upset, imagine what Jignesh's *haalat* is going to be when he finds out that his wife wandered off and had the baby among a bunch of strangers.' Nikita said wickedly. 'She's really something, that Pooja.'

'If I'm not wrong, Jignesh was the crazy-looking guy we saw running in when we were leaving,' Shilpa said grinning. 'Yes, that's a good thought actually. I should probably get Anuj to meet Jignesh. Let him know what he's missing.'

When she actually saw Anuj though, all thoughts of teasing him vanished from her mind. His face was still haggard as he said quietly, 'I'm so sorry I yelled at you, I was out of mind with worry.' His voice was steady, but his arms tightened convulsively around her as if he never meant to let her go. Unbearably touched, Shilpa reached up to cup his face in her hands. 'I'm sorry too,' she said softly. 'I'd put my phone on silent during the book launch, and I forgot to un-mute it. And after that things were so crazy, trying to get hold of Dr Merchant, and being with Pooja while she had the baby, it just didn't occur to me to call you and let you know I'd be late.'

Anuj didn't say anything, he just pulled her close again. After a few minutes, her hand automatically slipped into his as he led her to the bedroom, and then neither spoke for a long, long while.

◦∼◦

'I overslept!' Shilpa said the next morning. 'It's a quarter past six already. Oh well, I guess it doesn't matter if I'm going to be putting in my papers anyway.'

Anuj came and sat by the side of the bed. 'I need to talk to you about that,' he said. Shilpa's eyes flew up in alarm. 'London isn't happening?' she asked. Seeing Pooja's baby the day before had made her maternal hormones kick in even harder. She'd even dreamt the whole night about having a second baby.

'London's still an option,' Anuj said slowly. 'But there's been a development here. Rishi quit yesterday.'

'Rishi quit? But I thought he was doing so well?'

'There are rumours he was involved in an insider trading racket,' Anuj said. 'You remember that girl Diya? She'd got quite close to him over the last couple of months—she's quit too. Her dad is a fairly well-known stockbroker, and he's been on the fringes of a few shady deals.'

Shilpa sat up, looking horrified. 'But you were close to both of them!' she said. 'What does this mean for you?'

'Actually, I wasn't,' Anuj said. 'Diya and I were friendly once, but we fell out, and we haven't really been on talking terms for a while. And Rishi did these particular deals on his own.' He hesitated a little. 'I'm pretty appalled at what's happened, I've always thought Rishi was a straight guy. But as far as I'm concerned, the fallout is positive for me—they've offered me Rishi's job.'

It took her a few seconds to absorb the information, then she burst out, 'But that's wonderful! Why aren't you looking happier about it?'

'Because I admired and respected Rishi, and this isn't the way I wanted to get a promotion,' Anuj said, forcing a smile. 'I guess you're right, I've been trying hard to be a man-of-the-world, but I'm still that geeky Chandigarh boy at heart.'

'I rather like the geeky Chandigarh boy side of you,' Shilpa said, giving him a hug. 'You decide, Anuj. I'm OK with London, if that's what you prefer.'

'I think Mumbai is still the better option,' Anuj said. 'No disruption for you and Suraj, and after what happened to Radha Mausi, I'd feel better having my parents close by.'

∽

It was only when they emerged from their room ten minutes later that they discovered that Suraj was still asleep and Madhuri was missing. Her clothes were gone, and the bathroom she used was swept clean of her belongings. Suraj when shaken awake had no idea where she was. 'She didn't say anything,' he said. 'She was here when I went to sleep.'

'Should I call Ranjana?' Shilpa asked, but before Anuj could answer, the doorbell rang. Suraj pattered away to answer it. 'Hello, Vikrant Uncle!' they heard him say. Surprisingly, Suraj liked Vikrant, though Vikrant had made absolutely no efforts to ingratiate himself with the boy.

'Mom and Dad at home?'

'Yes,' Anuj said, stepping into the living room. 'Something wrong Vikrant? You look a little worked up.'

'I just need to talk to the two of you for a couple of minutes,' Vikrant said.

'Suraj, go play inside,' Shilpa ordered.

'But what about school? Don't I need to get ready?'

'You're already late,' Shilpa said. 'And Jai won't be coming today, so there's no one who can drop you. Take the day off, we'll do something fun together. Hopefully, when Ranjana comes in we'll know what's happened to Madhuri.'

Vikrant winced. 'I'm so sorry,' he said. 'God, this is embarrassing; I'll just come out and say it—Madhuri's with me.'

There was half-a-minute of stunned silence, after which, Shilpa asked carefully, 'Vicky, when you say she's with you, do you mean she's at your flat right now? What about her mother, does she know?'

Vikrant was evidently nervous—his American accent had faded in the past couple of months, but it was back now in full force. 'Yes, she's there, and no her mother doesn't know. But it's alright—I'm going to marry her,' he said.

'Marry our maid?' Anuj looked thunderstruck. Shilpa had explained the situation to him several times, but he'd dismissed it as a harmless crush Madhuri had developed with no encouragement from Vikrant. 'Are you serious, man?'

'Yes,' Vikrant said, and there was enough quiet dignity in his voice to silence even Anuj.

Shilpa looked at him with troubled eyes, seeing Vikrant as a stormy nineteen-year-old all over again. 'Vicky, I thought you didn't feel that way about her?' she asked. 'We discussed it, you said you'd let her be!'

'She came to say good-bye,' Vikrant said. 'She'd thought it over and decided she couldn't leave her family and go to London with you. Her mother's harsh, but she's had a tough life, and those two kids are all she's got. So Madhuri was planning to go to her aunt in the village, and come back whenever her mom let her.'

It had been an eye-opener for Vikrant, seeing Madhuri again. She was lifeless, all the spark and energy he'd admired about her wiped out almost overnight. She didn't reproach him at all; her mother had effectively killed whatever hopes she'd had of a relationship with him, and somehow that hurt him more than anything she could have said.

'I couldn't let her go like that, Shilpa,' he said, his eyes pleading with her to understand. 'It's not a whim. I'll marry her as soon as I can, and I'll make sure she gets the education she deserves and has a good life.' Unconsciously, his thumb was rubbing against the scar on his wrist, where so many years ago he'd slashed it with a razor blade. If his roommate hadn't come back unexpectedly to fetch a book, that would have been the end of his short life; and Shilpa would have borne the guilt for the rest of hers. In a way, she still felt responsible for him.

'Are you doing this because you're sorry for her?' she ased, trying to phrase the question as tactfully as she could. 'Because that isn't a good reason for getting married. You'll only start resenting her after a while, and you'll both be unhappy.'

Vikrant was already shaking his head. 'I do care about her,' he said, struggling to find the right words. 'It's not the same as it is for you and Anuj, but its there. I won't resent her. And if I let her go now, it'll haunt me for the rest of my life.'

'Then you should go ahead and marry her,' she said. 'No one else's opinions matter. Do you want me to let Ranjana know?'

'If you could,' Vikrant said. 'Thanks, Shilpa. And I don't like the idea, but Madhuri's offered to come back and work for you until you leave for London.'

'Well, as it turns out, we might not be going after all,' Anuj said.

Vikrant looked surprised. 'Oh, I'll tell her then. There's a girl Madhuri knows who's just brought her younger sister to Mumbai, she might want to work for you. The older sister works for someone you know—I think her name's Jenny.'

'Jenny, that's Madhuri's Chinese-looking friend,' Anuj said. 'That should work out well. And I hate to be practical and unfeeling, but I do need to go into work; maybe it'd be best if Madhuri came back now and made us breakfast. Then Shilpa could break the news to Ranjana, Jenny could send her sister over and you could go right ahead and marry Madhuri.'

Shilpa laughed. 'I'll make breakfast,' she said. 'But do send Madhuri over when you can, Vikrant.'

Anuj waited till Vikrant had left and said, 'I don't think much of that ex-boyfriend of yours, marrying Madhuri because of a crazy fancy like that. Do you think we should tell Ranjana to stop it?'

'Oh, they'll be fine,' Shilpa said. 'It's like the old Pygmalion and Galatea legend. A man can't resist the thought of being able to mould a young girl into the kind of woman he wants.'

'Well, I get the moulding bit, but I've no idea who the Pyg-person is,' Anuj said. 'I already know you're better read than I am, do you have to rub it in before breakfast? Maybe I should have caught you younger as well, when there was still scope for some moulding.'

'Yeeurgh, *kissing*! How totally gross,' Suraj said, wandering into kitchen a few minutes later. 'Can I have something to eat? And if Madhuri didi is going to marry old Vikrant, can you learn how to make chilli cheese toast from her? She does it really well.'

'Do you want to come home and change and shower, Jignesh?' Jai asked his brother-in-law. Jignesh shook his head vigorously. 'I'm not letting that woman out of my sight,' he said, looking at Pooja as she slept peacefully with her cheek pillowed on one hand, her short hair fluffed up around her face. 'She didn't even tell me she was going out, I almost died of worry when she vanished. She messaged me to say she was meeting you, and the next thing I know, some random woman called and told me that the baby had arrived! We had the best possible room blocked in the best hospital in Jaipur...'

'But she's fine now, and so is the baby,' Jai said, looking at little Aditi Shah nestled into her crib. She was wearing regulation hospital wear, but Jai's parents were flying down from Jaipur with the heirloom baby smock that generations of Singh babies had worn on their first day in the world.

'I know,' Jignesh said, sighing in relief. His rather haggard face softened as he looked at the baby. 'She's a miracle isn't she? She'll be just like her mom.'

'Heaven help you then,' Jai said unsympathetically. He loved his sister dearly, but the thought of a miniature version of her was scary. 'Let's hope she takes after you instead. I'll see you in a while, Jignesh—call me if you need anything.' Jignesh nodded, not taking his eyes off his sleeping wife; Jai went out of the room.

It was not yet seven, and as the weather was unusually good, Jai decided to walk home. Except for the usual hazards of dog poop and banana skins on the pavement, it was a pleasant walk. Prabhadevi was some five or six kilometres from the hospital, and it took him the better part of an hour to get there. It was around then that he realized he was starving. He'd had very little dinner, and no breakfast at all, and now that he knew Pooja was fine, his appetite was back with a bang. There was a little vada-pav stall near his building, and he went there to pick up something to eat. The stall had a reputation (completely undeserved in Jai's opinion) of selling the best vada-pav in the city, and there was a huge queue snaking on to the pavement.

He was still waiting for his turn when his phone rang.

'Have you read the papers?' Nikita demanded.

'Not yet, I've just got back from the hospital. Why?'

'There's an excellent review of your book. And there are heaps of articles online...one even says that it's good enough to be a Booker nominee! I think you've cracked it, Jaiveer Singh; you'll be India's next Amitava Ghosh, only less boring.'

About to spring hotly to Mr Ghosh's defence, Jai realized the conversation was getting sidetracked.

'I'm buying vada-pav for breakfast, want some?' he asked. 'You can give me your newspaper with the wonderful review in exchange.'

'What kind of question is that, is the Taj Mahal pink? Of course I don't want vada-pav, it's oily and loaded with carbs. You keep eating stuff like that Jai and you'll turn into Humpty Dumpty.'

'Getting you some, anyway,' Jai said. 'Don't go to work today Nikita, I need company to celebrate.'

He took the stairs two at a time, and was hammering on her door in a few minutes.

'What's the matter, you forgot how to work the doorbell?' Nikita demanded as she opened the door, but her lips curved up in automatic appreciation as she took in Jai's appearance. Still dressed in the dark-blue formal shirt and jeans he'd worn to the launch the day before, his hair was rumpled and his jaw was shadowed with a day's growth of stubble—he looked tired, but incredibly sexy in a grungy kind of way.

'So what are celebrating?' Nikita asked as Jai dumped the vada-pavs and two PET bottles of Pepsi on the dining table.

Jai counted the reasons off on his fingers. 'I've become an uncle. My book's finally been launched. The publisher's offered me a contract for two more books, and a ten lakh advance...' As Nikita gave a little whoop of excitement, he grinned and added, 'Oh, and Shilpa's giving me a job in her company.'

'Wow,' Nikita shook her head in disbelief. 'That's a lot of reasons. And all I get is an oily packet of unhealthy food?'

'And Pepsi,' Jai reminded her.

'And Pepsi. In a PET bottle, I might add, not even a can.'

Jai reached over and tweaked the Pepsi out of her hand. 'Materialistic to the core,' he said, shaking his head sadly. 'Here I come rushing across to celebrate with you, and all you can do is quibble about oil and PET bottles.'

'Hey, give that back!' Nikita grabbed at the bottle, as Jai backed away, laughing. 'Come on, Jai don't be mean...'

She grabbed at it again, and Jai sidestepped, neatly grabbing her wrists in a strong grip.

'Nikita...' he said, and she stopped laughing at his suddenly serious tone. He was gazing right into her eyes, and she felt her pulse rate go up automatically.

'I wanted to thank you,' he said quietly. 'For what you did for Pooja. If you hadn't been around...'

'She'd have got someone else to take her to the hospital,' Nikita said. 'Pooja's a survivor, and so's that baby of hers.'

A smile tugged at the corner of Jai's mouth. 'The two of you have a lot in common,' he said. He seemed to have forgotten that he was still holding her wrists, or that Nikita was imprisoned against his chest at a rather awkward angle. Nikita didn't feel inclined to remind him either—there was something rather exciting about being so close to him, even if he wasn't paying full attention to her.

'I've got it,' she said suddenly. 'I've been trying to figure out what's different about you today. You look happy. You've never looked really truly happy before, you always had that slightly brooding, Devdas kind of look about you. Or not Devdas, perhaps, something more modern...'

'Nikita,' Jai said, interrupting her so that she broke off and gazed up at him with her lips parted mid-sentence. 'Stop babbling,' he said, and leaning down, he kissed her.

It was a completely mind-blowing kiss Nikita thought dazedly as she emerged from Jai's arms a good eight minutes later. Jai was...well, Jai was just wow. Saloni must have been crazy to choose Naveen over him—at the thought, her hands clenched possessively over his arms. Her voice sounded shaky to her own ears when she asked, 'What was that all about?'

'You asked me once if I found you attractive,' Jai said. 'The answer's yes.'

'And?' If he was just trying to prove a point, she really would have to kill him this time. Her head was still reeling with the aftermath of the kiss, and Jai sounded like he was reporting the results of a lab experiment. Or no, maybe not, she thought, as she took a closer look at him. A pulse was beating strongly in his temple, and he was flushed with emotion.

'I'm crazy about you, Nikita,' he said after a brief pause, his voice slightly hoarse. 'I've spent all this time fighting against it because I thought it would never work, but I can't resist it anymore.'

'And why should you?' Nikita asked indignantly. 'What's wrong with me anyway, I'm pretty and I'm smart, and I'm in love with you too...' The rest of the sentence was lost against Jai's lips, and she emerged from the second kiss considerably more breathless than from the first.

'If that's the way you're going to behave every time I try to say anything, I call it pretty unfair,' she complained.

Jai laughed. 'I'm sorry,' he said, but his eyes were dancing with mischief. 'From now on, I'll send you a written application every time I want to kiss you...' This time, he was the one who wasn't allowed to complete his sentence, as Nikita launched herself at him.

'Are you going to make up with your dad?' Nikita asked after a long interval in which they murmured their own brand of endearments to each other and made complicated, impractical plans for their future.

'Probably. I haven't really thought about it yet,' Jai answered. 'Why?'

Nikita gave him a sunny grin. 'I was wondering...'

'Nikita... I'm *not* planning to go back and work for him if that's what you're thinking,' Jai said, sitting up straight, his expression grim.

'No, you idiot, of course not, you're going to be a multimillionaire author. I was just wondering—do you think your dad would give us a good discount on an engagement ring?'